THE
LONG STAFF

Book 1 in the Staff Wielder Series

By

CLARE WILSON

Published by Olida Publishing
www.olidapublishing.com

First printing: August 2010
Copyright © 2009 by Clare Wilson
All rights reserved.

All comment and pictures are attributed solely to the author. No part of this book may be used or reproduced in any manner whatsoever without written permission, except in the case of brief quotations embodied in critical articles and reviews.

For more information e-mail: olidapublishing@gmail.com

Printed in the United Kingdom

Cover illustration: Paul Gildea

Cover Design: Paul Murdoch

ISBN: 978-1-907354-06-9

ATTENTION: SCHOOLS AND BUSINESSES
Olida Publishings' titles are available at bulk order discount rates for educational, business or sales promotional use. They are also available for fundraising projects. Please e-mail: olidapublishing@gmail.com for details.

The Long Staff – *This book is dedicated to all those who, no matter what they do, always go the extra mile…*

ACKNOWLEDGEMENTS – *My thanks and appreciation go out to Paul Murdoch and Allan Sneddon for their patience and hard work and without whom, this project would not have been be possible. I would also like to thank my loving husband, who has always had faith in me...*

Chapter One
A New Beginning

Tom was dozing in the back seat as he and his mother drove through the endless pouring rain, deep into the Scottish countryside. He opened his eyes and looked outside at the many images which were passing him like a slideshow. The sight of the rolling hills threaded like a patchwork quilt, with stone walls and the fields full of bedraggled sheep, filled him with happiness even through the constant drizzle. It was mid July and Tom had his mother were travelling from Lanarkshire to visit his grandfather in the Highlands for the rest of the school holidays.

Tom loved visiting his grandfather. He was excited at the thought of having several weeks with him and hoped that the weather wouldn't be this bad the entire length of their stay. He was due to turn thirteen in a couple of days and couldn't think of anywhere else he would rather be for the occasion. Tom was a slim boy for his age, with mousy hair and a kind face. His large blue eyes were his most distinctive feature and he had been told that they made him look like his father. He was on the cusp of adolescence but still had the look of a boy about him. Sitting in the car in his woollen jumper and corduroy trousers, he let out a sigh and opened his book once more. He loved to read. He found no greater pleasure than when he could immerse himself in another universe. It was so much easier than it was speaking to other people. He was able to fight in great wars and have amazing adventures, all neatly contained within paper and ink. His mother sometimes worried about the amount of time he spent reading, but Tom knew she thought that a trip to his grandfather would bring him out of himself. If anything could force him to look at the world beyond the safety of his printed pages it was the thought of fishing with his grandfather.

'Don't worry darlin', it's not much further,' he heard his mother say. Tom could see her kind green eyes smiling at him in the rear view mirror. He smiled back although they had been driving for what felt like hours and he was beginning to feel rather bored.

Very soon they turned into the small village of Cairn Holme and Tom immediately noticed familiar sites such as McCulloch the Bakers and McKenzie's Tackle Shop. The village was deep in the Scottish Highlands and it was where Tom's father had been born and raised. In a strange way it had always felt like Tom's real home, despite that fact that he had been brought up just outside Glasgow. His grandfather Evan lived in a small farm house on the outskirts of the village, and Tom always felt there was something magical about the place. He had spent many happy days playing in the woods beyond his grandfather's farm, living out all the adventures he experienced second hand through his books. Now as he grew, it gave him somewhere where he could find solitude, somewhere without prying eyes.

As they drove up the muddy path to the farm, daylight was fading fast and Tom could see the warm glow from the windows of the old stone house. The farmland the house was on had been in the family for generations and had room enough to keep a few animals. However, none of the animals were visible at this time as they had all been put into the small barn at the rear of the farmhouse for the night.

They pulled up in front of the house and as they got out of the car his grandfather appeared at the front door. Tom smiled to himself. His grandfather always pretended that he wasn't excited when they arrived. But Tom knew that he stood by the window watching for their arrival.

'Well, come in, my lad, before you catch your death,' came the familiar booming voice from the doorway. Tom ran laughing through door and into the bear hug that was his grandfather's arms, while the old man's sheep dog, Molly, danced excitedly around them. His grandfather had the fire roaring and fresh fish and potatoes cooking for supper. The smell made Tom's mouth water as soon as he entered the house.

Tom loved his grandfather dearly. He was a remarkably tall man and had a full head of messy white hair. It gave him an unusual quality. Rather like an overgrown tree tousled in the breeze. The old man had the same piercing blue eyes as his grandson.

'So, Helen,' his grandfather said, releasing Tom from their embrace. 'How was your journey?' he cried to her, playfully ushering Tom towards the door so they could return to the car to help her with the bags.

'Not bad,' she said, closing the boot and heading back to the house, 'although this rain hasn't stopped all day.'

As they rushed to enter the house together, eager to get out of the rain, his grandfather took one last look outside. 'It's to be clear and crisp tomorrow,' he said looking to the skies, 'although we do always get quite a lot of rain in July.' With that he closed the door, shutting the bitter night outside.

They entered the main part of the house and immediately felt the heat of the fire coming from the living room. Tom quickly turned and made his way up the staircase to his left taking him and his mother's bags to their usual rooms, while Evan led his mother into the living room. Excited, Tom reappeared quickly, anxious to see his grandfather. As he entered the living room he saw two old leather armchairs and a small, surprisingly inviting sofa placed around the familiar roaring fire. The room was simple but cosy, and had photographs in silver frames showing members of the family long gone. It was the kind of room which never changed. At one side of the fireplace there stood a large bookcase containing many dusty old volumes. It had glass doors covering the front and Tom remembered trying to pry open the doors when he was younger. His grandfather always said that even then Tom had a hunger for books. His mother was helping the old man to set the large scrubbed wooden table at the far end of the room.

'I hope you're hungry, my boy, I had an excellent catch yesterday,' his grandfather beamed.

'I'm starved,' Tom said hungrily. He threw himself down on one of the chairs at the table trying his best to look like he may well die of hunger at any moment.

'It smells wonderful, Evan,' added Tom's mother.

'Well, best not waste any time. We don't want our boy here dropping dead with hunger,' his grandfather said sarcastically. Without another word he walked back into the kitchen to serve up the food.

After eating his fill Tom lay drowsily by the fire, while his grandfather sat opposite him in one of the leather armchairs smoking his pipe. Molly was curled up at his feet, and his mother was sitting with her head back and her eyes closed on the sofa.

'Tell me one of your stories, granda,' Tom asked quietly, trying not to wake his mother.

'Well, my boy,' replied his grandfather. 'I prefer to call my "stories" educational adventures, one of which I would gladly tell if it were not for the fact that you can barely keep your eyes open.'

'Granda…' Tom tried to interject. However, his attempt to convince the old man turned into a yawn.

His Grandfather slowly stood up and gave Tom a kind smile, 'Come on, there will be plenty of time for stories. Off to bed with you.'

This startled his mother who opened her eyes blearily. 'Is that the time?' she asked. 'Tom, you had best be off to bed.'

Tom, realising that he would not be able to convince his grandfather otherwise, heaved himself from his chair and kissed his mother goodnight.

After one last longing look at his granda, the old man winked. 'Sleep well, son,' he smiled.

Tom climbed the stairs to his room and as always stopped on each step to look at the photographs his grandfather had framed on the wall. There were pictures from fishing trips and family weddings long passed. Tom's stomach lurched as he saw the picture of he and his father on Tom's first fishing trip several years before. It had been two years since his father's death, but Tom still felt like he would appear at any moment at the bottom of the stairs and tell him to stop dawdling. He thought for a few moments about the day the picture had been taken. He loved fishing in Cairn Holme, in fact, even more since his father's death. Something about being here made him feel closer to his father, and he hoped that he and his grandfather would have time to go fishing during his stay. Longingly looking at the photograph, he reluctantly carried on up the stairs to get ready for bed. After washing and changing into his pyjamas, Tom climbed into the oversized bed which sat in the middle of the large room which had once been his fathers. The sheets were soft and warm and made him realise how tired he really was. Glancing around the bedroom it felt as though nothing ever changed here. He even spotted the snow globe from London he had left here on his last visit, sitting atop the tall wooden dresser. With heavy eyes Tom rolled over and switched off the bedside lamp.

Tom fell asleep almost instantly and had no idea how long he had been asleep when he was awoken by raised voices coming from downstairs. Slowly becoming aware of his surroundings, he recognised his mother's voice.

'You know that Tom and I would love for you to come and live with us,' he heard her say.

'This is my home!' his grandfather exclaimed.

Tom, slightly startled by the strained tone of his grandfather's voice, crept to the top of the stairs where he could see the shape of the old man through the open living room door. He was silhouetted against the firelight.

'Well, if you're set on staying here, Evan,' his mother continued, 'I think Tom and I should stay for a while. That fall last year really scared us, and besides, Tom loves it here.' She was desperately trying to defuse the situation.

Tom didn't hear his grandfather's muttered response, but the old man turned toward the stairs and winked. The boy was sure no-one could see him where he sat, but he smiled to himself at the thought of his grandfather. He always seemed to be able to sense things others could not. With that Tom slunk back to bed and fell back asleep, although not as quickly has he had only a few hours before. He did what he always did to help himself doze off to sleep. He went over what was happening in the book he was reading and then wandered off in his own mind with what he thought should happen next. These thoughts usually relaxed him and he drifted off to sleep dreaming of battles and adventures.

Tom awoke the next morning to the sound of birds singing outside and the sun streaming through the curtains. *Right again*, he thought. His granda was always right about the weather. The smell of breakfast wafted up the stairs, making Tom feel extremely hungry. He leapt from bed, pulled on his dressing gown and ran down the stairs two at a time to the living room below.

'Well, sleepy head,' his grandfather joked, 'we wondered when you were going to join us. Do all you lowlanders sleep until nine o'clock on a Saturday?' Tom laughed and followed his grandfather to the kitchen where his mother was preparing eggs and bacon.

'Morning, darlin',' she said as she gave him a kiss on the head. 'Take a seat. It's just about ready.' Tom sat down eagerly awaiting the food.

'How did you sleep, my boy?' his grandfather asked, casting a side glance at his mother as she sat the plates down on the table.

'Fine,' said Tom. He knew that they were worrying about whether he had overheard their discussion the night before. Tom decided it was best not to say anything and tucked into the food his mother had put down.

'If I know my boy, Evan, I would venture he slept perfectly well until his stomach woke him!' his mother laughed.

'Well he's a growing boy,' said his grandfather patting him on the back, 'and breakfast is the most important meal of the day. Besides you have a long one ahead of you. Eat up.'

After a delicious breakfast Tom washed, dressed and headed out into the garden with his grandfather. While the land the family had was not large, he kept some animals which included chickens and a couple of goats. He had told Tom before that the farm had once covered several acres, but that he had sold the land after Tom was born because he was too old to manage it. He had known after Tom's father had gone off to University that he was highly unlikely to return to Cairn Holme to tend the farm. Heading down the garden to a small chicken coop located near the side of the barn, they fed the chickens and laughed as Molly pranced around their ankles excitedly.

Tom stood looking at the old man. As long as he could remember he had always looked the same, had always had a mass of white hair. 'Granda,' Tom asked, 'how old are you exactly?'

The old man could sense that Tom was playing with him. After considering the question his grandfather simply said, 'Old enough, my boy.'

'Are you as old as that cane you carry?' Tom said sarcastically, looking at the ancient gnarled stick his grandfather leaned upon. It was a worn old thing, but it had always fascinated Tom. He could never understand why his Grandfather didn't get a new cane. The one he carried looked like it may snap in two if he put too much weight on it.

The old man looked at him for a moment and with a twinkle in his eye replied, 'This is a staff, Tom, and it's as old as our very family itself. For generations the MacKays have lived in this valley, and this staff here, has been passed down father to son. That means that one day it will be yours, m'boy.' Tom looked slightly bemused by his grandfather's response, so the old man continued. 'In answer to your question, I am old, but nowhere near as old as this staff.'

'How old is the staff?' Tom asked, now curious about just how old it could possibly be.

'As I said, it's as old as our family. There are records of MacKays being on this site in Cairn Holme for several hundred years at least.'

Tom's mind was now filled with questions about their family history, when pondering what to ask his grandfather next on the subject the old man interrupted his train of thought.

'Well lad, thirteen tomorrow. What would you like to do?' his grandfather asked.

'Erm, I want to go fishing!' Tom replied with very little hesitation.

His grandfather laughed as if somehow he had expected that to be what Tom wanted to do with his day. He knew that the boy loved spending the long summer days in Cairn Holme fishing. He was like his father that way. There was something about the tranquillity of sitting next to the water with the wind lightly blowing by. 'Well lad, you had best get a move on with your chores so we can head into town to pick up the necessary supplies,' the old man said with a glint in his eye.

That afternoon the three of them went in to the village for groceries and fishing supplies. While his mother went to the local store to get ingredients for a special birthday cake, Tom's grandfather took him to the tackle shop to let him choose bait for the trip they were to take the next day. As they entered McKenzie's Tackle Shop Tom looked around himself excitedly. The store always looked like a messy jumble of everything a fisherman could possibly need. It was dimly lit and as your eyes adjusted, you saw that there were nets hanging from the ceiling. Tom then turned to an entire wall adorned with so many different types of rods it was hard to count them all. Old McKenzie sat behind the counter reading a dusty old volume.

'Why, Evan!' McKenzie exclaimed. 'It's always a pleasure. Is this young Tom?' he asked shifting his gaze to the boy. 'You get bigger each time I see you, and more like your father than a son could be.'

Tom was used to hearing this and smiled at the man while feeling slightly distracted by his enormous shaggy beard. He thought it looked like there may be crumbs from the man's lunch lurking in its depths.

'What will it be?' he heard McKenzie ask.

Tom's grandfather patted Tom on the shoulder and smiled. 'Our young man turns thirteen tomorrow and we're going fishing to celebrate. Tom's been learning to fly fish so we'll need your best flies please.'

McKenzie went through the back and appeared with a box which he placed on the counter. He had an awed look upon his face as he put the box he carried down. Tom half expected that when the box opened, it would emit a golden light. *Who would have guessed that the Holy Grail was hidden in a Scottish tackle shop?*

'I have just gotten in some fantastic Woolly Buggers,' McKenzie said slowly opening the lid. 'No young man should be without these in his tackle box. Better still they are cheap at the price.' He held one of the flies up in his hands. To Tom, it looked like he handled them the way a jeweller would handle a delicate necklace.

Tom's grandfather laughed into himself, he could see the confused look on Tom's face. 'Don't worry boy, I'll explain about all of this tomorrow,' he mused. 'Tom here hasn't used a Woolly Bugger before, I think he was getting a little confused,' he added to McKenzie.

'Oh,' McKenzie boomed. 'You thought I was being a little rude did you? Not at all, my boy.'

Evan considered haggling with McKenzie on the price of the bait but thought better of it. He was an old miser and Evan doubted that anything in his shop would be cheap at the price. Nevertheless, they had been friends since they were children and he would not have gone anywhere else to buy his fishing equipment. He paid for the bait and they left the shop to meet Tom's mother and head home.

They arrived back at the house and Tom's mother prepared a delicious meal for the three of them. Feeling bloated after his feast of home made steak pie and dessert of rhubarb and custard, Tom moved over to the living area to sit by the fire.

After helping Tom's mum to clear up the dishes, his grandfather came to join him in the armchair opposite. 'I believe I owe you one story, laddie, now, which one to choose...' his grandfather pondered.

At this Tom's mother simply shook her head and moved back into the kitchen to make them all a cup of tea before bed.

Tom looked at his grandfather inquisitively. After a few seconds he decided to ask, 'Granda, can you tell me more about your staff?'

'Well, now,' said Evan, looking decidedly serious all of a sudden. 'Those are serious matters, but since you're turning thirteen tomorrow I believe that I could tell you a wee bit.' The old man lit his pipe and with the other hand held the staff at his chair. He was taking his time in order to build the atmosphere. Molly seemed to sit up as though she too had been waiting for this. He let a few moments pass in silence as though he was contemplating where best to begin. 'As I said, this staff goes back generations,' he said now looking stern. 'My father could never tell me exactly how many, but it is at least three hundred years. There have always been MacKays in this valley and we were entrusted with this staff to act as wardens. From this I'm sure you will have gathered that this is no ordinary Celtic staff. It was carved from the branch of an ancient oak and can be used to defend against evil.'

'Evil?' Tom said expectantly. His grandfather had never told him anything so far fetched before.

'Yes,' his grand replied abruptly. 'It is a very important role that our family plays, Tom. We all have a destiny, my boy, and our destiny as MacKays is to live in this valley and help to protect the land from evil.'

Tom's eyes were open wide; this was definitely more than he had expected. All he could do was nod and he simply mouth the word, 'wow.' He didn't know whether to believe the old man, or whether he was pulling his leg, but it was a great story none-the-less.

His mother had re-entered the room at this point with a tray holding cups and a pot of tea. She looked at Tom's grandfather and tutted. 'Evan, don't you go filling my son's head with nonsense.'

Tom was surprised that she didn't sound like she was joking.

The old man, who had decided to push his luck a little, winked at Tom and continued. 'Only a MacKay can wield the staff, and the next male heir must master its lore.'

'Does that mean you will teach me how to use the staff?' Tom asked, already imagining himself wielding it on a mighty quest.

'Yes, I suppose it does. But you're a little young to worry about all that, my boy,' his grandfather replied seriously. 'It is something we will discuss further when you come of age.'

'How old is that?' Tom asked despondently.

'Traditionally, that would have been sixteen. But in this case I would wager it will be when your mother deems you mature enough,' his grandfather said, looking warily in the direction of Tom's mother.

'I think sixteen is old enough,' said Tom. 'It seems so far away. I think I may be ready before that,' he added hopefully.

Evan, who could see that Helen was becoming more agitated, quickly responded. 'Come, lad. There will be no talk like that. Have you any more useful questions to ask?'

Tom thought for a moment. 'Have you had to fight evil with the staff?' he asked.

'I have been lucky, only once or twice in my lifetime has there been need'.

At this Tom's mother seemed to lose her patience, 'Enough!' she said. 'Tom, I think it's time for bed.'

Disappointed, Tom turned to his mother. 'I haven't had my tea yet, mum,' he appealed.

'I don't care, Tom. It's late. Now off to bed with you,' she said shortly.

Despondently he got up and headed for the stairs; he knew from the tone of his mother's voice that it was best not to argue with her.

Tom strained to listen on his way up the stairs and overheard his mother saying, 'I don't think it's appropriate for you to tell him such things. You know how I feel about this.'

'Helen, I'm sorry,' replied his grandfather. 'The boy asked. He will know all about his heritage soon enough. Be that as it may, I will respect your wishes and not bring this up around him until you think the time is right.'

'Thank you,' she said curtly. 'His head is already full of adventures and battles, I don't want him running off and getting himself hurt!'

At this Tom carried on up the stairs and into his bed. His mind was racing. What could this mean? Was he really in the middle of his own adventure? Could he really be a young warrior about to start his apprenticeship? Lying in bed he dozed off with dreams of him and his grandfather fighting off ghouls and monsters with their staff.

A little after midnight, as Tom slept, his grandfather came into his room and placed the staff next to his bed. 'Spend your first night as a MacKay man, my lad,' his grandfather whispered. 'Happy Birthday, son.'

Some time later Tom was awoken sharply by a bright light. He sat bolt upright in his bed. Confused, he thought to himself, *is it morning already?*

As his eyes adjusted he saw that the light did not come from the window but from the staff next to his bed, his grandfather's staff. An amazing blue light flooded the entire room, emanating from the celtic carvings which covered the staff. It pulsated and seemed to be calling to him. Tom was completely petrified and didn't think he would be able to move. After a few moments he took a deep breath, built up his courage and reached out a hand slowly to take hold of the staff. The instant his hand made contact with the wood there was an explosion which threw him from his bed. Surrounded now by the blue light he found that he could not let go of the staff. It seemed to burn white hot, welded to his hand, although he was in no pain. His head was spinning and he could see the room flying around him. The room moved faster and faster until Tom could no longer make out the details of what was spinning around him.

Only aware of the blue light surrounding him, he closed his eyes in the hope that he could shut it out. This made him feel even dizzier. Opening his eyes again he tried to find something in his room he could focus on, something which would bring him back to himself. Terrifyingly he found that he now could no longer see anything at all other than the light pulsating from the staff. At this he screamed aloud hoping that someone would hear him and come to his aid. Panic set in as he realised that no-one was coming to help him. After another couple of moments the build up of sensations was so overpowering that he passed out.

Chapter Two
The Learning Curve

When Tom came round he noticed that he was wet. Opening his eyes and sitting-up he found that he was outside sitting on the grass and it was raining. Still blinded by the light from the staff, he found it difficult to see in the darkness. Slowly, as his eyes adjusted he looked around and saw the familiar hills that surrounded Cairn Holme. He breathed a long slow sigh of relief. Somehow the familiar outline of the hillside made him feel safer. With his heart still pounding from his ordeal he slowly stood up and thought: *How on earth did I get outside?* His legs were still shaking as he turned round only to find that his grandfather's farmhouse was gone and in its place a small stone thatched cottage stood. The sight of this made him suddenly feel like he was going to be sick. *How had he gotten here?* he thought. At that he bent over and vomited on the grass.

By this time the blue light had completely gone from the staff which Tom still held in his left hand, and the only light Tom had left to guide him was coming from the windows of the cottage. He was extremely disorientated but thought that only thing to do was to try the house: he couldn't stay outside in the rain all night, and surely whoever lived inside would know his grandfather. Cairn Holme was not a big village, and his grandfather was well known to most people who lived in the area. However, for this same reason he tried to ignore the feeling in the back of his mind, that if he was not far from home, how did he not recognise the house and how far could he have been thrown to have landed in a different farm?

As he stood and made to start his way toward the door of the cottage, he saw the outline of a man appear from the shadows hobbling towards him.

'Who goes there? Be you the MacKay I seek?' the man asked. Tom, petrified, was afraid to speak. The stranger continued. 'Speak. I am not afraid of you. In fact, I am armed!'

Tom was scared in case the man had a gun. 'Please Sir! My name is Tom, Tom MacKay,' he proclaimed.

At this the man shuffled more quickly towards him, angrily spitting: 'A child! What devil's trickery can this be?' As he approached and saw that Tom held the staff he said, 'What have you done, lad? Where did you get that staff?'

Tom tried to explain, but the old man was cursing under his breath about impending doom and young thieves. It was at this point that Tom noticed that the man leant upon a very similar staff.

Although confused by this, Tom mastered his courage. 'I am no thief,' he said, hoping that the old man wouldn't sense the fear in his voice. His heart was pounding so loudly he felt sure that the old man would hear it. It felt ready to burst from his chest. 'Only a MacKay can wield the staff,' he said trying his best not to sound shaky.

At this the old man laughed a deep throaty laugh, 'Strong words. Wield you say?' he remarked smiling. 'I'm not sure you can call it wielding when you fly out of nowhere and land on your rump in the mud!' He shook his head, 'Yet what you say is true, none but a MacKay could have been summoned.'

'Summoned?' Tom questioned.

'Aye, summoned,' he continued. 'I am Torean MacKay, keeper of the staff in my time, and I summoned the strength of MacKay here this night. Tell me this laddie, if you do not know of such basic rights as the summoning, how did you come to be in possession of the staff?'

Tom thought about this for a moment and realised he actually didn't know. The staff had not been in his room when he had gone to bed. How had it come to be by his bedside? 'Sir, I cannot truly answer that question,' he replied. 'It's my grandfather, Evan MacKay, who owns this staff. He has told me of its heritage but nothing of how to use it.'

The old man once again shook his head and tutting under his breath he led the boy towards the door of the cottage. 'Forsooth, this is a right mess we are in, boy,' he said. 'I will need time to work out what we should do. There will be no further talk of this tonight. For now you are a lost child in need of shelter on this bleak night. Come.' Tom blindly followed the old man into the house.

As they entered the dimly lit cottage Tom felt the heat of the fire burning in the centre of the low roofed room. This appeared to be main chamber in the house with several doors to the back. He immediately felt that the house was a lot smaller than his grandfather's home. As Torean closed the door Tom became aware of the aroma within the house. It was a very homely smell, a combination of burning wood on the fire and cooking. There was a woman knitting by the firelight and a boy of roughly the same age as himself sitting at a large wooden table to one side of the room. The woman, small and slim with fair hair, sat on a rocking chair moving the chair back and forth to the rhythm of her clicking knitting needles. The boy, who resembled Tom remarkably, except for the fact that he looked slightly older, did not say anything as he looked across the room at the new arrivals.

In the light of the cottage he became aware of the different style of dress worn by the family. They looked like people from another time. Torean looked at Tom and seemed to come to the same conclusion about the boy's dress. In one swift movement he grabbed a blanket from near the fire and placed it over Tom's shoulders. He then removed the staff Tom was holding from his hands and leant it against a corner in the shadow. In the light Tom noticed that the man reminded him of his grandfather. He was short in comparison, but had the same shaggy head of white hair and large blue eyes. Tom was not sure whether this reassured him or made him feel slightly uneasy. *Who was this man, where was he, and more importantly, when was he?*

He led Tom further into the room and announced their presence. 'Adaira, here we have Tom. I came across him after checking the pigs. He was lost and needed shelter for the night. I told him we would oblige.'

The woman looked up, 'Poor lamb,' she sighed. 'Your mother must be sick with worry. Sit by the fire to dry yourself and I'll fetch you something warm to eat.'

As Tom sat down he suddenly realised that he hadn't thought of his mother and wondered whether she would have noticed his absence yet? He knew that he would need to get home somehow, before she noticed he was missing. He felt hot tears well up in his eyes as he thought of her, but forced himself to blink them away.

Torean then turned to Tom. 'Adaira, there,' he said, pointing to the woman, 'is my daughter in law and that is Aneirin, my grandson.'

The boy had not spoken at all, but sat at the table and eyed Tom inquisitively. Tom smiled at Aneirin, who returned his smile after a few moments. Tom got the impression that Aneirin didn't trust him.

'Aneirin,' said his mother, 'fetch Tom some dry clothes. He looks about your size. Poor lad must be soaked to the skin.' Aneirin returned with a nightshirt which Tom quickly changed into. Again he noticed Torean hastily disposed of his incriminating pyjamas. At the same time he also observed that Aneirin looked like he was making a great deal of effort not to take any heed of this occurrence. Aneirin was slightly taller than Tom, but could not have been much older than him. He had dark brown hair and the same blue eyes as his grandfather. The same blue eyes as Tom's grandfather too, as Tom. Unlike the jolly old man Tom was used to, he looked very serious. Tom felt like every time Aneirin looked at him, he was closely examining every detail about him. He made Tom feel guilty even though he knew he had done nothing wrong. His eyes had the appearance of someone who had gone through too much too young. It was a look which Tom recognised from his own reflection.

After a cup of broth Tom was sent off to bed in one of the back rooms with Aneirin. This was where they were to sleep top to toe in a small wooden single bed. As he lay in bed he heard Adaira question Torean about how Tom had appeared in the middle of the night, but Torean stuck to his story that he had come across the boy after checking the pigs. Tom, looking around himself, noticed that Aneirin was also listening. As their eyes met he considered asking Aneirin about where he was, but when the boy saw Tom looking he pretended to be asleep. Tom decided to try and sleep in the hope that he would wake up in his own bed. He hoped that surely this had all been a bad dream. As he lay with his eyes closed he longed for nothing more than his book to comfort him. *It's ironic* he thought. *I've always wanted to be in one of my adventures. It's not quite as fun when you're in your own. It's terrifying!*

As morning came Tom was awoken by the sun streaming through the small window by the bed and the smell of porridge. He smiled to himself and opened his eyes, but was taken aback as he found that he was not in his bedroom. Suddenly, the events of the night before came flooding back and once again he found his heart in his throat.

Torean then appeared in the doorway. 'Right laddie, if you want your breakfast it's on the table,' he said.

Adaira appeared at Torean's shoulder. She could feel that Tom was afraid and said, 'Don't worry son, we'll get you back to your mammy.' Tom smiled gratefully and rose from his bed to eat his breakfast.

At the breakfast table Tom thought about asking some questions but remembered Torean's words of the night before. It had seemed as though he could not mention to the rest of the family the circumstances which had brought him to their home. He would need to find a chance to speak to Torean alone to find out more about where he was and how he could get back. In a strange way he felt like he trusted the old man, this was probably due to the startling resemblance between Torean and his own grandfather.

After eating he returned to the bedroom and borrowed some more of Aneirin's clothes, even though they were a little too big. He quickly returned to the main room.

'Well, I'm going to take this boy to the field so he can earn his keep,' Torean said to Adaira. 'You stay where you are, Aneirin. When was the last time you had a morning off?' The boy looked puzzled and somehow disappointed as Tom and Torean left the cottage. Tom had the feeling that Aneirin had been desperate to question him about his sudden appearance, but wanted to get him on his own. He also thought that the boy was none too pleased at the prospect of Tom getting to spend the day with his grandfather in his place.

They left the cottage and walked for several minutes down a dirt track and into a field. Tom was startled by the fact that although everything had felt so alien to him since this had began, he still recognised all of his surroundings; the trees, the hills, even the fresh scent upon the wind. There was a reassuring familiarity to it all.

Torean was carrying what Tom had assumed to be farming tools wrapped in a large cloth. Tom soon became confused, however, when it appeared that the old man had no intention of stopping in the field. Instead, they left the field behind and started into a dense wood. Finally, they stopped in a clearing which had a stream running alongside. 'Are you going to send me home now?' Tom asked expectantly.

'I'm afraid not,' Torean sighed.

Tom felt his heart sink. 'Don't you know how to send me home? I need to get back, my mother and my grandfather...'

'It's not that simple,' Torean interrupted, holding his hand up. 'As I mentioned last night, the staff chose to summon you. You were sent here for a reason. While I can't fathom what that is, it's up to the staff now.'

'So can you tell me when the staff will send me back?' Tom begged, becoming desperate and trying his best not to cry.

'It will all become clearer as we work. For now I can only ask that you trust me.' Torean said, trying to reassure him.

Tom took a few deep breaths as he tried to take in what the old man said. He managed a nod and then asked, 'So what do we do now?'

'We're going to sort out what you know, and what I can teach you,' Torean answered. 'We'll need to work fast if we're going to survive.' Torean rolled out the cloth on the ground revealing Tom's staff and some farming tools. He passed the staff to Tom.

In the daylight Tom realised that you could tell the difference between the two because Tom's staff was worn in comparison to the one Torean carried.

'What did your granda teach you?' Torean enquired.

'Well,' Tom said, 'he really only told me that it's powerful and that it was entrusted to our family.'

Torean hung his head and took a deep breath. 'This is going to be harder than I thought. 'You had best sit down.'

Tom sat down on a boulder and wondered how he had gotten himself into this situation in the first place. *Next time you see a mysterious staff glowing next to your bed in the night, don't touch the blasted thing!*

'Now,' Torean began, 'the power of the staff comes from the power of nature itself. As such you are only as strong as your surroundings. The staff was given to our family generations ago, and came from an ancient oak which grew in these parts when the earth was young. The valley surrounding Cairn Holme is an area of great earth power. This means it provides great strength to a staff bearer, but it also attracts darker forces who wish to control such power to their own ends. There are many places throughout the world where the make up of the earth has caused there to be a shift in the normality of nature. It means that if you know how, you can use earth power to control your surroundings. In Cairn Holme this comes from the mountains around us. Although, we do not know exactly what it is about the hills that causes this phenomenon. If you were to take this staff to somewhere else in the country it would be nothing more than a carved piece of wood. It is because of our surroundings here it is a means of channelling the powers around us.'

Tom then asked, 'Do your enemies want to steal the staff?'

'No,' Torean answered matter-of-factly. 'The nature of the staff means that it will only work if used by someone from our bloodline. It will not respond in the same way for just anyone.'

'So it's my destiny to be here?' Tom asked, almost to himself. He was remembering his grandfather's words about how his destiny was to remain in Cairn Holme. *I wonder why my dad left?*

'Yes' said Torean solemnly. 'We are in effect wardens. I will show you an example of what the staff is capable of.' Torean then turned to face the water, raised the staff and said in a low voice: '*Cuairteag.*' Tom felt a sudden breeze rising among the trees. The water began to stir unusually and then began to spiral. Within moments the water had risen several feet in the air and was now in a perfect whirlpool suspended in mid air. Torean lowered the staff and the water fell instantly. 'Now,' Torean said, 'I want you to try to focus the power.' He picked up a pebble and put it in front of Tom. 'I want you to try to move this stone. The word you need to use is *amas*. It is a word which can summon items towards you. You will need to focus yourself as you say it. Close your eyes and listen to the wind, to the water, to the trees. I am going to go and work in the field for an hour and I will return to see if you've made any progress.' Without another word Torean turned and walked away.

Tom watched him go and felt a great sense of fear wash over him. *Could all of this really be happening?*

For a time Tom sat looking at the stone and listening to the wind in the trees. A sense of panic suddenly took over, he felt completely overwhelmed. It was at that point that he remembered it was his birthday. He should have been fishing with his grandfather; instead he was sitting in a clearing trying to work out how to move a pebble. Unable to hold it back any longer, a hot salty tear suddenly rolled down his cheek. After a minute or two he took a deep breath and thought: *Right, pull yourself together. Thirteen today, you can't cry. You're a MacKay. What would your granda say?* So he closed his eyes and listened to the trees and the wind. He knew this was pointless unless he could control his breathing. Trying to focus on the power of nature surrounding him and the pebble, he opened his eyes raised the staff and said, 'Amas.' Momentarily he felt the wind around him rise, although the pebble did not move. So, he let his mind clear and he tried again.

After several failed attempts that left Tom feeling rather drained and despondent, Torean appeared in the clearing. 'Well lad, how are you getting on there?' he mused.

'That can't have been an hour!' Tom exclaimed feeling extremely disappointed at his lack of progress.

'Aye boy, just over in fact,' he said motioning his hand to the sky. 'So come on, show me.'

I really hope he doesn't shout at me, Tom thought to himself. He closed his eyes, focused his thoughts and tried to concentrate on the pebble. He opened his eyes and said, 'Amas.' Again, as before the winds rose. This time he noticed that they were stronger than they previously had been. For a moment he thought he saw the pebble shake, but it did not move.

At this Torean moved forward. 'Not bad, boy,' he said. 'You're better than I was when I started my training.' Putting an arm around him he continued, 'For now we will go and work in the field before lunch. I want you to think of all that you have heard and learned. We will return this afternoon and try again. Unfortunately, we cannot afford to waste any time. If we are to be successful we must work quickly.'

'Can you tell me of the evil we face?' Tom asked, still feeling like he didn't fully understand what was expected of him.

'As we work in the field I shall tell you. Come.' Torean turned and Tom followed him from the clearing. The sun was bursting through the trees as Tom assisted Torean working with the crops.

After they had gotten into a rhythm working Tom decided it was safe to question Torean further. 'When did this evil show itself in Cairn Holme?' he asked.

'It started around a month ago,' Torean replied, 'when a new woman arrived at the big house. Apparently she is the Laird's niece but I sense ill in her. I believe that she has started recruiting others in the community to her cause. Through my searching with the staff I have felt the darkness steadily growing since her arrival. I can sense that she has also felt me, and this has been proven by the fact that our family has had several visits from the local sheriff when no others have. She knows that I am powerful, and that I am a threat. I believe that the Sheriff is one of the people she is using in order to achieve her goals without revealing herself directly. If my calculations are correct, we have until the next full moon before she moves.' Torean could see Tom looked confused by this statement. 'That's roughly two weeks, boy,' he said, in a tone which suggested he was extremely worried if the boy didn't even know the cycles of the moon.

'Two weeks!' Tom exclaimed.

'It's less than two weeks actually,' said Torean, unsure that this would help the situation.

'I can barely move a stone!' Tom now felt he was in a state of complete panic.

'Look, boy,' Torean said, holding up his hand to silence Tom. 'You are more promising than most; it took me six months to gather the wind. We must make the best of what we have. We will work on this every morning and afternoon and I'm sure we will be able to do enough to get through this. I'll obviously have to concentrate your training on what we will need rather than the usual course.'

'How long does it usually take?' Tom asked, although he was not sure that he really wanted to know the answer.

'Well,' said Torean, scratching the whiskers on his chin. 'A couple of years… but don't worry, you seem unusually gifted. Your youth may be an advantage; she won't expect a child to be a threat.' Torean said, in a tone which suggested he knew this was unlikely to make Tom feel any better.

The thought that Tom was going to have to learn the lore of the staff in just under a fortnight terrified him. 'Two years in two weeks! I won't be any threat at all!'

Torean smiled kindly, 'Don't worry, my boy. Come.' He motioned for Tom to follow him from the field to a place where there were large stones they could sit down upon.

After a light lunch, they worked on for an hour or so and then went back to the clearing. On the way there Tom asked Torean some more questions. 'Could they not attack now? Why will they wait to move with the moon?' he asked.

'The new moon is a time of power,' replied Torean. 'It signifies a time when the earth power here in Cairn Holme is at its height.'

'I can't believe how little I know,' said Tom despondently. 'Does your family know of your role with the staff?'

'No, boy,' he said, looking around them as though he expected someone to be listening among the trees. 'And I'd rather keep it that way for now. It may not always be possible, but I'd like to protect them as much as I can.'

The pair then walked on in silence until they reached the clearing. Tom thought over how he was going to be able to learn everything expected of him and keep it a secret from Torean's family.

When they set back to work in the clearing Tom tried his best to focus, although he was secretly terrified at the prospect of having to learn so much so quickly. His thoughts often drifted to his grandfather. Tom knew that he would have known exactly what to do in this situation. He would have been much better equipped to help Torean in his quest. *Did the staff know it was getting me? Or did it think that it was getting him?* 'Will my family be looking for me right now?' Tom asked.

Torean looked at him kindly and smiled, 'Don't worry, lad, the staff always has a way of returning you exactly where it took you from. They won't even know you've been gone.'

Tom at least felt comforted by this thought. He had worried that his mother would be frantic trying to figure out where he could have gone. 'Have you ever been summoned from your home by the staff?' he then asked Torean.

Torean leaned on his staff looking grave. 'Once, laddie, but it was a long time ago. I was taken from my time into, well, I don't know when.'

'What do you mean you don't know when?' Tom couldn't help but interject at this point.

'Well boy,' Torean mused, 'have you asked yet what year you are in?'

Tom thought about it. 'Well, I suppose not. What year am I in?' he questioned

'I was always told that it's better not to ask,' Torean said seriously. 'From the way you speak and dress, I would guess that you have been drawn into the past. When I was taken the MacKay who called me advised me not to ask. He said that it would wreak havoc with my judgement.'

'Why?' Tom asked surprised. He thought to himself, *surely part of the adventure would be to learn about a time other than your own?*

'I believe that I was in the future,' Torean replied. 'He probably knew that if I were to become consumed with the time I was in, I would lose focus on what I was there to do. And, as I was brought up, I respected my elders and did not ask. Although thinking about it now, I suppose I was technically the elder,' he said musingly. 'The point is, do not worry about when you are, you are in Cairn Holme. It is where your destiny will cause you to stay all your life. You are simply playing your role. We are people who have to belong to a place rather than a time. In fact, it is foretold that there will at one time be a great battle when we will all have to fight together. If that is so, all the MacKays across the generations will meet. It would be quite a sight.'

With that Tom resigned himself to the fact that he had little choice. He was in this predicament and if he wanted to get home he would have to focus all his energy on learning the lore of the staff. Nonetheless, he couldn't help but wonder about the prophecy Torean had mentioned. Like in one of his books, he wondered about this foretold last battle. When it came, would he fight at his father's side?

* * *

In a dim lamp-lit room Lady Anstruther was sitting at a lavish dressing table combing her long blonde hair.

A knock came at the door and a servant came slowly into the room. The young girl had dark brown hair tied back tightly into a bun, and large green eyes. Her appearance gave the impression that she was a very young girl who was dressed older than her years. 'Dinner will be ready in half an hour, m'lady. Would you like any help getting ready?' she asked, hardly raising her large eyes from the floor.

'No, Lizzy,' replied Naithara wearily. 'I shall be fine. I will be down shortly.'

As the door closed Naithara stood up swiftly, bustled over to a bureau in the corner of her room and opened the lid to reveal its contents. Within the bureau there were several candles, an ancient leather-bound book and some strangely shaped black stones. She smiled to herself. Since her first ceremony her power had grown immensely. She no-longer needed the book of power which had led her to Eiric, and was now able to summon him focusing her own strength. He had become part of her. She wanted to speak with Eiric;

she had missed his presence. He was a drug for her, his absence was like a gnawing hungry ache in her heart. In some ways it was the closest thing to love the strange girl had ever experienced. Laying the candles and stones out on the floor in an intricate circular pattern, she closed her eyes. '*Nathura Gathera Eiric,*' she said, in a hissing voice which didn't sound altogether human. Suddenly a wind rose and swirled around the room making the curtains billow as though someone had suddenly opened a window to the humid night air. As the breeze died down a heavy dark gaseous cloud seemed to fill the room. It was the type of atmosphere one could almost taste. It hung in the air, slightly sweet but had a musty feel like food-stuff which has gone bad.

'Why do you summon me?' said a deep disembodied voice.

'Forgive me, my Lord, but I wished to seek guidance on how best I may ensure that our plans are fruitful?' she quaked.

The voice, now raised, spoke angrily. 'You summon me for this!' It boomed. 'Do not forget who has given you your power, Naithara, I could remove it as easily as it came.'

Naithara cowered like a small animal, motioning to the air that she wanted to keep the noise of their meeting as low as possible. 'Again, forgive me, Lord,' she said quietly. 'I simply wish to know that I am doing everything possible to ensure your rise is successful. And,' she continued hesitantly, 'when we are apart I miss your presence.'

At this the voice seemed to soften slightly. 'Very well,' it said. 'You know that if we are successful you will not need to feel such an absence. The main obstacle we still face is the old man. If I am to return to my physical form we will need to remove him quickly. I sense that he has summoned more power to him in his fight against us. If we are to move with the moon we will need to remove him now.'

Naithara looked puzzled. 'What kind of power has the old man summoned?'

The voice replied pensively, 'That I cannot tell, the vision is blurred to me at this time. I do not know whether this indicates great strength which can block me, or whether it is insignificant. Either way, you must move soon if we are to succeed.'

Naithara thought on this for a moment. 'The Sheriff is coming to dine with us this week. I can feel him becoming seduced by my power. He should provide the easiest way to dispose of the man. I cannot remove him simply without exposing myself. At this point, it would be foolish for me to do so. I cannot afford to have people like my Uncle rising against me.'

'Simply make it happen,' said Eiric curtly.

Naithara, although in awe of her master, worried about his wrath should she be unsuccessful. She had always felt a mixture of exhilaration and dread in his presence. It was an addictive combination of emotions.

When the voice spoke again it sounded weaker than before. The tone of the voice was almost pained in some way. 'I grow weary now. Do not summon me again until the old man is removed. You must move quickly, Naithara, I cannot stress that enough.'

With this the atmosphere in the room quickly lightened and the candles suddenly extinguished themselves. The presence was gone. Naithara shook her head as though she had been in a daze or dream, then quickly put her things away and looked in the mirror. She composed herself, straightening her dress, and smiled. Her face which had once held great beauty seemed to be contorted slightly by cruelty and greed. Around her blue eyes there was a distinct look of malice. She tied back her long blonde curly hair and thought back to when she had first discovered the ancient lore in a book in her uncle's library. The old fool had not even realised it was there. She had taken it away years before and had only realised after a great deal of study what it was capable of. With the book she had summoned Eiric and learned of his dark arts. He had taught her that her family resided on a great source of power; a power so strong it was capable of freeing him from his current prison and could allow him to return to his former glory. With the help of Eiric they would take control of her birth right, harness the power of Cairn Holme and control the forces of nature themselves. With one last gleeful look in the mirror she swept from the room and proceeded downstairs.

Chapter Three
Dark Omens

Tom had spent two days in much the same way as he had when he had first visited the clearing and he was beginning to get extremely frustrated. On his third morning he could tell that Torean was also beginning to lose patience.

'Look, laddie, can you feel the earth power flowing through you at all?' he rasped.

Tom thought for a moment. He could feel an increased power around him. Closing his eyes he tried to focus on that. He listened again to the wind and tried to forget that the old man was there. He opened his eyes and said, 'Amas.' The winds rose around him as they had before and he saw the pebble tremor but that was all.

'Not bad,' said Torean, trying to sound encouraging. 'That was better than before.'

Tom made no response to this, he felt like a failure.

'Try again,' the old man continued, putting an arm on his shoulder. 'Do it again just as you did before, but this time, try to concentrate more.'

Tom felt angry, *how can I concentrate any more than I already am?* He knew that his negative attitude was not going to help. So he took a deep breath and tried to forget his anger and frustration. He tried again. This time the pebble began to rise slowly into the air. He suddenly became excited about this and before he could react to what was happening the stone flew through the air and hit him square between the eyes. 'Ow!' Tom exclaimed, rubbing the red mark in the centre of his forehead left by the stone. 'What use is a spell which does that?!?'

Torean laughed, 'That was almost as funny as the way you fell out of the sky and landed on your rump!'

Tom couldn't help but crack a smile.

'With the right concentration,' Torean continued, 'you would make the pebble float gently into your hand. As our little experience has just taught us, letting yourself get carried away can have consequences, like losing an eye,' the old man winked.

'Sorry, I just got excited when it moved.' Tom said sheepishly.

'Don't worry, boy,' Torean smiled. 'All that matters is that you've done it. Once you can focus your power you can learn anything!' He patted Tom on the back.

Inside Tom felt completely elated, he wanted to jump around the clearing. The success of the morning had given him an immense sense of achievement.

'We will do no more today. Tomorrow the hard work really begins,' Torean said, as he turned round collecting their things.

Even this omen could not bring Tom down from his high. They worked in the field that afternoon and as dusk began to fall Torean spoke to Tom of the ways in which evil had struck before. 'It always comes in different ways,' said the old man as he gathered their tools, 'but always wants the same thing. If they can use the concentrated power of Cairn Holme they can bring about a darkness that would cover the land. Many of them are disillusioned and do not understand the consequences of their actions. They only sense the power and do not understand how to wield it properly. In such circumstances this power consumes them and they ultimately destroy themselves. Right now I can feel that she senses the power, and that those she recruits will be used as fodder to achieve her ends.'

'What is her name?' Tom asked.

'She calls herself Lady Naithara Anstruther. However, such great forces of darkness are not usually in human form for long. Either she is not what she appears, or she is being used by a force she will not be able to control for long. I believe it to be the latter. I remember her as a child staying with her uncle during a time of illness, although, she does not appear to be the same person now. Evil distorts people in this way, sometimes the transformation is even visible.'

Tom seemed intrigued by this thought. 'Do they turn into monsters?' he asked, puzzled.

'No, my boy, evil just has a certain mark. When you gain more experience you will be able to see it too. Anyway, we need to concentrate on your training rather than fear of the enemy. You must always remember that they are weak because they lust for power. We simply allow power to use us as a vessel for the protection of the earth. Let's go home for the night,' said Torean, as he wrapped the last of the tools in the sacking he carried them in.

As they walked back to the cottage Tom felt that his success that morning made him more aware of everything around him. Every bird singing was suddenly so vivid to him that it was almost deafening. He felt the heat of the sun in a new way and the smell of the air around him seemed to be bursting with life. When they arrived back at the cottage Adaira was preparing dinner. Tom's senses were extremely alive and he felt hungrier than he could remember feeling before.

'Ah, the wanderers return,' Adaira said. 'Dinner is almost ready. Aneirin is out putting the animals back into the barn. Tom, would you be so kind as to go and fetch him?'

Tom agreed and walked out into the yard. He was slightly apprehensive about speaking to Aneirin as the boy seemed to have gone to great lengths to avoid speaking to him previously. He entered the barn and looked around. 'Aneirin, are you there? I've come to fetch you to dinner,' he said in a slightly sheepish tone.

Aneirin appeared from the shadows at the back of the barn. 'Thank you,' he said curtly. 'How are you and my grandfather getting on?'

Tom thought about this for a moment, 'Fine,' he replied. 'We are working in the fields. You have a lot more land than my grandfather has. It's hard work but...' Tom paused. 'It's fun,' he said smiling nervously.

Aneirin smiled sarcastically. 'Really? Well, hopefully you will be back with your own grandfather before long. How old are you anyway?' He asked this question in a way that made Tom feel belittled.

'I'm thirteen. Just,' Tom said feeling uncomfortable. He had almost forgotten that he had turned thirteen a couple of days previously.

'I see. Well I'll be fifteen when winter comes,' Aneirin said, as if this settled the argument. Without another word he brushed past Tom into the yard.

For a moment Tom felt hurt. Obviously Aneirin was not happy with the amount of time he was spending with Torean. He wondered how he would feel in the same situation. Aneirin was obviously used to having his grandfather to himself and Tom could understand his unhappiness. He sighed and couldn't help smiling to himself. He didn't want to let worrying about this spoil what he had done that day. There was nothing he could do to change the situation. Looking around the barn he realised he could even feel the energy of the animals surrounding him and wondered whether it was possible to turn off this sensibility once it had been awoken. *Will I always feel this aware of everything around me?* He imagined that in the wrong circumstances these senses could be overpowering. *What would it feel like to stand in the centre of a crowded room? Would it be deafening?*

That night as they sat down to eat, Tom couldn't believe how alive he felt. It was the first day since his arrival that he hadn't felt wracked with fear, the first time he had thought himself capable of mastering the lore Torean was to teach him. He then looked at Torean and thought once more of his own grandfather. He wanted to make him proud. He wondered what his grandfather would say when he returned and told him of where he had been. He could visualise the old man's smiling face. He then thought of his mother, disapproving at the danger Tom had been in and whether she connected it to how his father had died. He knew one thing: even if he made it back in one piece to tell his grandfather this awesome tale, nothing was ever going to be the same again for him or his family.

At this Adaira interrupted his train of thought. 'So Torean, is there any word of Tom's family?'

It's like she's reading my mind, Tom thought. He felt panic wash over him, *what is Torean going to say?*

The old man seemed to think over what she had asked for a few moments. 'From what Tom has said,' he said calmly, 'he must have hit his head, because he doesn't remember where he's from. I will take a trip into town tomorrow to visit the Sheriff's office to see if anyone has been looking for the boy.'

'You poor lamb,' she said reaching for Tom's hand.

He did his best to look like he was worried. 'I hope it won't be long before my memory returns. It's okay,' he told her. 'I feel like I was meant to be here, I like staying with you.'

She stroked his hair and smiled, *he's such a gentle little thing. Somehow he reminds me of my Abhainn.*

Aneirin looked livid. He didn't say anything, but Tom thought that he didn't want him staying with them any longer than was strictly necessary.

'You are welcome here, young man,' Adaira said returning to her food. 'Although I'm sure you have a mammy somewhere who is frantic looking for you.'

They carried on eating their dinner in silence. Tom hoped that as Torean had said, his mother had not noticed his absence. That he would be able to return from where he had left.

*   *   *

At the Laird's house Naithara was preparing herself for the evening meal she was due to have with the Sheriff, Michael MacDonald, and her uncle, Laird Angus Anstruther. She sat at her dressing table putting rouge upon her cheeks and an extra hint of perfume upon her neck. If she was to convince the Sheriff to act on her behalf to solve the situation with the old man, she would need to use all her feminine wiles. She smiled to herself as she put down the bottle of expensive perfume having been careful not to put on too much. Her mother always told her that a lady's perfume should whisper, not shout. She had to get this just right. Her bedroom was strewn with various dresses she had tried on and then discarded, trying to create exactly the right look. Finally, satisfied with her efforts, she stood, took one last look at herself in a full length mirror and left her room.

A few moments later the room door re-opened. Lizzy went into Naithara's room in order to tidy up the various things the Lady had left strewn around. While picking up various garments haphazardly thrown to the floor she had the feeling someone was watching her. She quickly turned towards the window, but no-one was there. The atmosphere in the room made the hairs on the back of her neck stand up. She quickly finished putting the clothes away and rushed from the room closing the door behind her. Something in her had made her want to flee in terror from the room.

As Naithara entered the drawing room her uncle was talking to the Sheriff by the large ornate marble fire place. The room was large and the soft lamp light showed many paintings on the wall depicting family ancestors. 'As you know,' her uncle said, 'the farmers on the estate are very important to me. Your father understood that well, I hope that you will…'

'Good evening, uncle. Sheriff MacDonald,' interrupted Naithara brightly. She smiled demurely at the two men. The Sheriff turned and gazed at her, mesmerised.

'Ah, good evening, my dear,' responded her beaming uncle. He was a small portly man with thinning dark grey hair. One could find him comical to look at as beneath his dark grey hair he had bushy white eyebrows and a jolly smile.

The Sheriff, who had been unable to take his eyes from Naithara, approached her hungrily and kissed her hand. 'Good evening, my Lady. Your uncle and I were just discussing the importance of the farmers on the estate. He is a very loyal Laird.'

'Yes,' Naithara responded, sighing with feigned weariness. 'He cares for their welfare very deeply. He is perhaps too generous. There are those who do not appreciate the kindness. The MacKays, for example, seem a lazy bunch. One wonders if they could be deemed farmers at all. I think the grandfather actively encourages his grandson to poach our fish and fowl.'

'Come now,' said her uncle shaking his head, tired of hearing this from his niece. 'Since the death of his son, Torean has done his best for his family. The MacKays have resided in this valley for generations; I would not begrudge them food on their table.'

Naithara sighed and looked at the Sheriff. 'Still, the law is the law. Is that not so, Sheriff?'

Before the sheriff could respond the bell rang for dinner. He was greatly relieved that he had been spared from answering Naithara's question, and they proceeded into the auspicious dining room. The long, slightly narrow room seemed to be illuminated by the silverware; from the gleaming cutlery on the table to the ornate pieces in the cabinets around the room. Lizzy scurried around the long table making final adjustments to the three place settings that seemed slightly out place on the enormous table which on many occasions had seated large numbers of guests.

As they ate their meal of smoked salmon followed by rich venison, conversation roamed from subject to subject, mainly concentrating on issues of taxation and fishing rights. Naithara, picking at her main course, did her best to appear reserved and not overly involve herself in the discussions of the men. She knew she would need to choose her time carefully to broach the subject with the Sheriff. If possible, she would need to do so without her uncle in the room. It was so tiresome to sit there and listen to them drone on when she had important matters to discuss.

It was fast approaching ten thirty when they retired to the drawing room for a dram, and Naithara's uncle quickly fell asleep by the fire. As the fire crackled in the dimly lit room, the Sheriff idly discussed with her the flowers coming into bloom for the season. Naithara un-subtly brought the conversation back round to that which she had been waiting to discuss all evening. She had no interest in wasting this opportunity discussing such silly women's things. 'I sense, Sheriff, that we are of kindred minds,' she started.

'Well,' said the Sheriff blushing, obviously flattered by her words. 'I do feel drawn to your company.' He lifted the poker next to the fire and began to stoke the flames in order to distract from his obvious embarrassment.

'With regard to our earlier conversation, if we are to grow closer, I would appreciate if the MacKay situation could be… brought to a close, shall we say?' she said, no longer sounding innocent or demure. 'My uncle is too kind and permits people to take advantage of him. If I, or should I say, if we are to develop our relationship further I need such "generosity" to end.'

The Sheriff was slightly flustered by the choice of topic and almost dropped the poker. He had hoped that they could discuss more romantic matters. 'My Lady,' he sighed gently, clumsily putting the poker back in its place. 'I have visited the farm on several occasions at your request and have found no evidence that they are poachers.' While he desperately wished to impress Naithara, he did not see how he could get her to see reason on this subject. The MacKay family had never been in trouble before and it was beginning to look suspicious with him having already made several visits to them on behalf of Lady Anstruther.

'That is unfortunate,' she said shortly, examining her finger nails. 'Let me think for a moment upon the problem.' At this she put her hands together and began to mutter under her breath. The atmosphere in the room suddenly changed; it became warmer with a sweet smell - almost sickly. It was similar to the one which appeared earlier in Naithara's room and it seemed to intoxicate the Sheriff. As Naithara spoke the fire seemed to dim and a haze of pleasure came over him. 'I can share great things with you, Michael,' she whispered in silky tones. 'I am a very talented woman. Still, I need you to remove Torean MacKay from this estate permanently. He offends me.'

The Sheriff, who now almost appeared to be in a trance, simply nodded like a dog, 'I understand, my Lady,' he said. 'I wish nothing but to make you happy.'

'Thank you, Michael,' she said, smiling at him like a cat with a mouse. 'If they are not poachers, I will need you to find another reason to remove them. However, it will not be enough to simply evict them from the farm. You must find a way to remove the old man permanently, a tragic accident perhaps?'

At that moment there was a noise outside the drawing room which sounded like someone had dropped something. Naithara's uncle stirred in his chair and the atmosphere was instantly broken. The Sheriff, who looked a bit like he had just woken up himself, looked dreamily across the room at Naithara. She knew this look as she too felt the hunger for power. It was an addictive and exciting feeling. She knew that he was experiencing what she had long ago and loved the power she felt from ensnaring another to do her bidding. She was unaware that the Sheriff's thoughts were driven more by his lusts for her, than by his hunger for power.

Her uncle, completely unaware of anything which had transpired, leaped from his chair. 'What on earth was that?' he yelped.

'It was probably Lizzy being clumsy with the silverware again,' said Naithara impatiently. She hoped that this interruption had not distracted the Sheriff from what she was trying to impress upon him.

'Good Lord, is that the time?' yawned the Laird, looking at the grandfather clock in the corner. It was now past eleven o'clock. 'We had best all be off to bed.'

At this they rose and Naithara offered to walk the Sheriff to the door. On the way out she stopped in the hall to admire another cabinet containing silverware. 'A handsome collection, yes?' she asked.

The Sheriff was slightly confused by her comment. 'Yes. Indeed, my Lady.' He had been in the house on many occasions throughout his life and the extensive silver collection of the Laird was not new to him.

She beckoned for Lizzy to open the front door. 'Come to me again when it has been done,' Naithara said softly. She then leant in and kissed him on the cheek.

The Sheriff felt his heart leap as she touched him, her scent made his head feel fuzzy. As he stood on the step dumbstruck, she briskly closed the door in his face and ascended the stairs with a smile on her face. The fool would do exactly what she wanted him to do; the seeds for the next phase of her plan had been planted. This felt like progress, surely they could not fail now. Soon she could summon her master with the good news that their last barrier had been removed. She wondered what rewards he would bestow upon her for such an achievement. Would he increase her power? That would probably have to wait until his ascendance; he was growing weak waiting for the new moon. At least if she could report such momentous news the wrath she had encountered from him recently would stop. She wanted to prove to him everything she was capable of.

Meanwhile, as the Sheriff made his way into the night, he wondered about how he was to achieve what Lady Naithara requested of him. Putting these doubts aside he then thought of how she made him feel, with a woman like her he could achieve great things. With this in his mind he strode along and set to finding a way to make her happy and remove the MacKays. Suddenly he heard something clinking in his pocket, reaching down to feel that it was heavier than normal. He stuck his hand in and discovered that he had some cutlery with the Laird's family crest upon them. He didn't remember picking them up and wondered whether Lady Naithara had slipped them into his pocket when she kissed him on the cheek. By the time he had arrived home an idea had began to form in his mind. Like a puppet, he was acting exactly as Naithara had hoped. He thought to himself, *Michael MacDonald, you had better be sure about this. There is no turning back if you take this path*. He shook his head to clear his thoughts; he couldn't disappoint Naithara. She was the most intoxicating woman he had ever met. He knew if he didn't take this chance he would regret it for the rest of his life.

Chapter Four
The Dark is Rising

Back at the cottage all of the MacKays were sleeping. There came a rattle at the front door and Torean rose from his bed to find out who was knocking. He was muttering to himself about un-godly hours as he opened the front door to find a hooded figure in the doorway.

Tom, awoken by the noise, couldn't make out what was said, but he could tell it was a woman. He moved to try to leave the bed and the sagging wooden frame creaked loudly. Aneirin stirred in his bed. Tom sat perfectly still until Aneirin rolled over and began to snore. Then crawling like a cat from the bed trying not to wake Aneirin, he looked through the crack in the bedroom door. This wasn't easy, the figure in the doorway was cloaked and he could only see Torean's back from his position. Plus Aneirin's snoring was making it very difficult to make out what was being said.

'Thank you for taking this risk, lassie,' he heard Torean say. 'Go safely now and do not stop until you are home, do you hear?' With that he closed the door.

By now Adaira had risen from her bed and was walking into the living room sleepily. Pulling her nightclothes about her, she drowsily enquired what was happening.

Torean looked round as she entered. He no longer looked sleepy, all colour had drained from his face. 'Wake the children, we must talk,' he said seriously.

Torean's words seemed to rouse Adaira from her sleepy daze. Without a word she turned towards the room the boys were sleeping in with a worried look upon her face.

Seeing this Tom quickly scuttled back to bed and only just made it back beneath the sheets as the door creaked open. He pretended to be asleep as Adaira came to them and shook her son awake.

'Darlin', you need to wake up,' she said softly. 'Your grandfather wishes us to gather in the living room,' she leant over him, lovingly stroking her son's hair.

Tom sat up and rubbed his eyes, trying his best to look as though he too had just woken. 'What's happening?' he enquired, yawning. She lingered on him for a moment and he hoped he wasn't overdoing it.

'I'm not sure, dear,' she said, crossing the room to fetch Aneirin's house coat. 'I think Torean will need to tell us that.'

As they all sat down together at the table in the living area, Adaira busied herself putting on a pot of tea. She always did this when she was nervous. It was easier to be busy than to be sitting imagining what on earth could be wrong.

Torean looked around at them all unsure where to begin. 'We are in great danger,' he said solemnly. 'It is now at the point where I can no longer protect you from the truth.'

'What is all this?' Adaira interrupted. 'Does it relate to why the Sheriff has been visiting us so often?'

'Please,' Torean replied. 'It would be best if you let me explain first, then ask questions.' Torean took her hand and gave her an imploring look. She accepted this and poured them all a cup of tea. Torean took the cup gratefully. 'It's hard to know where to begin,' he said. 'I suppose it all comes down to this.' He rose and fetched his staff from the corner.

Tom felt his heart leap into his mouth. *Was the old man about to reveal the secret's of the staff? That would also mean he would need to reveal the reason for me being with the family. Will they still want me here once they know we have been lying to them?* He felt physically sick.

'This is no ordinary walking cane,' Torean continued, sitting back down at the table. 'It's been in our family for generations. It can channel great power and here in Cairn Holme the MacKays have used it to protect the land from evil.'

Adaira was looking at him as if he had gone mad, while Aneirin had a look about him like he had been waiting on this information for a long time.

'Torean, please, it's late. What is this nonsense?' Adaira said doubtfully. Nothing that the old man was saying made sense to her. He was beginning to frighten her, *has he lost his senses?*

Torean held up a hand to silence her. 'Young Tom appearing here isn't a co-incidence either,' he continued. 'I summoned him with the power of MacKay and brought him from his own time here to us. He too has a staff.' At this he motioned for Tom to fetch his staff from the corner.

Tom, unsure of what else to do, simply stood up and brought his staff over to the table. He couldn't look either Aneirin or Adaira in the face; he knew they were staring at him in disbelief.

Adaira and Aneirin were now looking from Tom to Torean both wondering what else the old man was going to reveal.

Adaira could not sit silent. 'Do you mean you have stolen this boy from his family? Do you know how to send him back? How would you feel if…'

'Please, mum,' Aneirin cut in. 'Let granda continue, I'm sure he will answer our questions.'

She was not happy, but sat in silence, her arms now folded.

'There have been times,' Torean continued solemnly, 'when I have had to fend off great evil. This is one of those times. Tom has come here to help, he will return to where he belongs once this is over. A friend, at great personal risk, has come here this night to inform me that we are to expect another visit from the Sheriff. However, this time he will not simply be poking around as he has before. He has orders to remove us in whatever way he can find. As such it is no longer safe here. Adaira, I would like you and Aneirin to leave tonight and seek shelter in the hills.'

At this they both looked appalled. Adaira put her arm around her son. 'If what you say is true,' she said firmly, 'I wish to stay here and defend my home. We have done no wrong, why should we run?'

'They are strong words,' Torean said softly, 'even so, you are my family. I wish to protect you. You do not know what we are up against.'

Suddenly Aneirin cut in, and Tom thought that this was the most talkative he had seen Aneirin since their conversation in the barn. 'I too shall stay,' he said. 'Although I am hurt that you have not been training me to help in this fight, is this stranger more important than me?'

A tear rolled slowly down Torean's cheek. 'No, my boy, please do not say such things. You know how important you are to me. You must also remember that Tom is family. He is a MacKay, even if he is not familiar to us. It is a fault of mine, but one which you must understand has come from love. I have tried to preserve your innocence, and, since your father's death, I have put off bringing this burden upon you.'

At this statement Adaira looked up sharply, a defiant tear fell from her eye. 'What are you trying to say Torean? Do you mean Abhainn died fighting this?'

The old man looked down at his cup of tea, ashamed. 'It is our destiny lass. We have no choice! If I could have died in his stead I would have gladly done so.'

She new this was the truth, but still she felt betrayed. 'Tell me what happened to him, Torean,' she demanded tearfully. 'I believe I deserve that much.'

Torean looked at her with great sorrow; he seemed to hesitate. 'It was a different threat to that which we face now. Abhainn took up the staff when I was injured in battle. Trying to fight our enemies and protect me he was overcome. A stray spell which he had not blocked sent him flying over the edge of the rocks up by Dawson's Watch.'

'You told me he fell trying to rescue a stray sheep from the edge?' Adaira said, feeling a mixture of confusion and anger.

'I know, my dear,' Torean whispered, tears now rolling freely down his face. 'Anything I have said to you both has only been to protect you. I couldn't bear to lose another loved one because of this responsibility which I bear.'

The group sat in silence for several minutes after the old man had finished speaking.

'Can you forgive me?' Torean said quietly.

Adaira looked up at him as though his voice had woken her from a dream. 'I'm not sure Torean,' Adaira responded frankly. 'I can't take this in. You're telling me that my husband's death was a lie. I don't know how you expect me to feel?'

Torean looked at the floor, he could not expect forgiveness.

'Nevertheless, I love you,' Adaira continued, 'and if what you say is true, I will need to put this aside for now in order to protect my son. We will need to discuss this later Torean, I am not happy about being lied to.'

'Mother!' interjected Aneirin. 'You cannot be suggesting that we leave our home!'

'Did I say that?' Adaira said matter-of-factly, looking her son squarely in the eye. 'We will not be chased from our home like frightened animals,' she turned back towards Torean. 'For now everything else I feel will simply have to wait.'

Torean smiled at her hopefully. 'I cannot ask anything else for now.' She was such a strong woman, and in the last couple of years since Abhainn's death, he had felt like she was his daughter in more than just name. He needed her now more than ever. Deep down he was glad that they wanted to stay with him. 'I think if you are set on staying we should get some proper defences in place,' he said almost cheerfully. 'Adaira, my dear, please prepare some bags for travelling in case we have to run.'

'How many days should I pack for?' she said.

'Well,' replied Torean thoughtfully. 'I would hope we won't have to run at all. Although if we do have to flee from here. It would mean travelling for some time, at least a week? Pack as much as you can within limits. The main things will be blankets and food.'

She nodded and rose from her chair eager to get the bags prepared. As before, she always felt a little better when she was able to busy herself with something.

'Aneirin,' Torean continued, now turning to his grandson. 'I want you to gather the animals and take them to Wilson's farm. Old Wilson has been a friend of mine since boyhood and will understand.' Now looking to Tom he said, 'Tom, come outside with me and we shall place some protective enchantments around the farm.' He stood and ushered Tom towards the door.

As he opened the door Aneirin said, 'Surely Wilson will ask me why I am doing this? What shall I say?'

Torean turned to him and smiled, 'I know this is hard, boy. Tell him that we may need to go away for a short time, and that you cannot reveal any further information to him at this time. Tell him that the situation is serious and that I will explain to him upon our return.'

Aneirin shrugged his shoulders and headed for the back door.

Tom and Torean went outside the cottage, 'Face the house,' the old man said.

'Are you okay?' Tom said warily. He thought that Torean looked drained by what he had been forced to reveal to his family.

'I am fine boy,' snapped Torean. He couldn't afford to get upset again, they must be ready. 'We must leave such talk for now and concentrate on preparing ourselves. Face the house.'

Tom did not argue with the old man, and they both stood with their staves and faced the building.

'We are going to raise an enchantment which will alert us to danger,' he said motioning to Tom to hold his staff aloft. 'I don't want you to worry; you are perfectly capable of such a task. Close your eyes as before and sense the power.'

Tom closed his eyes and listened to the wind.

'When we cast this we must both turn in opposite directions so as to cast a circle around the farm,' said the old man. 'Now, after me say, *rabhadh*.' There was a moments silence when Torean raised his staff and then said, 'Rabhadh.' Blue light flowed from Torean's staff and flowed out around the cottage.

Tom felt a great sense of tension. 'Rabhadh,' he said a few moments later. He was worried that he wasn't experienced enough, in spite of this, the power flowing from Torean helped him to focus his own. Slowly they placed a protective charm around the farm.

'There,' Torean said.

'How does this enchantment work?' Tom asked.

'Well,' Torean replied, 'if anyone other than a MacKay penetrates the boundary of the enchantment we will both know.'

'How can we?' Tom enquired, puzzled.

'My father told me that the sensation can be slightly different for each person. It will be a sensation which is out of the ordinary, something which distracts you.'

'What do you feel when it happens?' Tom asked, starting to worry that he may not recognise the sign when it came.

'For me, my boy,' Torean said smiling and trying not to laugh, 'it's my nose.'

'What do you mean your *nose?*' Tom asked, now visualising smelling some horrid aroma or bursting out in nose bleeds.

'My nose tickles,' he smiled.

'Tickles?' Tom asked thoughtfully. 'It's a little less dramatic than I was expecting.'

'Well, my boy, it is the nature of the staff. The staff learns to know its wielder, for each of us it is slightly different, as we have different strengths and weaknesses from one another.'

Tom looked worried.

'Don't worry yourself. When it happens you will know. When you become more accomplished with the lore of the staff you will recognise the ways in which it reacts for you.'

Tom hoped that Torean was right. 'What will we do when they come?' he asked changing the subject.

'Well,' said the old man, 'there are some protective spells I can show you if you would like?'

'Yes please,' said Tom. 'I feel so helpless right now.'

'Don't,' Torean said, trying his best to comfort him. 'Let me see, some protective spells,' he mused. '*Srad* is the word used to summon fire; it can also be used to manipulate fire. Therefore if you are in a situation where you need to escape flames or if you need to create flames it is extremely useful. Then there is *Amail*. This incantation puts a barrier between you and a foe, and as with all the powers of the staff this enchantment will use whatever is to hand whether it be the wind or the trees. When accomplished you can also combine words so that you can determine what form they will take. By combining the two words I have told you, you could create a barrier of fire between yourself and a foe, very formidable.'

Tom was now moving his staff through the air obviously imagining wielding such power.

'Nevertheless,' Torean added quickly, conscious that he did not want Tom trying to run before he could walk. 'You should not try such things at this stage. Also, if possible, I would rather keep you out of sight when the Sheriff comes. At the moment you are a bigger asset to me if they do not know you are here at all.'

'Why?' Tom asked, feeling slightly hurt.

'Well,' said Torean, sensing Tom's insecurity. 'This isn't the final battle, and if Lady Naithara doesn't know you exist it could help us in the long term. Plus, young man, right now I would spend more time worrying about you trying to wield your staff than protecting the farm. If you were to try combining incantations without the proper guidance you could end up destroying the place yourself. '

'I understand,' Tom said, feeling a mingled feeling of disappointment and relief. He wondered what they were about to face, and despite his initial feeling of annoyance he felt shamefully relieved that he would not be expected to join this fight.

Having completed their task of protecting the farm they both went back inside the house and Torean wasted no time showing Tom a secret entrance to the hay loft in which he could hide safely from the coming enemy.

Dawn was fast approaching when Aneirin returned from Wilson's farm looking exhausted.

'Thank you, son,' said Torean, patting him on the shoulder as he fell into one of the chairs around the kitchen table.

'Don't worry, granda,' Aneirin said, wearily touching the old man's arm.

'Did Wilson ask questions?' Torean asked warily.

'He was curious why we needed his help with the animals,' Aneirin said, shrugging his shoulders. 'But when I said that we may have to go away for a while, and that I couldn't tell him any more than that, he seemed to accept it.'

'He's a good friend,' Torean said thoughtfully. 'Although I'm sure he will not rest until he knows exactly what is going on. Hopefully today will be a success and you can fetch the animals back tomorrow.'

Aneirin feigned a smile at this thought, although he was not convinced that things would go so well. He also sensed in his grandfather's over hopeful tone that he did not believe this either.

Torean now gathered the three, 'I think we have done all we can tonight. For now we should all get back to bed and try to catch up on some sleep. If they come, the wards Tom and I have placed around the farm will soon alert us.'

Too weary to argue with the old man they all trooped off back to bed to try to catch up on some much needed sleep.

Tom found himself lying awake for a long time after the others had all gone off to sleep. Although he was exhausted from their exploits the night before, he could not help himself from worrying about whether the protective charms he had help Torean place around the farm would be effective. He did not doubt Torean's ability, but worried whether his own weakness could lose them the advanced warning they would desperately need. Could he be sure he would know the warning when it came? What if his sign was subtle and he slept through the whole thing? Concluding that this was too big a risk he rose from bed and went to sit in the living room. He decided to try to stay awake and keep watch so that he could warn the others if trouble arrived before they were ready. He sat looking into the low burning flames of the fire. *What would a great knight do? He would keep watch over his camp and protect his friends. That is what I must do now.* Despite his good intentions, as the embers of the fire slowly burned out, his eyes grew as heavy as lead. He tried several times to force them open, but tiredness soon overcame him and he dozed off.

His dreams were full of flashing images. He could hear people screaming in fear and saw heavily armed men destroying the farm. In his dream he was trying to run, but no matter how hard he tried, his legs would not move. His legs rooting him to the spot like he was trapped in mud, he felt a great sense of panic, a sense of hopelessness. Then he suddenly felt a warm feeling come over him, everything was going to be alright. This made his dreams subside and he passed into a deep dreamless sleep. He felt safe again.

As Tom had slept Torean and Adaira had woken and seeing him, Adaira placed a blanket over him in his chair. 'Poor lamb. It looks like he decided to try to keep watch over us,' she said, stroking his hair the same way she had her son.

'My dear,' Torean said sombrely. 'I fear that today we'll need God himself to watch over us.'

Adaira reached out and grasped Torean's hand firmly. 'I think you are right Torean. But God is on our side, so what do we have to fear?'

He squeezed her hand in return. He was so grateful for her strength. In a strange way it felt like a great burden had been lifted from him because he was no longer expected to do this alone. He hadn't felt this since he had fought with his son at his side. He hoped that this saga would not end the same way his son's chapter had.

Chapter Five
The Phoenix Flight

Tom thought it only felt like he had dozed off minutes earlier when he woke, but it had been several hours since they had all gone off to bed. Confused, he lifted off the blanket covering him and stiffly rose from his chair next to the fire place. It was now mid afternoon and Adaira had decided that he and Aneirin dare not sleep any longer. They arose and ate a meagre meal since a lot of essentials were now packed up in case they would have to make a hasty escape. During this time the group barely spoke to one another, and the room felt like there was a heavy fog hanging over it. They were all gripped by the fear of what was to come.

The afternoon passed very slowly during which time Torean tried to break the tension by talking to them of where they should meet in the hills if they were separated. 'Adaira and Aneirin know well enough where Longford's Pass is, boy,' he said to Tom. 'I shall need to show you so that you know where you are going.'

'While I have spent my time with you feeling as though I know absolutely nothing,' Tom said, finding himself laughing, 'I too know how to get to Longford's Pass. You forget that while I am not from your time, I am still a MacKay from Cairn Holme.'

The old man smiled. 'Yes, my boy, I do forget that you are still one of us. Well, at least we know where we are going.'

Adaira could not take comfort in this. 'It is all well and good that we all know the hills surrounding us, but are you sure it will come to that? We have done no wrong; I cannot see that the Sheriff will be able to find a way to remove us from our home.'

'Adaira,' said Torean kindly. 'You speak the truth, we have done nothing wrong. But if the Sheriff has been seduced by Lady Naithara he will not care about right and wrong. He will only care about serving his mistress. We, or I, am a threat to her success.'

Tom felt extremely nervous. This was the first time that he would come into direct contact with the evil which Torean had described. Again he felt guilty that he was secretly relieved the old man did not expect him to be involved in any form of combat. He didn't know what to expect from the Sheriff's visit. *Would he use the evil powers which Torean had talked of? Would he march to their home like an evil mage from one of Tom's stories, bent upon wreaking havoc and destruction?*

Several hours passed, and as the sun began to set Tom found himself feeling like there was no real danger at all. He had been waiting so long, that he had begun to feel that no evil would ever come. Watching the light change in the room with the early evening sun; his vision of evil warlocks marching to bring about their destruction seemed childish. Just then he began to feel a strange buzzing sensation in his head, it was the wards they had put in place the night before. He jumped and looked outside. There were people approaching the farm from a distance carrying torches. He was amazed by the distance the protective spells covered.

Torean had also sensed this and stood by him. 'Go to your place and hide, I will warn the others.'

Tom, now feeling a fear which made him want to be sick, nodded, turned without saying a word and went to the corner to fetch his staff. He knew that he may need it with him in case of an emergency. Up in the hayloft above the cottage was a good vantage point; he could hear both inside the house and out because of a vent in the roof. He could also partially see outside through the small opening. He felt slightly frustrated by the prospect of simply hiding away and watching events unfold, as it also made the situation seem slightly unreal. His fear had made him feel almost numb, as the scene outside began to unfold he felt more like he was watching a scene from a film rather than crouching in fear for his life only feet away. It was almost like sitting on the edge of his seat reading an exciting chapter. He could feel fear for the characters involved, but did not feel like he was one of them.

Downstairs Torean spoke with Adaira first. 'It is time,' he said. She looked pale, but said nothing and went to stand by her son in the hallway. The three were all ready and the house looked as normal as possible when the door was knocked loudly.

'Torean, open up,' a voice said from outside. 'This is the Sheriff, Michael MacDonald.'

Torean slowly got up and opened the door. Trying to look casual, he leant on his staff like a wizened old man. 'Sheriff, what can I do for you this evening?'

The Sheriff didn't flinch even though he knew that the old man was playing with him. Looking very serious he said, 'I believe you know why I'm here. There have been further allegations of illegal activity on your farm and I have a warrant to search your property.'

'I feel we are becoming friends, you and I,' said the old man sarcastically. 'These visits are becoming so regular, and there is no more illegal activity going on here now than there was the first time you called.'

The Sheriff didn't smile, instead he signalled to the four men he had with him to enter the property. Torean stood aside and let them enter, motioning for the men to look around wherever they saw fit. The Sheriff looked around the cottage from the doorway. 'While we have previously had reports of poaching, today's visit regards a more serious matter,' he said sternly.

'Oh?' Torean enquired, curious about what they could have concocted to try to escalate matters.

'Yes,' the Sheriff replied, smirking as he pushed past the old man into the house. 'Some items were stolen from the Laird's house in the past couple of days and we have reason to believe that your lovely grandson was involved.'

Torean knew that Aneirin had been no-where near the Laird's house for over a week. Since the situation with Lady Naithara had been deteriorating, he had found ways to avoid sending him there on errands.

The Sheriff disappeared into kitchen area. He quickly reappeared from the shadows holding some silverware aloft which had the Laird's family crest upon them.

Aneirin started to protest, but one look from his grandfather told him to hold.

'Look, Sheriff,' Torean said, having now dropped his pretence of being a feeble old man. 'We both know that you had that silverware on you when you entered this house. Why don't you tell us why you're really here?'

Torean could tell that the Sheriff's men were now slightly confused.

The Sheriff turned to Torean looking angry at any suggestion of wrong doing. 'I believe we both understand the situation,' he said, his blood boiling. He then turned to face his men. 'As thieves this family must have their farm confiscated. I will also be taking the boy for further questioning.'

'No! You can't!' Adaira cried out. She instinctively put her arm around her son.

Torean, stony faced, stepped in front of Aneirin. His voice now sounded very different to that of the old man who had opened the door. 'I think we both know that isn't going to happen,' Torean said. He then turned and made a gesture to Aneirin.

'Look, old man,' said the Sheriff stepping forward. 'Don't make this difficult. There are five of us and one of you. Are you going to take us all on?'

In one motion Torean raised his staff then slammed it off the stone floor, '*Buireadh!*' he shouted. There was an extremely loud bang and the cottage was immediately filled with smoke.

In the confusion which followed Adaira and Aneirin dropped to the floor. Putting their hands over their mouths to avoid suffocating in the smoke they crawled to the back of the cottage. Wasting no time, they crept out of the back door. As they stepped outside they had to put up their hands to shield their eyes from the sunlight which was so bright in comparison to the dark house filled with smoke. Aneirin had been smart enough to keep one of the horses *Onero* tied to tree outside. He was a strong and loyal beast and Aneirin had made sure that the horse was saddled and had their supplies on his back. The two moved swiftly as they needed to be on the horse quickly. 'Move!' Aneirin yelled.

'I'm right behind you,' Adaira said panting.

'Onero, my friend, we need your help,' Aneirin whispered, stroking the horse's mane. He quickly leapt onto the horse and pulled his mother up behind him. 'Heeya!' he shouted and gave the horse a kick to signal that they needed to move off quickly. The horse took off out of the farm gates at a tremendous speed. The wind rushed in their ears as they made their escape. Adaira couldn't help but look back towards the cottage fearful for those left behind.

The men had re-grouped from the confusion in the cottage and were running out of the cottage to stop Aneirin's escape. On foot they had no chance to stop the two of them on horseback. After watching Aneirin and Adaira fly past them and disappear into the distance, they ran back into the house to see the old man and the Sheriff struggling with one another.

'Don't just stand there staring you fools! Help me!' shouted the Sheriff.

One of the men grabbed a pan from next to the fire and hit Torean around the head with it. The blow made Torean lose his balance and fall to the floor. This allowed the Sheriff to switch positions with the old man and hold him down.

'I want this place burned to the ground!' the Sheriff screamed, absolutely livid.

His men momentarily looked from one to the other.

'Now, you fools!' he bellowed.

They quickly lit their torches in the fire and set the thatched roof alight.

The Sheriff made for the door with his men and slammed it shut behind them. His men barricaded the door and windows quickly to ensure that Torean would not escape.

Inside, Torean coughed and looked around himself in the darkness. He then turned and started making his way to the back of the house away from where the fire was spreading rapidly through the cottage.

Tom started towards the ladder from the hayloft as he heard the front door close behind the Sheriff. Adrenalin pumping through his veins, he decided to try using the word Torean had taught him to control fire. He somehow found the strength to control his power and made his way through the burning loft to the cottage below. He was totally blind and was relying on the staff to protect him from the rising flames. The loft was completely engulfed in smoke and Tom tripped over some tools which were stacked up on the floor. He had hurt his leg, but knew that he must keep going. By the time he made it down the ladder the entire cottage was full of smoke. Looking around frantically, he struggled to find Torean. Suddenly he noticed a light near the back of the cottage. It was a piercing blue which made it stand out against the darkness. Choking and spluttering he made his way blindly towards the light. Behind him a ceiling beam to the front of the house collapsed and sent debris flying everywhere. It was inches from where Tom had been standing only moments earlier. As it fell the blast knocked Tom to the floor. He raised his head and saw the blue light growing distant as the old man moved towards the back of the house. Crawling along the ground, he found Torean and grabbed his ankle. Torean helped Tom to his feet and taking his hand led him to the back of the cottage and into a hidden doorway which led into a dark tunnel. Tom was coughing and spluttering as they stumbled through the dark passage.

The two emerged from a hatch hidden in the undergrowth further down the garden. Torean helped Tom out of the hole and quickly covered over the exit so as not to reveal its whereabouts.

'What was that?' Tom asked, pointing to the tunnel they had exited from.

Torean turned to him and motioned for him to be silent. He let the light fade from his staff and slowly led Tom further into the undergrowth. They moved a short distance away from the house and waited. Torean pointed and Tom noticed that the Sheriff and his men were positioned strategically to try to ensure no-one escaped the cottage. He whispered in Tom's ear, 'We will have to remain here until they leave.'

They sat there for what felt like hours watching the cottage go up in flames. In a strange way Tom was surprised at how quickly the old house was destroyed. Eventually they saw the Sheriff and his men move off.

'Come!' shouted the Sheriff, motioning for his men to gather round. 'No-one could have survived that fire. We should head back.'

The men were looking from one to the other unsure about what had just taken place.

'Do not be troubled,' the Sheriff said to the group. 'Remember that this man was a criminal. We gave him every opportunity to come with us quietly. We had no choice.'

The men stood looking at one another in silence. Tom got the impression from the tone in the Sheriff's voice that he was trying to convince himself as much as the others. With that the group turned to head back towards the town. Torean, after ensuring that they had gone a safe enough distance, led Tom slowly through the undergrowth and onto a track leading into the hills.

After a short time Torean decided it was safe to talk turned to face Tom. 'I'm glad you found me, boy,' he said. 'I don't think I could have gone into the loft after you.'

'I remembered the word for controlling fire and used it to clear a path and find my way down. Did the others get away?' Tom asked.

'Well done! They did get away, thank God. We should set off now. This light won't last long. I believe that they got away safely; hopefully Adaira and Aneirin will be waiting for us at Longford's Pass. We can shelter for the rest of the night at least.'

They walked on in silence through the dusk, unable to make small talk because they were both so shocked by the day's events and tired from lack of sleep. After climbing up through the hillside they reached the clearing as night fell across the valley and Tom noticed a horse tied up outside a cave. They sped up, desperate to know that the others were alright. As they reached the cave entrance they saw that Adaira had a fire lit and looked to be preparing a meal. Aneirin stood up and ran to his grandfather.

'I'm so happy you're okay,' Aneirin sobbed, embracing the old man tightly. 'Mother and I feared the worst when we saw the smoke rising from the farm.'

At this Adaira simply looked up. 'Is our home destroyed, Torean?' she said. Her eyes had the look of one who was completely in shock.

He nodded. He knew that if he said the words aloud he may not keep his composure. He could not quite believe what had happened himself.

Tom, sensing the unease between the members of the family and feeling a little awkward, spoke next. 'We were lucky to get out alive. I think the Sheriff wanted Torean to die in the fire. He wasn't interested in arresting him.'

'The boy is right,' Torean added. 'He is more consumed than I thought, and the fact that he has now involved Aneirin means we have to stick together. I doubt he will go directly to his mistress this evening. If that is the case, we have until tomorrow before they realise that I am not dead. We will need to move around the hillside and make camp at different places throughout the valley.'

Adaira looked crestfallen at the thought. 'How long shall we be living like this, Torean?'

'Don't worry, my dear,' he said softly. 'They shall make their move upon the next new moon which is roughly nine or ten days from now. We must be here in Cairn Holme for the final attack. Until then they will keep looking for us. For tonight we should try to enjoy our meal and get some rest. The coming days will not be easy, but we are strong.' As he said this he put a hand on Aneirin's shoulder, showing his belief in his family. The boy returned the gesture and gave his mother a smile to try to reassure her.

While Adaira finished preparing the meal Tom and Torean walked around the camp using *rabhadh* to place wards around them as they had done the previous night with the farm.

The four settled down to a stew which Adaira had made using the supplies they had managed to take with them from the cottage. None of them felt particularly hungry, although the act of doing something which was normal and routine seemed to help them come back to themselves.

After their meal Tom stood looking out over the valley. The cottage was no longer alight, but he could still see smoke rising from where the house had been. He didn't think he would get much sleep and he found his mind wandering back to that night at the farm. *Who was the mysterious lady who had provided their warning? Were they going to be able to survive for nine days in this hillside alone?* He felt terrified and for the first time since he had achieved control of his power, he wished for his grandfather. He understood now why his granda had said he would need to wait until he was older to learn the ways of the staff. After everything they had been through Tom felt like nothing more than a confused child.

As they lay down to bed Torean sat by the fire, he could tell that they were all shocked by the day's events and were unlikely to get to sleep easily. As an act to help both he, as well as the group he leaned back and sang a song in a soft lilting voice.

In years gone by when times were dark,
I often thought upon my home.
The place I lay my head to dream,
the place my heart is free to roam.

My love is far from where I lie,
though I can see her bonnie smile.
For she is close within my heart,

within slumber deep tis ne'r a mile.

So home is never far away,
For in my sleep I see her eyes.
So in my dreams I see my home,
I see the hills and glens arise.

Torean stopped singing and lay down to his bed, a tear rolling down his cheek. The song had allowed them all to grieve for the losses of the day.

Tom also believed that it had given them hope. While they may have lost the farm, they would never lose their home. They would rise to this challenge, and once they had defeated the evil which had driven them to such extremes, they would return and rebuild the life they had previously lived. As Tom dozed off to sleep he shed a tear for his own home and his family so far away. In his dreams that night he was back with his grandfather and mother. He could not speak with them. He could see them sitting around the table in his grandfather's garden laughing. Yet, no matter how hard he tried he was stuck, unable to reach them or make them hear him. It felt like he was looking at them through a screen, watching them from far away.

Chapter Six
The Ears that Hear

The Sheriff lay in his bath in front of a roaring fire soaking after the trials of the day. Staring at the flames, his mind flashed back to the cottage ablaze. As he lathered up some more suds he didn't want to have to think about what he had done. He rose from the bath and drying himself crossed the room to his bed. The picture of his father on his bedside table seemed to be staring at him. Putting the picture face down, he stood, lifted his clothes from a chair next to the bed and put them into the bath water. His clothes and hair had smelled strongly of burning wood and smoke. While he was easily led, the Sheriff had until now always been in essence a good man. In order to distract him from the thought that he had knowingly burned a man alive, he fanaticised about what Lady Naithara would say when he told her his good news. He imagined her running into his arms and him kissing her passionately. He found that such thoughts were enough to remove images of the burning building. *She is worth anything,* he thought. With such deluded fantasies he changed into his night clothes and went to bed.

The next morning he hurriedly completed the tasks required of him and retired back to his quarters to change into his best clothes. He wanted to look perfect for Naithara. He looked into the mirror and thought that he didn't look at all like he had been involved in a fire the previous day. The Sheriff had always been quite a cowardly man with a somewhat gentle face. If he hadn't been so pleased with himself he would have noticed the slight change around his eyes. Where they had once been big open brown eyes there was now a slight cruelty around the edges. With his head full of thoughts of love and passion he left his abode and headed to the Laird's estate.

He was excited as he walked up the long gravel drive to the large house. The air seemed sweet to him and he stopped to smell the flowers and looked out over the lake at the front of the house. All thoughts of guilt and insecurity were gone. As he rang the bell his mind drifted back to thoughts of Lady Naithara throwing herself into his arms. He was so engrossed in lustful thoughts that he didn't notice Lizzy open the door.

'Can I help you, Sheriff?' she enquired.

He started when he saw her. 'Ah,' he stuttered. 'I'm here to see the Laird and Lady Naithara with news of the utmost importance.'

Lizzy ushered him into the reception room and went to fetch the Laird.

Lady Naithara had come out of her room at the sound of the door bell. 'Who was at the door, Lizzy?' she enquired.

'It was Sheriff Macdonald,' she replied, climbing the stairs to the Laird's study. 'He wishes to see yourself and the Laird regarding some important news.'

At this Naithara pushed past Lizzy and went down the stairs.

Lizzy took a deep breath to calm herself at Naithara's rudeness and went to the Laird's study door. She knocked on the door and entered. 'My lord, Sheriff MacDonald is here to see you with important news. Lady Naithara has already gone down to greet him.'

The Laird who could see the look of annoyance on Lizzy's face simply smiled and shook his head. 'Don't worry. That girl is too nosy for her own good. But she only does so in order to protect me. Young ones these days just don't understand how things aught to be done. Apart from you that is.' At this the Laird rose from behind his large desk and went down the stairs.

Lizzy advised that she would run along and fetch them some tea.

As the Laird entered the reception room he noticed that Naithara was almost bursting with excitement while Sheriff MacDonald was trying to suppress a grin. The Laird was puzzled by their happy expressions. 'What's all this?' he questioned. 'This is a serious matter I understand? Was I mistaken?'

'Yes, a grave business,' the Sheriff replied, suddenly changing his demeanour and looking more like a professional than a love sick school boy. 'It regards the MacKays. I was informed that the boy was involved in stealing. When I went to arrest him he fled the scene. There was a struggle and during the confusion the house went up in flames. My men and I managed to escape, however we believe that Torean MacKay was burned alive.'

The Laird dropped into his chair in shock. 'My God!' the colour had drained from his face. 'This is appalling!'

'Yes,' Naithara interrupted looking smug. 'I told you they were trouble, uncle.'

'No!' the Laird exclaimed, looking at her as though he could not comprehend her response. His expression looked like he wasn't sure who she was. 'I find it appalling that a good man is now dead. How heavy handed were your men for there to have been such an outcome? What did the boy even steal?' He couldn't take in what he was hearing.

'Well,' responded the Sheriff. 'I have the utmost confidence in my men. There was no heavy handed behaviour on our part. Also with regard to the stealing, if you must know it was silverware from this very house. We found the goods at the cottage. It was an open and shut case.'

The Laird, still in shock, looked even more puzzled. 'Silverware… I have no memory of anything being reported missing?'

At this Naithara once again interrupted and said in a very forthright voice, 'Uncle, it was I who reported the crime. I did not wish to worry you and thought it could be dealt with quickly.'

'Worry me?' the Laird said, bemused. 'It is my property. I would ask that you do not take such liberties in future my dear. While I understand your intentions, you should know your place.'

Suddenly Naithara had become aware that Lizzy was hovering in the corner taking a great deal of time to arrange the tea cups. 'Lizzy, dear,' she said looking over at her impatiently. 'I will take care of that, you run along.' Naithara knew she did not need the staff gossiping about such affairs.

As Lizzy left the room she felt like she was going to faint. She couldn't believe what she had heard. She also thought to herself that she was not aware of any missing silverware. It had been used for the dinner with the Sheriff two nights before and Aneirin MacKay had not been to the house in over a week.

Back in the reception room the Laird was enquiring after Adaira and Aneirin. 'Where are the boy and his mother now?'

'When the boy absconded his mother went with him,' the Sheriff replied. 'I suppose that she could even be declared an accomplice.'

'Well!' the Laird exclaimed. 'If you can prove your charges against the lad, all well and good, but that woman has gone through enough. She does not need further pain. In fact... can you charge the boy with theft if I do not wish to press charges?'

'Uncle!' Naithara burst in. 'It is a crime which I reported!'

'Well, young lady,' her uncle said angrily, 'it was not your property to report stolen in the first place.'

Naithara was livid at the Laird's scolding tone but sat in silence.

'As such,' said the Laird now turning to the Sheriff. 'I appreciate your "enthusiasm", however, in future I would hope that you will not arrest people for crimes against myself when I have no knowledge of it. The same goes for you, Naithara. I understand that you only do these things out of fondness for me, even so, if you had consulted with me on this matter earlier perhaps a good man would not now lie dead.'

By this point the Sheriff was also livid at being treated like a naughty child. 'As you wish,' he said curtly. He then rose from his chair. 'Now if you can excuse me, my Lord, I have other business to attend to.'

'Of course,' said the Laird gesturing towards the room door. 'I am sure Naithara would be happy to see you out.' The Laird rose from his chair and left the room without another word. He could not believe what he had just heard. Torean MacKay had been a close friend of his since childhood and now he was dead. Dead for no better reason, than that of petty theft. That was also something which he could not imagine young Aneirin to be capable of. *I have known the boy all his life. Could he do this?*

Lady Naithara led the Sheriff out. Before she opened the door she turned, pressing herself against the wood. 'Do not let such foolish words perturb you,' she said softly. 'While the boy may be free it was Torean MacKay who was the threat. You have proven yourself most capable, Michael. If you would like to understand more about what we can achieve together, meet me at midnight in the clearing beyond the aviary.'

The Sheriff merely nodded excitedly as Naithara opened the door and ushered him out. As he walked away from the house he felt like he was dancing down the street. In his head he fantasized about what he was sure would be a romantic rendezvous in the clearing. It had all been worth it. How could he have doubted her affection for him? That night it would be the two of them alone, talking and deciding how they would rule the estate once the old man was gone. Now completely carried away, 'Laird,' he said aloud. He thought to himself, *I always knew I was destined for greater things.*

* * *

Unbeknown to Naithara, Lizzy had overheard her conversation with the Sheriff while being very conscientious about polishing the banister in the hall. As Naithara went upstairs to her room thinking that everything she wanted was happening as expected, Lizzy was thinking of a way to get to the clearing at midnight undetected.

That night after finishing her chores for the evening and checking that neither the Laird nor Lady were in need of anything else, she hurried up the stairs to her room in the attic to prepare for the task which lay ahead. It was ten to eleven. Quietly closing her room door behind her she crept over to her small cupboard in the corner and retrieved her full length travelling cloak. It had been a gift from the Laird a year earlier, since she often had to go on errands to other towns and villages for him. It had been an old cloak which had belonged to the Laird's late wife, but Lizzy had been grateful for such a generous gift. She loved the way it flowed around her; she had never owned something so grand. Donning the black cloak she quietly descended the stairs to her usual exit at the back of the scullery. Moving quickly and quietly through the dark grounds she arrived at the clearing at around eleven fifteen. It was around a quarter of a mile north of the main house. Looking around herself hurriedly, she picked a tree close by and decided to climb it so that she could hide out of sight among the branches. She was cold and terrified, but could not think of any other way to get further information regarding what the Lady was doing. It was awkward to climb the tree wearing her cloak, yet it gave her the best protection against being seen. She found a branch halfway up the tree which seemed comfortable enough and settled to await the arrival of Naithara and the Sheriff. It was a chilling place. Surrounded by a circle of trees, it was private, but was strangely lit by the moon above. The birds, now asleep, left the place eerily quiet. After a time, when her body stopped shivering, she started dozing off. With a shake, she forced herself to stay awake. *Lizzy*, she thought, *you cannot afford to lower your defences at a time like this.*

Lady Naithara was the next to arrive in the clearing some forty minutes later. She lit torches and placed them in a circle, then disappeared into the shadows to await her guests. Soon Lizzy noticed figures appearing out of the darkness to gather in the circle. There were six people standing among the group when Naithara made her entrance appearing slowly from the shadows. 'My, friends, thank you for coming,' she said in a booming voice. 'We have made a great step forward in our mission. I would like to thank those of you who have been patient waiting for this moment to come.' The men looked around the group nodding in satisfaction. 'Tonight I will welcome a new addition into our band,' Naithara continued. 'It is thanks to him that we are now in a position to tell my master some very exciting news.' At this the Sheriff appeared in the clearing. He was the only one who was not cloaked and he looked rather confused. The expression on his face was a mixture of bewilderment and disappointment. He was sheepishly hiding some flowers behind his back.

'Welcome, Michael,' Lady Naithara said, taking no notice of his confusion. 'You have proven yourself worthy to join our group. Let me introduce you to our friends.'

One by one the people removed their hoods. Lizzy had to stop herself from gasping aloud when she saw who stood in the clearing. Among the group were the most important people in the county: people like the Lord Provost and the local Church Minister. She even saw the local butcher Ruthven McDermott among the group. He was a large man with a limp, but had fists which could floor a giant. The Lord Provost stood at Naithara's right hand. She couldn't help but think that he was her apprentice. He had a definite air that this was what he was born for. He was a proud peacock of a man, and Lizzy was now sure of the fact that he was no good. She had always feared him, but had thought that he intimidated her because of his position. He was a man who looked at you like a cat looked at a mouse. She noticed that this was how he looked at the Sheriff and she somehow felt sorry for him.

'As I promised,' said Naithara, now addressing the group, 'we are now in a position to call upon my master and inform him that the last obstacle to his rise to glory has been removed. I know that you have all waited for this as long as I have, and soon with all your help we will take control of such great power that none shall be able to stand in our way.'

Michael couldn't help himself, 'Lady, what power is this?' he said. 'You make it sound almost supernatural?'

Lady Naithara laughed. 'Well of course it is. You must have felt the power between us lately. We are all drawn to the banner of power.' She then turned away from the confused Sheriff to address the group as a whole. If he was such an idiot then he at least had served his purpose. 'Now, I will waste no more time. I have longed to be in the presence of my master for too long. If you will all join in the chanting he will use your collective energy to sustain him. 'Hamish,' she said turning to the Provost. 'Can you please lead the group?'

'Of course, my Lady,' the Provost said with a subservient bow.

The group began to chant *Nathura Gathera* to a strange rhythm. At this Naithara raised her hands and chanted atop of their voices, calling for Eiric to come forth. The winds rose and soon that same heavy atmosphere which had been in Naithara's room came over the clearing. It swirled like a whirlpool until the entire clearing was enveloped with its stench. Lizzy had to cover her mouth to stop herself from retching.

'You called me?' a deep voice said. 'I hope it was not in vain, Naithara?'

'Yes, my Lord,' she responded eagerly. 'I have great tidings. We have removed Torean MacKay, the last obstacle to your ascendance.'

'Really?' said the voice almost sarcastically. 'Can you tell me how this was done?'

'Yes, my Lord,' she said bursting with excitement. 'Our new recruit, the Sheriff here, had him burned alive in his home.'

The words and the joyous way Lady Naithara said them, combined with the nausea already caused by the atmosphere, made Lizzy physically sick inside. She raised a hand automatically to her nose as though stopping herself smelling something foul.

'Is this a joke?' Eiric said angrily. 'Do not play such games with me, Naithara,' he boomed. 'He lives still! Are you so incompetent that you do not ensure a task is carried out fully? Did you see a body?'

'Well...' Naithara hesitated, 'I did not actually see a body, but Michael assured me that he and his men stayed at the farm to ensure no-one could have escaped.'

'Where is this *Michael* of whom you speak?' Eiric said, in a voice so full of acid it would have made the bravest man quake like a frightened animal.

Michael, who had never been more terrified, simply stood there struck dumb. His head felt fuzzy, like he was listening to the scene from a distance. His mind was trying to protect itself from what he was hearing. He had completely shut down.

Lady Naithara glared at him. 'Speak, maggot!'

This broke the spell and brought him crashing back to the clearing. He was starting to see that Naithara did not feel the same affection for him as he did for her. 'I am here,' he said feebly, feeling bile rise to his mouth.

'Well,' said Eiric, 'how thorough were you and your men?'

'Erm,' Michael replied, unsure of where he was supposed to direct his answer. 'We waited for over an hour as the farm burned to ensure that no-one had left the building.' As he spoke he looked upwards, directing his voice into the night air.

'You obviously do not understand who you are dealing with,' Eiric said impatiently. 'He is not an ordinary old man. He has great power. Did you destroy his staff?'

'His staff?' Michael stammered, completely confused. 'No-one mentioned that it was of any importance my... Lord.' The word stuck in his throat. 'I...'

'Enough!' Eiric shouted, 'Naithara, I hold you responsible for this. You should not send a blithering idiot to carry out such an important task. Torean MacKay still lives. I can feel his sickly goodness in the air as we speak. You must go after him and destroy him. Most importantly you must destroy his staff. The time until the new moon rises grows short. I expect you to have this problem eradicated before then, or our chances of success are greatly diminished.'

'My Lord...' Naithara tried to interject.

'I do not want excuses, Naithara. I will speak with you alone.' All of a sudden everyone in the clearing froze; it was as though Eiric had frozen time. Even the flames in the torches stood perfectly still. Naithara was the only one still moving. Eiric obviously wanted what he had to say next, to be for her ears only. There was one other creature in the clearing who had not been frozen by Eiric's power, and that was Lizzy. She sat petrified in her tree above the group listening to every word. She was afraid to breathe in case they heard her, the silence was absolute. Her heart was thudding in her chest. To her it seemed like someone shouting *over here, over here!*

Suddenly it was broken. 'There is a word which you must use to kill Torean, this is *Bas*. Use it carefully Naithara, the word commands great power. If it is used incorrectly, or by one who does not have the control to channel it, it can bounce back upon the caster. I need you to take care of this personally, Naithara. The time for trusting others has passed.'

The clearing began to move again. 'Thank you, my Lord,' Naithara said bowing her head. With that the presence was gone. Everyone in the clearing seemed visibly relieved.

Lizzy gasped for breath, trying quickly to steady her breathing. She did not want the men to notice her in the tree, but in her terror she had forgotten to breathe as Eiric had delivered his final message to Naithara.

'Well, everyone, it would appear that Michael did not achieve his task as we had hoped. We will need to work together quickly to smoke them out. I know that they will stay within the valley, the old man dare not leave else we strike. Sheriff, you have a chance to redeem yourself. I need you to find Torean MacKay and bring him to me. Speak to my colleagues and formulate a plan, I wish to hear from you by sundown tomorrow with your progress.' With that Naithara strode out of the clearing and did not look back. 'This time, do not forget his staff!' she shouted as she walked away.

All faces turned towards the Sheriff. 'Well... I suppose we had best get to work,' he said, uncomfortable at being the focus of the group's attention again. 'Unfortunately it will be difficult for me use my official resources to seek out the pair, as the Laird has made it clear that he does not wish them prosecuted. I will need you all to help me in this task. I suggest that you go home and consider where you would take refuge within the valley. We will meet at dawn tomorrow to discuss how to begin the search.'

The gathered men muttered amongst themselves. They were not happy to be following the Sheriff's lead when he had been so unsuccessful the last time, especially the Provost. Despite this, no-one spoke with any other ideas, and with that the group broke up.

Lizzy could not believe what she had heard. She knew that the Lady had been involved in something untoward, but had no idea that it was this evil. She sat in the tree for half an hour after everyone else had left to ensure that she would not be noticed dropping from the tree. The rain had begun, and by the time she reached the house she was sodden. Upon entering the house she went straight to bed. She didn't sleep. Instead she tossed and turned in the dark thinking of how to approach this subject with the Laird. She knew one thing; there was no time to lose. She would have to move tomorrow morning, before Torean and his family were harmed. The whole situation felt unreal. How could this be happening in Cairn Holme? Her disbelief was mingled with a great sense of relief that Torean was still alive. She would have to move if that was to remain so. As she pulled her pillow over her face and tried to blank out the fear, she could not believe that so much of what she had believed to be the reality of her existence in Cairn Holme had been a lie. The safe rural community where she had been born and raised was actually the home of vile creatures like Naithara and Eiric. Not to mention it being defended by powerful *watchmen*, like Torean. She couldn't think of a better word. Did not want to use words like wizard or warlock, he was the man who had been a father to her since her own father's death. She tried to put these thoughts out of her head, tried desperately to get some sleep.

Chapter Seven
Alone in the Hills

After a discussion they had spent the next day at Longford's Pass. Torean had decided that it was safe enough for them to stay for one more night. He could tell from the fear in Adaira and Aneirin that if forced to move too quickly they may reach breaking point. This wasn't surprising given what had happened in the past couple of days. Tom had spent some time during the day trying to practise with his staff, but it was rather difficult in the cramped conditions.

That evening, the same night that Lizzy was hiding in the clearing, Tom was lying awake. He had struggled to sleep the night before; somehow the thoughts of his stories didn't help him now. He couldn't control this story himself and found that the uncertainty made him extremely restless. Tom was in an adventure that had a life of its own. He couldn't close the book and be okay, and knew that he would never look at the characters in his stories in quite the same way again. The boy hadn't realised how difficult it could be to be stuck in the middle of an adventure.

Suddenly he became aware of a movement among the trees. He felt a rush of panic, thinking that their enemies had found them, but then he realised that the movement was too low to the ground to be human. A few seconds later he saw a head pop out of the long grass. He couldn't believe his eyes; the creature was quite unlike any animal he had seen before. It was no taller than a small dog and had extremely large jet black orbs for eyes. Tom found it hard to tell if the large reflective surfaces were focusing on him. It slowly crept from the undergrowth and walked towards the place where Tom lay, peering in the dim light. Its movements were slow and awkward, like it wasn't meant to walk on land. It was creeping, arms bent, hoping not to be seen. As it came closer, by the dying fire light Tom could see that it was leathery and dark grey in colour. It walked on two legs, both of which seemed very short for its body. At the bottom of its stumpy legs, was a pair of large flat feet. Tom noticed that the creature's toes were webbed. They made a light slapping sound as they hit the earth. Its head also seemed out of proportion, it was shaped like an American football on its side and with large floppy ears that waggled steadily as it walked.

Tom began to sit up as it drew closer and for some reason he did not believe that the creature meant him any harm. His new found senses told him that the creature was not an enemy. However, as he moved it seemed to frighten the creature that started back several paces. The animal was frozen in a state of panic. Tom then stayed perfectly still hoping that this would show the creature that there was nothing to fear. After a few moments of tense silence it again began towards him once more.

Once it was within a few paces of where he lay, it looked up into his eyes. 'Shassy saw?' the creature said.

Tom wasn't sure how to respond.

'Shassy saw?' the creature then repeated.

'I can't understand you,' Tom said quietly, trying not to wake the others. As he spoke the saw the creature's face fill with terror. He tried his best to gesture to the creature not to be afraid, but it simply turned on its heels and fled, ears flapping wildly as it ran.

Tom quietly rose from his bed and walked towards the undergrowth. He spent several minutes rooting around trying to find the creature in the darkness, but it was gone.

Although Tom tried his best to be quiet, Torean opened his eyes and quickly had one hand on his staff. He then noticed it was Tom in the undergrowth, 'What are you doing, boy?' he asked groggily.

'Erm, nothing,' Tom said, feeling rather foolish somehow. 'I needed to go to the bathroom.'

'Back to bed with you!' the old man said grumpily as he rolled over. 'This is no time for creeping around.'

Tom contemplated waking Torean to tell him about what he had seen, but looking at the old man's back hunched among his bedding made him think better of it. He climbed back into his bed and tried to get to sleep. He could not stop thinking about the small creature. *What on earth was it? What was it trying to say?* He was frustrated that he had been unable to find out what the creature had wanted with him. Somehow he didn't think of it as an animal which had randomly wandered out of the bushes. It seemed like a creature which had determinedly wanted to communicate with him. It was not a coincidence. It was as though its strange words meant something.

As they awoke the next morning, Torean tentatively advised them that they would have to move on. They all felt rather down about the prospect of finding somewhere else in the lonely hills to take shelter. Grimly the four sat down to finish their meagre breakfasts and decide where it would be best to go next.

'It would be folly to stay here any longer,' Torean started. 'While Longford's Pass is well equipped for our needs, our enemy will currently be discussing where they believe we would hide. This place would be top of the list if I were thinking in the same manner.'

'Well where should we go?' Adaira asked downheartedly. 'Shall you have us dying of cold in the wilderness?'

'We will need to go somewhere they wouldn't expect,' Torean said, trying to be as patient as possible. 'Somewhere which will be hard to reach and will probably not provide the kind of shelter we require, but somewhere they would rule out,' Torean answered. He knew that this was not what they wanted to hear, but it was not going to be easy if they wanted to survive. Their best chance was to pick somewhere unlikely, that way they wouldn't be caught out by their enemies.

There was silence for a few seconds as the group tried to consider all the possibilities. Tom found himself thinking of a place. In spite of this, he wasn't sure whether they would think him mad for suggesting it. 'I have an idea,' he said plucking up his courage.

'Well, boy, said Torean hopefully. 'Out with it.'

'What about Devil's Ford?' he suggested, expecting to be shot down. When no-one spoke he continued, 'I've never been myself because I hear it's a treacherous climb, but no-one would volunteer to go there.'

'There's a reason for that,' Aneirin said sarcastically.

'No,' Torean interjected thoughtfully. 'The boy may be onto something. We will definitely struggle to get the horse through, but no-one would think we would dare such a steep climb through the hills. Plus it actually gives quite a good vantage point over the valley, although we would need to be careful lighting fires.'

'I'm not leaving Onero,' Aneirin said. 'Not now.'

'I wouldn't ask that of you, son,' said Torean. 'I don't think I could part with him myself. He is more responsible for saving us than he can know. If we can pull this off, Devil's Ford actually provides more cover than I would have thought we could hope for. There are caves which could provide us with shelter.'

'Torean, we will follow where you lead us,' Adaira said sternly. She had a tone in her voice which suggested she had set herself to this course and would have to see it through. Her tone also told her son that he had best do what his mother told him to do. Aneirin was a loyal boy, and knew when his mother was pulling rank. As such he did not pass any further remarks regarding their decision to start the difficult journey through the hills, even though he thought it completely insane.

With that they started to pack up their camp, and tried to remove any signs which would show that they had stayed there. Torean drew Tom aside from the group. 'I will now show you how we can use the power of the staff to disguise the fact that we have been here,' Torean said, gesturing to Tom to hold up his staff. 'The word we use is *cleith*. It is a word used to reveal things which are hidden. By the same token, it also if used properly, can hide things which would be seen.'

Tom looked confused.

'This is a good lesson for you to learn my boy,' Torean said smiling. 'It shows you that what the staff can do differs greatly depending upon your intention.' He motioned for Tom to raise his staff and said, 'Cleith.'

The winds began to rise around them and Tom closed his eyes and also said, 'Cleith.' When he opened his eyes again the winds were beginning to settle. The clearing was now clear of all foot and hoof prints. The area where they had burned a fire inside the cave mouth was now completely clear, and even had grass growing where the ash and wood had been. Tom smiled at the sight.

'Yes,' Torean said, seeing his face. 'It is amazing what we can do.'

When they started the long treacherous journey into the hills it was still just after dawn. Tom asked Torean if they could train as they walked. They had managed a short training session the day before, but it had been very cramped and they hadn't achieved much. The conditions of their present journey didn't make things any easier.

Adaira was riding Onero up front with Tom and Torean walking behind. Aneirin was walking to the back of the group hoping to listen into any conversation between Tom and the old man.

'Since we are struggling with this,' Torean said inquisitively, 'might I ask you what you were doing in the undergrowth in the dead of night?'

Tom felt flustered for a moment. 'I told you, I…'

'Boy,' Torean said smiling. 'We both know that you were not going to the bathroom. I could tell by the expression on your face when you saw me.'

Tom thought it was probably best to be honest with the old man, even if he would sound like a fool. 'I was struggling to sleep,' he began, 'when I saw something move among the trees. I know you will think I'm crazy, but a small creature appeared from the undergrowth. I cannot say what it was, for I have never seen its like before. It crept towards me and said something, but I could not understand what the words meant. They were not English, or Gaelic. When you teach me the words of power, I know them from my grandfather speaking Gaelic, but the words this creature used were completely foreign to me.' Tom was surprised to see that Torean did not look at him like he was a lunatic.

'Strange,' said the old man. 'Tell me, what did this creature look like?'

Slightly taken aback by the old man's response, Tom described the creature, 'It was small and grey. Its skin looked almost leathery, its legs were a little too short and it had an overlarge head.'

'Hmm,' said the old man thoughtfully. 'What did it say?'

'I can't remember,' said Tom racking his brains. 'The second word sounded like *saw*.'

'It sounds like you encountered a Nuggie, my boy,' the old man said smiling.

'What on earth is that?' Tom asked, confused.

'It's a water dwelling sprite. Quite why it would have been up in the hills I am not sure. Nevertheless it must have been drawn to you because of your staff. Magical creatures can sense these things. There are some springs and falls around here, so I suppose there could be Nuggie tribes in the area.'

'Tribes?' Tom asked, amazed.

'They do not commonly show themselves to ordinary people, but the staff makes you stand out. Think of yourself as a beacon. They tend to come forth when there is trouble coming. They will sense the dark forces at work as much as we do. What happened after it spoke to you?'

'I tried to tell it I couldn't understand what it was saying,' Tom replied. 'Although when I spoke it was startled and fled back into the undergrowth. I rose to see if I could find it and that was when you woke.'

'Well,' said Torean. 'Given the nature of our conversation and the fact that we are limited as to what we can do on the move, I should probably teach you more of our language, and hopefully as we pass various things upon our way you can try out your knowledge and control.'

'Thank you,' Tom answered. 'Right now, I think I could really use something to focus on. But how would it relate to our conversation?'

'Well, there are enchantments which can help you to communicate with animals and other creatures. If you had used your staff last night you may have understood what the Nuggie was saying to you.'

'Do you mean that there are other creatures out there attracted to magic?' said Tom curious.

'Yes,' said Torean nodding. 'There are your typical mystical creatures. We have wood fairies, they can be nasty little creatures. There are also Kelpies, a kind of water sprite you would do well to avoid.'

'Fairies,' said Tom, now feeling as though any logic he had managed to gleam from his current situation had just been turned on its head. 'What do the fairies look like?' He wanted to know so he could look out for them among the trees.

'Well,' Torean said thoughtfully. 'They are small with wings. They resemble a dragon fly, but if you look closely you can see that they are not. They are brown and green, as these colours allow them to be camouflaged among the trees.'

'Amazing,' Tom whispered, now wanting to see all the creatures which must have been hidden from his eyes before.

'Indeed,' Torean said smiling. 'For now we should get back to discussing our words of power. If you wish to communicate with any of these creatures you must know what you are doing.'

'Yes, and it may enlighten the rest of us with regard to how this whole thing works,' added Aneirin.

'Yes, boy,' said Torean, 'you're right. It would not do you any harm to hear us talk. If we survive this conflict, it has shown me that I must start your training with haste.'

'I'm glad you think so,' Aneirin said grinning.

Tom hadn't seen him seem so positive since they had met. It was almost as if he relished this challenge.

'Now, where to begin,' the old man said musingly. 'We have gone over the use of the word, amas. I used it as a tool for you to hone your control. It can be most useful in a battle situation, as it allows you to call any item you desire to you, as such, this could mean many things, even the weapon in the hand of one attacking you. Obviously this can be risky, but with the right control it can be invaluable. Also, I have told you of the word, to control and produce fire, srad and amail which can put a barrier between you and a foe. We have used the word *rabhadh* on more than one occasion now. We will need to use this word every time we stop to make camp. It is imperative that we are aware of anything breaching our defences. Also, I am not sure how much you heard, but when the Sheriff attacked I used the word *Buireadh*. This uses whatever is around you to create a distraction. In those circumstances it used the smoke from the fire to block the Sheriff's vision momentarily allowing Aneirin and his mother to escape.'

'So does that mean that in circumstances similar to ours right now it would use the wind or the trees to make a distraction?' Aneirin asked.

'Yes, son, exactly,' Torean said smiling. 'You would be most surprised at what can come to your aid when you are using the staff. It can be wonderful what nature provides. Even the animals are on our side. I was once rescued by a flock of gulls. Believe me, there is nothing more formidable than a flock of them swooping down at you!'

Tom noticed how proudly Torean looked at Aneirin for asking such a vital question. 'Will any of these words be able to defeat someone like Naithara?' Tom's question was asked doubtfully.

'No, boy, you are right,' Torean said, his brow furrowed. 'To defeat someone at the centre of so much evil will take something far greater. Although the words we have discussed could be invaluable when fending off her allies. You need to remember that we are not killers. People who are consumed with evil always forget that the simplest incantation can be their undoing. We are not here to learn about such occult arts. We are here to find their weaknesses. The best heroes always use defence as their attack.'

Tom suddenly felt like he was back in one of his favourite stories. One of his heroes would not have slain a man in cold blood. They would use defensive spells to best their enemies.

'There is one phrase which will remove her,' said Torean, knowing that he would have them in suspense. 'I would ask you to remember it, but never to use it until absolutely necessary. It is *Aicheadh Coirbte*. The words denounce evil, but it will probably take both of us saying these words for them to have the desired effect. That is why I summoned the power of MacKay. I could sense that the evil was too strong for me to take on by myself.'

What does the phrase do?' said Aneirin.

'Well,' the old man said, 'it basically draws any evil from the person you are fighting and leaves them without their strength. When this happens they either run or end up consumed by the force which has possessed them. Therefore if they die, it is not our doing. It is the evil power within them which brings about their end.'

'Well, hopefully I'll be enough.' Tom said despondently.

'Don't worry, my boy,' said the old man. 'You have shown great resilience and you must believe in yourself. Also, do not forget that the staff that you wield is very powerful, and our power does not rely upon strength but upon control. MacKays are not known as muscle bound heroes. Our success depends upon our wits. If you are smart of mind and quick of tongue you will prevail.'

Tom wasn't sure if this made him feel any better about the situation. *Would they get the chance to exorcise the evil within Lady Naithara? Or would they be hunted like animals where they slept among these lonely hills?* Yet again, Tom found himself wishing that his grandfather were with them. He was sure that like a hero in one of Tom's books, he would have defeated Lady Anstruther already.

They had now been walking for about an hour and a half and had reached the point where the road became more treacherous. 'Well, here we go,' Adaira said, dismounting Onero. 'Be sure of foot, my dear friend, we don't want to lose you now,' she said patting the horse on the rump kindly.

The horse seemed scared as though he knew where they were about to lead him. Torean approached the animal and raised his staff. 'Suaimhneach, Onero. We will ensure your safety,' he whispered. The horse seemed visibly calmer and started the climb up the narrow pathway which led to Devil's Ford.

'I imagine that's another word I should remember?' Tom asked Torean.

'Yes, *suaimhneach* calms animals. It is also the word which can be used to communicate with them, although when I say communicate I mean it in its crudest sense. You will not be having a conversation with them about the weather, but it allows you to understand emotions and see images. In cases such as our Nuggie, it should help you understand their speech because they use language.'

'Do you think I'll see it again?' Tom asked hopefully.

'Probably,' Torean replied. 'It sounds as though it was trying to communicate, so I would wager it will return at some point.

As Tom now started the climb at the back of the party he found himself thinking that he had a great deal to remember. He decided to use the climb to go back over the words in his head. He hoped that when they made camp he could try a few out depending upon their surroundings. Silence had fallen upon the group as they apprehensively climbed the steep path into the hills. It was a narrow path with a sheer drop on one side. One wrong footing could mean death, so concentration was paramount. Several times as they walked rocks gave way at the edge of the path and tumbled down to the gully below. The countryside surrounding them was beautiful, although treacherous. Tom stopped for a moment to catch his breath and looked out over the valley towards the village of Cairn Holme. The sky was a piercing blue and it made the green valley below look vibrant and alive. Tom could see the stream coming down from the mountains to the loch at the far end of the village. It was a peaceful morning and the water looked like a sheet of glass in the distance. Tom suddenly realised that the others had stopped to wait on him, and so picked up the pace to keep up.

Chapter Eight
A Problem Shared

Back at the Laird's house, Lizzy had been unable to sleep all night. She rose before dawn and decided that she would sneak back to the clearing where the band was due to meet. If the Laird was going to help her she had best know what the group intended to do about Torean. Deep down, she was also putting off the inevitable conversation with the Laird, because she was sure that he would think her utterly insane. While he was aware that his niece was precocious, he was hardly likely to believe that she was in league with an evil being and was plotting to commit murder.

She donned her cloak and headed out of the house while it was still dark. The birds had started to stir, but no-one else had yet risen for the morning. The path she followed on her route to the clearing was hidden in a thick morning mist. While this helped to keep her hidden as she walked, it also made the journey difficult as she couldn't see more than two feet in front of her. As she reached the clearing she climbed the same tree as before. Part way up the tree she caught her cloak on a branch. In a moment of panic she had to try to free the fabric, she was petrified that one of the men may arrive and see her in the trees. She had no choice but to rip her cloak in order to free it. As she did so, a small piece of fabric fell to the ground. She knew she didn't have time to go down to the ground to retrieve it and hoped that it would not be seen by any of the group. All she could do now was wait patiently.

Before long the Sheriff arrived in the clearing, he looked as though he too had not slept well the night before. His hair was unkempt and he had not changed his clothes from those he had worn the night before. Dark circles under his eyes, he was mumbling to himself. 'What to do… You got yourself into this, Michael… I didn't want to be involved in evil!' He paced around the clearing looking like an animal in a cage.

Soon more people began to arrive and as they gathered together it was clear that the Sheriff was not going to be allowed to control this discussion. The group had obviously decided, without him, that his previous incompetence made him unfit for the task. The Sheriff looked visibly relieved that he was not expected to mastermind any plan to resolve the situation.

The Lord Provost seemed to be taking the lead. 'Well, I believe it's obvious that from the position of the farm they would head to Longford's Pass. If Torean is as powerful as Lady Naithara believes, then he is unlikely to still remain there after all this time. However, I think we should all head for the Pass and search for any clues of their whereabouts. From there we can split into groups and search for them. We cannot afford to fail gentlemen; Lady Naithara will not be best pleased if we do not have good news for her this evening.'

'I agree, and if we are to proceed with this tactic,' the minister cut in, 'may I suggest that we all go home and dress as though we are a hunting party? If someone were to come across us they would be most suspicious, especially of the Sheriff here who looks like a crazed man who has been out all night.'

The Sheriff looked down at his waistcoat, trying to straighten his shirt and flatten his hair.

A man Lizzy did not recognise spoke at this point. 'Yes, I concur. I suggest we separate and meet back here in an hour. From there we can head for Longford's Pass. It should take no more than two hours to reach our destination. Hopefully, by lunchtime we will have made some positive progress.'

The Sheriff spoke sheepishly at this point. 'What if we are unable to stop him? He obviously wields great power if he can escape a burning building unharmed and un-noticed. Will we be capable of killing him?'

The Lord Provost responded in a voice which showed he was already tired of the Sheriff's company. 'Sir, those of us who have been party to Lady Naithara's cause for a little longer have more knowledge than you. We know of certain spells that can be used in a fight. Plus, I believe that we must have two goals. It would be good to have the man dead. Nevertheless, we must make our primary objective to destroy his staff. It is my understanding that without the staff he is as good as dead anyway. Besides, we have not been charged with killing him, since you failed so miserably last time. Lady Naithara asked that we bring him to her. I believe she wants to take care of this business personally.'

The crowd seemed to be murmuring in agreement. 'Well,' said the Minister. 'Shall we meet here at seven o'clock?'

The men all nodded to one another. The group did not linger and after a short time went their separate ways.

Lizzy terrified by the events she had witnessed stayed in the tree until she was sure that the group had completely cleared the area. Once she was sure that they had all left she quietly lowered herself from the tree and headed swiftly back towards the house. Lizzy was struggling to contain herself and as soon as she had left the clearing broke into a run. Again, she felt a mixture of fear and relief that Torean was still alive. Sweating by the time she opened the scullery door, she closed it behind her as quietly as possible and had to lean against the door for several seconds trying to catch her breath. She slid to the floor shaking and sat there on the cold stone for several minutes trying to calm herself. After she had slowed her breathing and stopped trembling, she removed her cloak and made to leave the room. It would not do to bump into someone in the house looking like she had already been out that morning, so nervously she crept up the stairs to her attic room.

After depositing her cloak she returned downstairs to start her chores for the day. Turning to look at the kitchen clock on the wall she saw that it was past six. She could not start her chores and pretend that nothing was happening. She would have to do something. Lizzy was unsure about waking the Laird at such an hour, but she couldn't see that she had any choice now. What more could she achieve on her own? As she tiptoed towards the old man's bedroom door and gently knocked, she realised she was shaking. She took a deep breath in order to steady herself and entered the darkened room. Afraid of waking him too suddenly, she approached his bedside and touched him on the shoulder. 'My Lord?' she said quietly.

'Hrrmmph?' was the only noise which came from the depths of the enormous bed. It was a large wooden four poster bed, and even the Laird, who was not a small man, seemed to be enveloped by its size.

'My Lord,' repeated Lizzy gently.

The old man grumped and rolled over to face her.

'It's Lizzy,' she continued, 'I apologise for waking you so early. I have something which I must discuss with you urgently.'

By this time the old man had begun to come round and slowly heaved himself into a sitting position in bed. 'Well, my dear,' he said groggily. 'What's all this? What in God's name can you have to tell me that cannot wait until a more gentlemanly hour?'

'Well, my Lord,' she said, now hesitant from his grumpy reaction, 'it regards your niece and the incident with the MacKays.'

'What's this?' The mention of Torean's family seemed to have sparked the old man's attention. 'Has something else happened?' he asked, now suddenly looking awake. 'Are Adaira and Aneirin okay?'

'They are fine, my Lord,' she said, trying not to panic him. 'Or they are fine for now, as far as I know.' said Lizzy, anxious to get to the point of her story. 'Nonetheless something has happened. What I am about to tell you will sound improbable, or even insane? I'm sure that you won't believe me, but I must tell someone. I could not live with myself if something happened to Torean and I had not told you.'

'Torean?' the Laird muttered, now thoroughly confused. 'My girl, I hate to tell you this, but Torean MacKay is dead.' The old man said gently and touched her hand.

'My Lord,' Lizzy said, beginning to feel frustrated and impatient. 'He is not dead. But if we do not act quickly he soon will be.'

The Laird looked deeply disturbed by Lizzy's words and the conviction she seemed to have. He had never seen her so full of passion.

'You see,' Lizzy said speaking quickly. She was determined to finish her story now she had begun. 'Your niece and the Sheriff planned the attack upon the MacKay family. Their intention was to kill Torean MacKay. But, I discovered last night that their mission was unsuccessful, and that shortly, a band of men will hunt him and his family in the hills to finish the job they started at the farm.' Lizzy seemed to visibly sag now that she had managed to get this statement out. Her cheeks highly coloured, it had taken a great deal of effort to tell another human being of what had been troubling her.

'Lizzy,' the Laird said in a voice which sounded both serious and also held a hint of pity. 'Those are very serious accusations. Even if what you say is true, why would my niece and Sheriff Macdonald wish to kill Torean MacKay? I realise that she believes him to be a poacher, but it is quite a leap to then suggest that she would wish him dead?'

'Sir,' said Lizzy, now trying desperately to make him understand, 'I believe that your niece has become involved in something which is far more serious than poaching. I have had suspicions about her behaviour for some time now. When I overheard her and the Sheriff talking, I decided to try to find out more in order to help Torean. The night after the Sheriff's visit with us for dinner, I left the house and crept to the MacKay farm so that I could warn Torean that they would be coming for him. He was not surprised, my Lord. Then, after the visit from the Sheriff when he advised you that Torean was dead, I...' Lizzy's voice broke. She wanted to get through this without getting upset. 'I overheard him and Lady Naithara arranging a meeting.' Lizzy was now becoming so worked up telling her story that she was close to tears.

'There, there, my dear, take your time.' The Laird held her hand, encouraging her to continue.

'I hope you understand,' she said, 'that because of the information I had become privy to, I had no choice but to go to the meeting myself to try to ascertain what was happening. I discovered that your niece is working with some very powerful people and together they summoned something, something evil.'

'Lizzy, forgive me,' said the Laird in as patient a voice as he could muster. 'But you must see that this all sounds a little far fetched.'

'I understand, sir,' she said bowing her head. 'I did not expect you to believe my tale straight away. I ask only that you dress and come with me now. The men of whom I speak are going to meet in the clearing by the aviary in less than half an hour. If you come and hear what they are saying, it will prove my story to be true.'

The old man looked concerned. While he found it extremely hard to believe, he too had felt a similar uneasiness around his niece since her return to Cairn Holme. 'Well, Lizzy, I will come with you. You must realise that if what you say turns out to be false, we shall need to seriously consider the consequences.'

'My Lord, I will gladly face any consequences you wish if I am speaking falsely. If I do speak untruly, I will be in need of a physic for I have heard and seen these things as truly as you hear and see me now. A great part of me wishes that none of this were true.'

With that the Laird ushered Lizzy from the room to give him privacy to wash and dress. He advised her that he would meet her downstairs as soon as possible. He quickly dressed and hobbled down the stairs muttering that his bones had still to wake up, and that no man should be dragged from his bed at such an ungodly hour. Then together they headed out through the back as Lizzy usually did when leaving the house alone.

As they reached the clearing, Lizzy ushered them to hide behind some boxes near the aviary. It was slightly further away from the clearing than the tree in which she had previously hidden, but she knew that the old man was not of an age where climbing trees was a good idea. A small sparrow was fluttering above their heads and singing to them excitedly. Lizzy tried to shoo the bird away but he kept circling the pair. 'Away you!' she shouted in a loud whisper.

They were not long in the clearing when some of the men began to arrive. As planned they were dressed as though they were going hunting for the day and muttered to one another in voices too low for Lizzy and the Laird to make out.

The Laird turned to Lizzy, 'These men are dressed for a hunt,' he whispered. 'Are you sure you were not mistaken when you heard them talk earlier? This is very serious Lizzy.'

'My Lord,' said Lizzy in hushed tones. 'They are dressed for a hunt, but not the sort you would usually embark upon. Hopefully this bird will not stop you from hearing their plans.' She did not say another word and faced the group, eager for them to say something which would make their intentions clear to the Laird. She kept scowling at the bird who flitted around them, at best he would stop them hearing what the men were saying. At worst he would end up giving away the position they were hiding in.

'We will depart in a couple of minutes,' the Provost said. 'If our friend Sheriff MacDonald is tardy he can explain his actions to Lady Naithara tonight. We do not have time to waste gentlemen. You would do well to remember our discussions earlier. Remember, if you cannot eliminate the man, you must at least destroy his staff. Without this, he is powerless.' He was an evil looking man. With slicked back dark hair and an overly groomed moustache, he looked like he greatly enjoyed his position within the community, and not for the right reasons. He had an odd obsession with time keeping and greatly enjoyed beating his servants if he thought they had been tardy bringing him his afternoon tea.

Suddenly Sheriff MacDonald then came running into the clearing looking very flustered. 'My apologies, gentlemen,' he attempted to say, bent over double and huffing loudly. 'I was detained by some official business. Shall we be off?' Clutching his side, he couldn't recall having a stitch like this since he was a boy. He hated how this situation made him feel. It was like being back at school, when you knew that the boys didn't want you on their team.

The Lord Provost scowled at him. 'Yes, now that our "friend" has chosen to arrive, we shall be off.' he said shaking his head. 'I trust that you will not hinder this mission further? From the colour of your face I would say that you do not exercise regularly. Perhaps upon our return you should seek a good physic? I find that a good regular exercise regime is essential to my well being.'

The Sheriff merely looked sheepish, but he knew that there was no point trying to argue back with such a man. He knew the Provost would be able to whip him with his tongue as easily as he did his servants with his belt. 'Let us be off about this business,' he said. 'Torean is cunning. He will not sit waiting upon us to pay him a visit. I think we should approach Longford's Pass from the direction of the old man's farm. If he has left any evidence during his journey we shall find it.'

As the last of the men finally left the clearing, the Laird turned to Lizzy. 'My girl,' he said. 'I'm sorry for doubting you.'

'It's okay,' she said beaming at him. 'I'm just glad that you now know the truth.' She couldn't help but smile. She felt like she had already helped Torean just by getting someone like the Laird to believe her.

'This seems to be a very dark business,' the Laird said, rubbing his fingers on his unshaven chin. 'However, I'm unsure how to go about fixing the matter. If the men in charge of the law are involved in this matter our resources are very limited.'

At this Lizzy physically sagged looking crestfallen. She had hoped that the Laird would know exactly what to do, as she was already painfully aware that she, in her position, could do very little. 'Is there nothing we can do?' she asked desperately.

'Well,' the Laird said thoughtfully. 'There is one man I would like to speak to upon the matter. He is an old friend, an old friend of Torean and mine in fact. If anyone can help me figure out a way to fight this, let us pray that he can.'

Lizzy looked hopeful once more. 'Thank you, my Lord,' she said bobbing a little curtsey. 'I couldn't live with myself if we didn't do something. Torean was always so kind to me, especially after my father died. I may not have gotten my position in your house if he had not introduced me.'

'Well, my dear, let's not dwell on such things. We must take action if we are to save Torean and his family. Also, if we are to get embroiled in this endeavour together, I think it is time you started to call me Angus.'

Lizzy blushed and nodded, unsure whether she would be able to bring herself to speak to the Laird as if she were an equal. It didn't matter however. All that mattered was that she had hope. Hope that they would be able to find a solution. Wasting no more time the two set off with Lizzy following the Laird towards a dirt road which led to the outskirts of the estate and to dense farmland. Lizzy was confused by this but decided to trust the Laird's judgement. As they left the clearing, the little bird who had been circling them headed off in a different direction. As fast as the wind, he flew off towards where the group of men had embarked, and towards the hills.

Chapter Nine
An Unexpected Ally

As Torean and the group reached Devil's Ford it was past nine o'clock in the morning. They were a sorry sight as they lowered their packs to the ground. The group was weary from their climb and sat down to rest. Out of breath, Torean looked around at them. 'Well, I think we did well. It is not an easy climb and should provide us with some safety for a day or two.'

Adaira looked up exhausted. 'I hope so Torean. I don't know if I have the strength to keep this up.' She felt close to breaking. How had they ended up here? She was a simple woman, who had been reduced to being homeless hiding in the hills.

'Don't worry, mother,' Aneirin said putting an arm around her. 'We must trust the path where grandfather leads us. We have no other choice. If we wish to regain our home, then we must survive such hardship.' The two seemed to change between backing Torean and feeling despondent. Luckily, when one of them was down, the other one managed to pick them back up.

'My boy,' Torean said emotionally. 'You speak like a man much older than your years. I had wished to spare you such hardship. Unfortunately fate has landed us in this situation and, as you say, we must endure.'

At that a small bird flew into the clearing, chirping at the top of its voice and circling the four. It landed in front of Torean and stood perfectly still as though awaiting instruction. Onero also seemed to have stood forward as though awaiting information. The group couldn't help but smile at the sight of the little creature. He was like a sentry standing to attention, although he was far too excited to keep up such a pose, and was soon hopping from one foot to the other with impatience. Torean mumbled to himself and lifted his staff.

'Are you going to communicate with him?' Tom asked expectantly.

'Well,' Torean said, 'it may be nothing, but I have a feeling that this little one is not purely excited about his breakfast.' Torean then raised his staff and whispered gently to the creature, 'Suaimhneach.' The bird began to chirrup and squawk in a repetitive pattern.

After a few seconds Tom decided to lift his staff and also tried saying, 'Suaimhneach.' He then realised that as the bird sang, a sense of understanding came over him. He did not hear words or sentences, but instead saw images. He saw a group of men standing in a clearing and understood that they were coming after the family. He also saw an old man and a young woman cowering in the background, and he felt that they meant to provide them with aid. The bird then rose up into the air and the connection between them was broken.

Torean turned to Aneirin and Adaira. 'We have been brought another warning,' he said. 'There is a company of men who seek us out. From my understanding they will head to Longford's Pass to start their search. It also appears that the Laird and our friend Lizzy are aware of our plight and seek to help us. I only hope that they do not endanger themselves in this endeavour.'

Lizzy? Tom thought to himself. 'Is that the woman who warned you of the Sheriff's visit that night?' he asked Torean.

'Yes, my boy, it is,' he replied. 'She has been around our farm since she was a small child, and she is a very brave girl to try to help us.'

'What do you think they'll do?' asked Aneirin worriedly. 'I don't want Lizzy putting herself in danger for our sakes.'

'Well, if I know the Laird,' mused Torean, 'or I suppose I should now say, Angus, he'll visit an old friend of ours for council. We were always close as boys and he'll not want to embark upon such a venture without support.'

Adaira couldn't help but look visibly relieved. 'I know that they may not be able to help us against the kind of evil you have spoken of, but it comforts me to know that we have people on our side,' she sighed.

'Yes,' replied Torean. 'It's nice to know that not everyone in Cairn Holme can be seduced by power. Unfortunately, they are not best equipped with the powers to contact us, but after our last visit from our little friend, I hope that Mother Nature will find a way to keep us abreast of their endeavours.'

The morning's events had given them all a lot to think about. They spent the next couple of hours setting up camp and talking with one another about what they thought the Laird and Lizzy could be doing. Torean and Tom went around the area setting up their usual wards to warn them of any strangers breaching the camp. Aneirin followed them round like a puppy, and as they walked the three talked of the staff.

'Granda,' Aneirin said, 'while I cannot learn the way of the staff when we are in such peril, can I listen as you and Tom work, so that I may start to learn of the language you use?'

'Of course you can,' Torean replied. 'This is your heritage as much as anyone else's and I would like for you to start learning of our lore.'

'So, where shall we begin today?' Aneirin asked excitedly, looking at Torean with a large grin. He was happy his grandfather wasn't going to keep him out of this important training any longer. He secretly wished that he could take Tom's place at his side.

Tom looked at Aneirin and couldn't help but feel bitter and slightly sad. A part of him wished that he had been given the opportunity to learn about the staff before having to use it. He resented being thrust into a situation he had no control over. He quickly put those thoughts aside, feeling ashamed of having even thought them. 'Are there any words I can use to heal people or mend things?'

'Very good question, boy,' Torean smiled. Despite the situation they were in, the old man was enjoying himself. It had been a long time since he had been able to speak so freely about the staff to others. This made his thoughts turn to his son; he would ensure that he did better this time.

'Well, granda?' Aneirin asked impatiently.

'There are words,' Torean said, shaking his head at Aneirin with a smile, 'you can use for such things. *Càirich* can mend or repair items, and the word *ioc* can be used to heal others. These are good words to know, but, ioc can only be used when a wound is not too serious. As you would expect, there is no way to bring someone back from a fatal injury. It goes against nature to undo such things. Also, if a wound is serious, the staff can call upon the life energy of the wielder in order to heal someone, so it can be dangerous. As you would expect, you can use the life around you to heal people, although this should not be done lightly. We are not here to kill the creatures which surround us. I also would like to suggest two very useful words you must remember. The first of these is *beathaich*; this may be crucial in our battle. It is a word which uses your strength to sustain another's enchantment. Using this word, even if you did not know what spell I was using as a defence, you could help me to fight the enemy. I believe that this could be an important tool in your arsenal, since I will only have time to show you the very basics of our lore. The second is *coimhead*. This is a word which can be used to look at what people are doing. To use it you must be next to water. The water provides the reflective surface to look into, but also allows the power of nature in the water to provide the strength for the spell. It is limited by what you use. If you use a bowl of water you will not be able to summon a lot of power and so will not be able to cover a great distance, although if you are next a lake, you can usually summon the power to cross several miles.'

'That sounds amazing,' said Tom. He then looked down sadly. 'If only I could cross time boundaries, I could see my family.'

Torean looked at Tom sympathetically. 'Unfortunately it would take a great deal of power to cross such a divide. I am not sure even the great mountains surrounding Cairn Holme can cross the boundaries of time itself. I understand that you are missing your family. But, I would ask you to take comfort in the fact that we are, in a way, also your family. We are all MacKays and through fighting with us here, you are preserving the safety of those you hope to return to.'

Tom liked this thought. He was fighting for his family. He also liked the thought that when he returned his grandfather would be proud of him.

Aneirin cut in at this point, 'Tom,' he said almost sheepishly. 'Hearing you speak, I feel that I have been too harsh with you. I forget that you are no older than I am and you have been separated from those you love to be here with us.'

Tom smiled. 'Don't worry. We have more in common than you think. I too rely upon my granda to be my best friend. Like you I also lost my father, in fact, after this trip I will be asking my grandfather some questions about how that happened. Somehow the likelihood of him dying in an accident while being away on a fishing trip seems a little less likely now.'

'Well, lad,' Torean said kindly, 'unfortunately it is a dangerous path we are chosen to tread. But we are blessed. Few get to have adventures quite like those of a guardian.'

'A guardian,' Tom liked the phrase. For a moment he felt like he was back in one of his adventures. Somehow, standing with Torean and Aneirin in sunlight discussing such matters made the fear he felt at night seem silly. He was a brave knight fighting his own crusade. He almost felt that if he turned round right now King Arthur would be beside him.

The three returned to the camp and Adaira was preparing a light meal for them for lunch. As they sat and ate some bread and cheese, Tom went over the words that Torean had taught him in his mind. He knew that he would need to know these words like they were second nature to him if he was going to be able to use them in times of great peril, especially *beathaich*. If he was to help Torean, he knew that it would be with Torean leading the fight in the end. The afternoon had filled him with hope. They had friends who were trying to find a way to help them, and he knew now that even if he did not know all the ways of the staff, he could help Torean in a battle simply by lending his strength to the old man's enchantments. Part of him couldn't wait to get home. He wanted to know what adventures his father and grandfather had experienced.

* * *

Meanwhile, Lizzy and Laird Anstruther were walking towards a farm. Along the way they had passed close enough to the remains of the MacKay farm to see the burnt down cottage. They stopped for several moments and just stared at the ashes, the harsh winds blowing the lingering smell of smoke into their faces, and the grass surrounding the house now blackened and burned. Somehow, it felt like they were stopping to show respect at a graveside, even though they now knew that Torean had not perished in the flames.

The Laird looked at Lizzy. 'You know,' he said, putting his arm around her, 'after this morning in the clearing I had accepted that something very wrong was happening, but it was not until this moment, seeing my friend's home, that it became real. We will have to move quickly if we are going to help Torean and his family survive this.'

'Yes,' Lizzy said, with her eyes glistening yet set sternly upon the ruin. 'The MacKays were good to me, and from what those men said Torean has power to fight them. We will make sure he knows that he is not fighting this alone.'

The two did not speak again until they reached their destination. The sight of the destroyed farm had galvanised their conviction to fight whatever had caused such destruction. Even if at that moment the whole situation seemed to fill them with more questions than answers. Not only did they not understand what Lady Naithara had gotten involved in, but neither of them, no matter how much they thought they had known Torean, could understand exactly what had made him such a target.

As they walked down a dirt road towards another farm, Lizzy recognised it as Old Wilson's farm. 'Can Old Wilson help us?' she asked perplexed.

'As I said when we set out,' the Laird replied, 'he has been a friend of both Torean and me for many years. While we went our separate ways when I was sent off to school, there has been a bond between us which could not be broken. Torean was always in trouble, he seems to attract it.' The old man was smiling as he spoke to Lizzy. He was imagining the scrapes they had gotten into as youngsters. 'Wilson always seemed to know what Torean was doing, if anyone can guess where they are hiding and to what purpose he will know.'

Lizzy smiled, relieved by what the Laird had said. Surely Old Wilson would be able to help them work out what to do next.

At that, they turned a corner into a farm yard with a large house surrounded by several outbuildings which formed a sort of courtyard. Wilson had seen the two coming up the drive and was waiting for them at the front door. He was a large man, who looked as wide as he was tall. He had rosy cheeks and thinning ginger hair, which was currently covered by his usual bunnet. 'You had best come in,' he bellowed, ushering them to hurry towards the house. 'I was not expecting such an unlikely pair, but I think I know why you're here.'

Lizzy looked at the Laird and he gestured for her to enter the house in front of him. They went straight through to the large, warm kitchen and Wilson signalled for them to sit down.

'Mary, my love,' said Wilson, turning to his wife who was standing in the corner of the kitchen. 'Would you put on the kettle for a cup of tea? Our two visitors look weary from their walk here.'

Mary beamed at her husband. She was the opposite of him in that she was a small woman, but she too was rather rotund. Like her husband she had very red cheeks, and a large kind face. She turned to lift a giant kettle which hung in the centre of a large fireplace. 'Of course, it is as always lovely to see you again, Angus,' she said smiling. 'I am sorry that we were not better prepared for your visit. If I had known…'

The Laird smiled. 'My dear lady,' he said looking around the kitchen, 'your home is always the perfect welcome. Thank you for having young Lizzy and I here.'

'Well,' said Wilson impatiently. 'Enough with the formalities, I assume you are here because of our friend, Torean?'

'Yes,' the Laird said sombrely. 'You will be aware of what has happened to his farm, I presume?'

'Yes, that I am, but am I to take it from your visit that you were not party to any of this business?'

'Of course not!' said the Laird clearly shocked.

'Forgive me, Angus,' said Wilson, embarrassed by the reaction he had received from the Laird. He regretted the words as soon as he had said them, but had been worried about Torean and his family for some time. 'You see, Torean has been troubled by the Sheriff quite regularly recently, and was repeatedly accused of crimes against yourself and the estate.'

'Well,' said the Laird looking angrily at the floor. 'I have only recently been made fully aware of the situation in that respect. I can assure you Sheriff MacDonald was not working under my instruction.'

'May I ask for whom he was working then?' said Wilson, now curious as to what could have been happening.

'It appears my niece, was involved in those visits that Torean received,' the Laird said. 'Lizzy and I will get to that matter shortly,' he added, feeling uncomfortable discussing that part of the situation. 'We came here because we need to help Torean and his family, and we need to know what you know of their plight.'

'Well,' Wilson said, removing his bunnet and rubbing his balding head. 'Several days ago in the early hours of the morning I received a visit from young Aneirin. He came bringing the majority of Torean's livestock with him and asked if they could be stored here. I obliged, but could not get much from the boy about why Torean needed this help. He simply said that there was a serious situation, and that the family may need to go away for a few days.'

Mrs Wilson reappeared at the table and set down a tray containing a pot of tea, some cups and some fresh toast. Lizzy set about helping her serve the tea.

'Thank you, my dear,' Wilson smiled at his wife. 'Angus, you will know as well as I do that Torean has been in some scrapes in the past. He has never told me the true nature of how he ends up in these situations, but I would trust him with my life and so do not ask.'

'Yes,' the Laird said thoughtfully. 'There was always something about the MacKays. Torean's father died very suddenly, and there were similar mysterious circumstances around the death of Torean's boy, Abhainn. Thanks to young Lizzy here I have some information regarding what has happened to Torean's family and their farm.'

At this Mary sat down and the whole group seemed to gather towards the centre of the table, silent in anticipation.

'It appears,' continued the Laird, 'that my niece and some *others* in the community have become involved in something unseemly.'

Wilson and his wife looked puzzled at this statement. Lizzy simply looked down into her teacup. She knew that it was hard for the Laird to reveal such information and somehow felt partly to blame for the situation.

The Laird, taking a deep breath, forced himself to carry on. 'Torean somehow stands in the way of them accomplishing something, and they therefore seek to remove him. They burned down his home.'

Wilson and his wife gasped, they couldn't take in what they were hearing. Although they had known that someone in the community must be responsible for what had happened, they had never imagined that it could be anything to do with the Laird's niece.

'From what I have gathered,' the Laird said, now visibly upset by the whole subject, 'Adaira and Aneirin escaped on horseback and Torean was believed dead. However, Lizzy here overheard the group in a conversation which suggested that Torean had escaped the fire and must have gone in search of his family and shelter. As we speak a group of men have headed into the hills to seek them out.'

At this Lizzy spoke, for she knew that it had taken great strength for the Laird to say what he had. She had felt the same way when she had tried to explain things to him that morning. 'They are headed for Longford's Pass to start their search. They believe that they have to remove the threat of Torean by destroying his staff.'

'Well,' said Wilson with a look of confusion on his face. 'This all sounds very far-fetched. Although, thinking about it, there has always been something about the family. Think about his staff. I never understood why he carried one as such a young man. He said that it was tradition in his family and that he had to carry the staff and then pass it on. I doubt there is obviously more to it than that. When you say that your niece has become involved in something *unseemly*, what sort of crime are we talking about?'

'It appears from what Lizzy has told me,' the Laird said looking slightly sheepish, 'that this business may be something of a supernatural nature.' He could see the pair looking at one another in astonishment and held up his hands to silence them. 'As yet, I have seen no proof of this, but whatever it is, it's not good. Also, what you mentioned about the staff is indeed important. The men Lizzy and I overheard this morning seek to kill Torean, but their primary goal is that they should remove his staff. They seem to believe that it holds some kind of power.'

Lizzy looked towards Wilson and his wife. 'Do you know where Torean would go in times like these?' she asked worriedly.

'Unfortunately I would say that Longford's Pass is a good place to start,' Wilson said thoughtfully, once more putting his hand to his thinning head. 'But knowing Torean, if he knew that people would go after him, he would not stay there to be found. He will have started at such a place and used it as a place to formulate a plan. From what you say, he obviously stands in the way of this group achieving an evil goal of some kind and this makes him unlikely to leave the valley altogether. While he will want to save his family, he will also want to ensure that they do not succeed. He will have gone somewhere which is not an obvious place to hide. Somewhere secure and somewhere which would provide a good place to defend yourself.'

'Can you think of such a place?' The Laird asked.

'Well, Angus, I can think of one place,' Wilson replied in a tone which suggested that he believed his idea to be outlandish. 'But I am not sure if even Torean would be mad enough to go there. The journey is perilous and Torean is not as young as he was. It would also be difficult if they are, as you say, travelling with a horse.'

'Where is this place?' asked Lizzy impatiently.

'My girl, the only place I can think of is Devil's Ford,' Wilson replied matter-of-factly.

The Laird looked shocked. 'Surely not?'

Silence fell on the group for a moment.

'Although,' the Laird then said thoughtfully. 'While it is difficult to reach, it does have all the attributes you mention, and from the West side could provide a good vantage point over the valley.'

'Exactly,' replied Wilson. 'Do you think he would be mad enough to attempt it?'

'How could we get there?' Lizzy asked. She did not want to sit and debate matters. The girl wanted to do something to help Torean and his family.

'Lizzy, lass,' Wilson laughed. 'That is a different matter altogether. It is a dangerous journey to the Ford, and even if we get there, it would be made more perilous by the fact there are a group of men with a head start on us.'

Mary was now looking from her husband to the Laird hoping that one of them would now say that it would be impossible for them to attempt such a thing.

'All that being true, how would you go about getting there if you were not coming from Longford's Pass?' Lizzy enquired.

'Well, coming from the West side of the hills, could it be approached from Moore's Glen?'

'Yes,' said the Laird. 'If we set off just now, and went straight for Devil's Ford. We could be there before sun down. I would be willing to bet, that even with a head start, the men who seek Torean would not go straight for Devil's Ford. Wilson, will you join us?'

'Are you sure about this?' Mrs Wilson said looking worried. 'Neither of you are as young as you were. And if it is true that Torean has power able to defend himself, perhaps he doesn't need you.'

Wilson looked kindly at his wife and touched her cheek. 'Unfortunately, I think he will need help. I doubt it will involve us staying there and fighting with him. But we need to speak to him of what we know and then offer what assistance we can. I know this is hard for you, lass, but he would do the same if we were in danger. Could you pack us some provisions for our journey?'

'Of course,' she said emotionally. With a tear rolling down her cheek she rose from her chair and walked away to prepare the provisions her husband had requested.

'We should be off as quickly as possible,' Lizzy said. 'I fear that every moment we waste, Torean and his family are in greater danger.'

'She is a brave young girl, Angus,' Wilson remarked to the Laird.

'Well,' the Laird replied, 'Torean and his family mean a great deal to her. They have been like family to Lizzy.'

Lizzy simply looked at the floor as the Laird spoke. She could not bare the thought of losing them.

Within half an hour the group had set off towards the hills. They by-passed Torean's farm on the way towards Longford's Pass and headed into the village of Cairn Holme itself. On the opposite site of the town was a bridge leading over to Moore's Glen; from here they could start an ascent in to the hills from a different angle than that the group heading for Longford's Pass would have taken. They would have to walk quickly if they were to reach Torean in time. The three did not speak much as they set off about their climb. They could all sense that there was a foreboding among the group, and all knew that what they were about to attempt was insane. Unfortunately, they did not have a great deal of choice if they wished to help their friend live through this. They had all found themselves in a situation which was like something out of an adventure story.

Chapter Ten
The Dark Group Moves

At the same time as Torean's friends were setting out to make contact, the group of men who were hunting him was arriving at Longford's Pass. They searched the area looking for clues as to whether Torean and his family had been there. Torean had covered their tracks well, and to the naked eye you would never have known that anyone had passed that way.

The Sheriff turned to the group. 'Well,' he said, 'we must have been wrong. It does not look like anyone has been here.' He felt slightly relieved.

The Lord Provost shot him a look of disgust and laughed. 'Yet again, you show your ignorance, Michael. I have no idea why Lady Naithara thought you worthy of this quest. There is no obvious evidence to the naked eye. Although if the right incantations are used we can see traces that no-one can erase.' He was enjoying this opportunity to show that he was Naithara's chosen one. She had taught him some of her magic, and he loved showing the group that he was her most faithful servant. He took a dark stone from his pocket and held it in his hands. After a few moments he closed his eyes. 'Cleith!' he yelled. The stone seemed to glow in his hand as he spoke, a dark red glow emanating from his fingertips. The wind rose in the clearing and suddenly things became more noticeable. Footprints appeared in the ground and marks where hooves had trodden. The Provost laughed a low and evil laugh. 'With their own magic they are undone. The spell they use to conceal can also be manipulated to allow those with the right eyes to see. Gentlemen, make haste. Examine these tracks!'

'There!' shouted one of the men. 'They have headed this way, the marks are unmistakable!'

The Sheriff looked at the marks on the ground. 'They cannot have headed that way,' he remarked, 'there is nothing there. No fool would take that path seeking shelter.'

'For once I feel that the Sheriff is right,' the Provost said, frustrated. 'Perhaps they have deliberately set tracks hoping to send us in the wrong direction.' The Lord Provost walked away from the tracks on the ground. 'You two,' he said, pointing at the local minister and the butcher from the village, 'I want you to check the cave. Sheriff, you will come with me and we will check the opposite direction to where these tracks lead.'

The Sheriff looked despondent at the thought of having to follow the Provost anywhere, but walked behind him slowly hoping that he would not cast any more blame on him for the situation they had found themselves in. They wandered down a path from the clearing. The two men did not talk and the Lord Provost looked around the surrounding area trying to figure out where the family could have gone in this direction to seek shelter.

'I'm not sure where they would have gone from here,' the Sheriff said, rubbing his chin thinking. 'If they were to take this path it would lead them down from the hills. Do you think they may have taken this route in order to leave the valley? I cannot believe that the old man would leave.'

'Perhaps,' the Provost said musingly, looking down the route which led them from the valley. 'Although taking into account the nature of the threat which Torean poses, I agree that he would not run away. If he has, then he will be unable to stop us and Lady Naithara has nothing to worry about.'

'It may be that he is not the threat that Lady Naithara supposes,' the Sheriff said hopefully. 'Perhaps burning down his farm has scared him away. Regardless of the power he has to fight us, he will surely wish to protect his family.'

'Surprisingly, Michael, the Provost said in disbelief, 'you make a good point. However, I do not believe that he would abandon this fight. From what we have learned of Torean so far, this power he possesses is used to stop people harnessing the power of this valley. It may be that he has sent his family this way, but that he alone has stayed among the hills. If he has done this, travelling alone he would be able to hide out in areas which would not be so obvious to us. Let us go back to the pass. I think we may need to go about this differently.'

After one last look around, the two men turned and walked back towards Longford's Pass. The Sheriff was relieved that he would not need to spend more time alone with the Lord Provost. He scared him. He had the look of a man who greatly enjoyed partaking in a man hunt. It was something the Sheriff had never particularly enjoyed, even when it was in the pursuit of his normal business of law enforcement.

'Men!' The Lord Provost shouted as he re-entered the clearing, 'Gather round!'

The men slowly appeared from various parts of the clearing and gathered around the pair.

'We have been discussing this situation,' the Provost boomed, 'and believe that the family may have separated, which is why we are getting conflicting information from this place. I would like two of you to take the path down from the hills and seek out the woman and the boy. While they pose no immediate threat, they may make good leverage if we were able to capture them. I would then like the rest of us to follow this path which has the footprints. I think that Torean may have set-off in a more dangerous direction alone in order to divide our attention.'

Two men volunteered and headed off towards the path that the Sheriff and the Provost had just come from. 'Ruthven,' the Provost shouted after them as they left, 'you know some of our incantations. If you are successful in your mission I would like you to find a way to contact us. We are meeting with Lady Naithara tonight, so if you are not back by then, I will pass on details of your mission to her. Go quickly.' At that the two men left at speed down the path. 'Everyone else, follow me!'

The Provost, swinging his cloak, strode to the front of the group and led the men towards the path which Torean and his family had taken earlier that morning.

The Sheriff hesitantly looked about himself. *Michael, this is ridiculous. This idiot is going to lead us to our deaths if he makes us walk along these narrow paths.* He was correct of course, the path which led along towards Devil's Ford was treacherous and many unsuspecting walkers and found themselves stranded when the weather had changed suddenly. Even in the summer time, the weather in the valley could be unpredictable. Anything from heavy rain storms to sudden fogs could leave the group stranded. He also knew that it was too late for him to turn around and leave the men. From what these people seemed capable of, they may not allow him to even if he did pluck up the courage to speak. A sudden thought then occurred to him. *Am I really any better? When I felt seduced by Naithara I deliberately burned down a man's home and left him for dead?* He felt a great sense of shame wash over him.

It was now early afternoon and the men would only have two to three hours before they would have to start their journey back to meet Lady Naithara in the clearing at nightfall. They would have to work very quickly if they were to find the family. It was looking more and more likely that this goal would not be achieved in one day. Although none of the men spoke, they all felt an apprehension at the thought of how Lady Naithara may respond to further bad news. No-one wanted to be the one deemed responsible for failure.

* * *

With the MacKay's camp secure, they all sat down looking over the valley.

'It is beautiful,' Adaira said, gazing out across the blanket of green in front of her.

'Yes, it is,' Torean replied. 'We must hope that we are successful or it may not always be so. I wish I knew what Lizzy and Angus were doing,' he said with a distracted look into the distance. 'I fear that they may be in great danger if they try to contact us.'

Tom had been thinking about this as they all had. He wondered if there might be something they could do to find out. 'If we can communicate with animals, would it be possible to ask a bird to go and look for them? I know it sounds silly, but if that little bird could come to us with information when we didn't even ask it to, couldn't it work the other way?'

'Yes,' said Torean thoughtfully, 'I suppose it could, but in order for that to be successful it would be best if we could commune with the same small sparrow that came to us earlier. We know that he knows who they are, and that they are trying to reach us.'

'That isn't a problem, granda,' Aneirin said, pointing lazily upwards. 'He's been watching us all morning from that tree.' He pointed to a tall aspen which was further down the hillside.

'Well done, my boy!' Torean said excitedly. 'It's been driving me crazy sitting here worrying about what they must be doing.' Without a moments hesitation Torean stood up and raised his staff. '*Suaimhneach*,' he mumbled. At this the bird flitted from the tree to the ground and hopped slowly towards them. 'I will need your help for this one,' the old man said turning to Tom. 'Can you use the word we discussed earlier to provide extra strength to my incantation? It is, unfortunately, harder to ask such a creature something than it is for them to relay images to us. I will need your strength.'

Tom nodded and raised his staff ready to help Torean when needed it.

'Suaimhneach,' Torean said again, and gestured to Tom.

'Beathaich,' Tom said raising his staff. He felt warmth pass through his body and into the staff. The power seemed to be released from the end of the staff and surrounded Torean in a pale blue aura. Taken aback by how the incantation looked, he had to concentrate to keep his focus until Torean lowered his staff and sagged to sit down.

'Are you okay?' Adaira asked worriedly, rushing towards the old man.

The enchantment seemed to have weakened Torean and everyone including Onero had gathered round him to ensure he was not injured. Tom found this strange, but for some reason the MacKay's horse seemed to have a heightened sensitivity to what went on around him. It was perhaps being surrounded by the power of the staff.

'I'm fine, my dear,' Torean said tiredly. 'I'm just not as young as I was, and communicating with creatures can be difficult, especially when the bird is so small. It is harder to gain their level of understanding and takes a great deal of concentration and strength. Thank you for your help, Tom, I could not have kept that up without you.'

Tom smiled at Torean's words, and then realised that the bird had not waited around. He had vanished at the end of the communication he had shared with Torean. Then looking up, he noticed that the small bird was circling the group and singing at the top of his voice over the valley. Watching him as he flew, he hoped that the little creature had understood the message Torean had tried to convey. A great deal depended upon it.

Torean had to go and lie down for a short while to recover from the enchantment he had cast upon the creature. Tom felt guilty that he had suggested the spell which had drained him so badly.

'Don't worry,' Aneirin said, trying to comfort him. 'My granda is very stubborn. I'm sure if you had not suggested the spell he would have thought of it anyway. Hopefully our little friend flies fast and can return quickly with news for us. It's very hard just sitting here. I feel like we're hiding from these people, from the people who ought to be hiding themselves.'

'Well,' said Tom. 'In a way we are hiding. From what I can gather we will fight them, but we can't do so until they make their move. I don't think the staff can be used for attacking people without provocation. It must be used only as a form of defence. That's what makes us the heroes. We don't act, we stop others acting.'

'I hadn't thought of us as heroes,' Aneirin said smiling.

'When they destroyed your home,' Tom continued, 'they removed the place we could wait. So unfortunately we must spend the next few days hiding out in the hills. I suppose we have to be patient.'

'Patient,' Aneirin said shaking his head. 'It's a little easier said than done unfortunately. Can I ask you something?'

'Of course,' Tom replied.

'If you think it is appropriate,' Aneirin said tentatively, 'would you mind showing me what you have learned from my grandfather so far? I know that he wishes me to take this training slowly, but something about this whole situation makes me uneasy. I would not ask him to train me with his own staff right now. But perhaps if we both work together it will serve to help me build knowledge of these things, and also help you to continue your training?'

Tom thought for a moment, 'Perhaps. You don't think your grandfather would be angry?'

'What he doesn't know won't hurt him,' Aneirin said with a wink. 'I just feel so helpless.'

Tom looked at Aneirin for a few moments. It made him feel a bit better that he was not the only one feeling helpless. 'Okay. But we should probably find somewhere to work where we won't be easily overheard.'

Aneirin grinned. 'Mother, we are going for a stroll,' he said, loud enough for her to hear. 'We're feeling a bit cooped up and we don't wish to disturb granda's rest.'

His mother did not look particularly happy at this thought. 'Make sure you don't go far, you must not be seen. You must also make sure that you can hear me if I call on you.'

'Very well, see you soon, mother.' Aneirin smiled and led Tom away from the camp and into the trees. They found a small clearing and sat down.

Tom began to tell Aneirin everything that Torean had taught him since his arrival. It felt good to talk to someone other than Torean about these things. He also felt good about himself when he realised how much he had learned in the short time he had been with the family.

'Can I try the incantation with the stone?' Aneirin asked after a short time listening to Tom.

Tom suddenly felt strange at the thought of passing his staff to Aneirin. He couldn't believe how attached to it he had become. However, he then realised that this was silly because technically the staff must have already belonged to Aneirin in the past. He slowly handed the boy the staff and selected a small stone. 'You need to listen to the wind in the trees. It helps you to focus your energy.'

Aneirin closed his eyes. 'Amas,' he said quietly. The wind rose around the two the way it had when Tom had first tried to focus the power of the staff, but as it had with Tom, the stone stayed exactly where it was.

Tom laughed. 'Don't worry. I was exactly the same. It seems like if you can learn to do this, it means you can focus the energy of the staff, and well, pretty much do anything.'

'I have been thinking,' Tom said wistfully. 'Has anyone ever written down what the staff is capable of?'

'Well,' said Aneirin, 'I doubt it. I can read, my granda taught me. He said that the Laird taught him as a child, but we are not wealthy enough to afford books.'

'Don't you think it would be a good idea?' Tom suggested. 'My granda is an old man, and so is yours. What if something happened to them before they could teach us?'

'I hadn't thought about it,' said Aneirin. 'I suppose we're both in generations where it matters. Most MacKays have probably learned from their fathers, not their grandfathers. Perhaps when you return home, you should write everything down.'

Tom found the idea intoxicating. It would be like he was writing his own adventure, a hero's handbook. He was daydreaming about such a text written down in ink, bound in thick leather with a metal clasp, when he suddenly noticed Aneirin.

Aneirin looked very disgruntled. '*Amas,*' he repeated. Again the wind rose and the stone shook slightly where it lay.

As the wind fell Tom thought he heard Adaira's voice. He looked up. 'I think that was your mum,' he said, looking back towards the camp. 'We had best get back.' The two boys leapt up and Tom awkwardly took his staff back from Aneirin before they headed back to the camp. Although it had been hard to give Aneirin the staff, it somehow also felt strange to ask for it back.

When they arrived they saw that the sparrow had returned and was bobbing up and down on the ground as though he was anxious to give them his news.

Torean had awoken and was sitting watching the bird expectantly. 'Where exactly have you two been?' He said without looking up.

'Sorry, granda. We just went for a walk,' said Aneirin, his cheeks blushing with shame as he lied to the old man. He knew that his grandfather knew him too well, and somehow he would know exactly what the two boys had been doing.

As Tom watched this he thought that his granda would be the same. He now understood why his grandfather could foretell the weather. Tom had now started to feel more of what was going on around him. He was also starting to feel people's emotions.

'Well, we shall have to keep an eye on that sort of behaviour. Impromptu walks are not good for your health when you're on the run,' Torean said, still sounding exhausted and trying to hide his face so the boys wouldn't see him smiling. 'Tom, come and sit next to me, I still feel a bit tired. Could you please cast the spell and I will join in behind you to share your vision?'

Tom felt slightly nervous at the thought of taking the lead. He took a deep breath, sat down next to Torean and said, 'Suaimhneach.' He could feel the link with the little creature rush through him, and then noticed that Torean must also have said Suaimhneach, because he could also feel the link between the two of them. He saw a vision of the same old man and young woman climbing through the hillside. They now also had another older man with them. From the surrounding area it looked like they were headed for Devil's Ford coming from the West. Tom tried to communicate to the bird that he was grateful for his help and severed the connection. He turned to Torean.

'Well, boy, it looks like our friends are on their way to see us after all.'

Aneirin and Adaira looked at one another with mingled apprehension and joy. They had been so worried about the Lizzy and the Laird, but they couldn't help but feel excited at the prospect of seeing the pair.

'They look like they are an hour or so away,' continued Torean, 'but are approaching from the opposite side of the valley from the path we took. This suggests to me that the men who are tracking us have gone via Longford's Pass.'

'Do you think we are safe here?' Adaira said suddenly looking concerned. It was easy to forget the evil band out there looking for them when they were focusing on their friends.

'We should be for now,' said Torean, settling back down among his bedding. 'I don't think this will be the first place they will think to look. Although how Old Wilson and the Laird managed to think of this place I will never know! This was your idea Tom, I guess we are more alike than I realised.'

'So what do we do now?' Aneirin asked.

'All we can do, my lad, is sit and wait,' Torean replied wearily. 'They have come this far without being harmed, and hopefully they will be with us soon and we can discuss where to take things from here.'

Adaira stood up and went to make them all some tea. It was the late afternoon and was starting to cool down. She thought it would be a good idea to get a fire started. Torean dragged himself from his bed to follow her and advised that they set up their fire away from the edge of the camp. The vantage point they had over the valley also meant that any fire they lit could be easily seen, so she set up a fire in a small cave near the camp.

'I do have some enchantments which can provide heat and light without also providing a beacon for where we are,' Torean told Adaira. 'If we end up sitting out in the camp at night I will use this to sustain us rather than fire.'

Adaira nodded and went about her task, and she was grateful to have something to do. As always, she found it best to busy herself doing something which made things feel normal, routine.

'Torean?' Tom said thoughtfully. 'Can I ask you about Onero?'

'Of course, boy,' Torean said, sitting down painfully with Aneirin's help. 'What can you possibly want to know about our old friend here?'

'Why does he seem more aware of what is going on around him than a normal horse?' Tom asked. 'I may be imagining things, but it seems that he gathers round when we talk as though he understands what is happening. I keep expecting him to join in the conversation!'

'He is special,' Torean said chuckling. 'He has been in our family a long time, as was his father was before him. I think that over a couple of generations, the constant exposure to the staff has made him more than just an ordinary horse. In spite of this, he will not, as you say, join in our conversations. He can sense when we are worried, and can even find us sometimes when we need him. But he cannot talk.'

'I see,' Tom said thoughtfully. 'I knew there was something about him. I will need to get you to tell me about a time when he has come to find you. It sounds very fitting for a hero to have a magical horse.' Tom was now off in his own imagination. He was again envisaging himself as a hero astride a great talking horse.

Torean shook his head, unaware of Tom's wild imagination. He was about to launch into the story of the time when Onero had come to his rescue, when Adaira returned with the tea and the group's conversation turned from such things towards speculation about their friends and where they were. It was hard for them focus on anything other than the thought that they were out there, coming for them. Tom didn't know Lizzy or the Laird, but he couldn't remember feeling this impatient in a long time.

Chapter Eleven
A Friend in the Dark

Lizzy, the Laird and Wilson had been walking for hours and she was starting to weary. 'Is it much further?' she asked them while wiping the sweat from her brow.

'Not too far, Lizzy,' the Laird replied. 'We should hopefully be there very soon. We just need to hope that Torean will not be too shocked by our arrival. I am sure that he will be nervous of any visitors approaching him right now.'

'Yes,' Wilson said nodding. 'We shall need to be careful when we get closer. If I know Torean, the old goat will have set up traps to stop people sneaking up on them unawares.'

Lizzy tried not to think about this, as she looked forward to seeing Torean and Aneirin. The thought of surprising them was the only thing stopping her from dropping to the ground to rub her blistered feet.

As they made their final approach the light was beginning to fade. They heard someone speak out of the gloom.

'My friends,' said a familiar voice. 'You are fools, but I am glad to see you!'

'Torean, is that you?' The Laird said peering into the growing darkness.

'Yes,' Torean replied chuckling, appearing from the undergrowth with a large grin on his face. 'Now follow me and we will talk where it is safe.' The old man had sensed their arrival through the wards that he and Tom had placed around the camp earlier that day, and was able to meet them upon their approach in order to lead them safely to the camp.

They walked for several more minutes and reached the place where the family was staying. As they entered the clearing the first thing Lizzy could see were two figures sitting around a fire set back into a cave front. Suddenly they turned and she saw that it was Adaira and Aneirin. She felt a great rush of relief run through her as she looked at them and saw that they were well and smiling. She noticed another boy further inside the cave although she had no idea who he was. Aneirin rose from his place next to the fire and rushed to embrace her.

At that she stumbled slightly. 'I hadn't realised how tired I was,' she explained. 'My feet are killing me.' She couldn't stop smiling at the sight of Aneirin.

Torean looked round at the three of them, concerned. 'Come, sit. I believe we have a great deal to discuss, my friends.'

The group sat down and Adaira began to fix a pot of tea for them all. 'You look weary. I'm sure a nice hot cup of tea will sort that out,' she said, looking physically refreshed simply by the presence of these new allies. 'We don't have milk I'm afraid.'

'Ah,' the Laird said removing his shoes. 'That sounds just the ticket, my dear.' He stretched his feet out in front of him and flexed his toes. It was a great relief to sit down, he never thought he would find sitting on rough ground so comfortable.

'I'm so glad you're safe,' Lizzy said looking at Torean. 'After I warned you, the Sheriff told us that you were dead! I was distraught! I couldn't stop thinking that I should have gone to the Laird before. Perhaps if I had, then I could have saved you...'

'Listen, dear Lizzy,' Torean interupted, putting an arm around her and stroking her hair softly, 'there is no need to dwell on such things. We all survived which is the main thing. And we would not be here if it hadn't been for your advance warning. Now it is more important to concentrate on how we are to survive the coming week.'

'Torean,' the Laird stated seriously. 'They are looking for you now. Lizzy and I saw them set off for Longford's Pass this morning at first light.'

'It is as I thought,' Torean said, his face showing resigned grief. 'You must tell us everything you know.'

'We shall my friend. But after this I think you will also have to share some of your information with us. We will do anything to help you, but we must understand the nature of the peril you face,' the Laird said.

'Of course, Angus,' Torean replied feeling ashamed. 'I cannot keep the truth from you now. Our survival may depend upon you being able to help us along this path.'

'Very well,' the Laird mused. 'I believe that Lizzy should start. She was the first one to become aware of this and has been privy to information which neither Wilson or I have.'

'Lizzy, please speak,' Torean said kindly.

Lizzy looked nervous at the thought of addressing the group, but she knew that she would need to tell them everything that had happened since the night that Sheriff MacDonald had come to dinner at the house. Torean must also know what she heard in the clearing the night after his farm burned down. 'I became aware that the Sheriff and Lady Naithara were planning to hurt you when he came to dinner at the house. She asked him to remove you in any way possible. And, as you know, that night I came to your farm and passed on this warning.'

'As Torean mentioned, my girl,' Adaira said fondly, 'we would not have our lives if you had not done so.'

Lizzy smiled, and Adaira's words seemed to give her more confidence to continue. 'It was two days later when the Sheriff arrived at the house with the news that your farm had been burned to the ground and you were believed to be dead. As he left, I overheard Lady Naithara advising him to meet her in a clearing at midnight in order to discuss things further. I was scared, but I knew that I would have to go to this meeting in order to find out why they had taken such action. I thought that if I knew more of why they were doing this, I could go to the Laird and seek his help with the matter.' She meekly took a tin cup from Adaira and nodded gratefully.

'You're welcome my dear, carry on,' said Adaira.

'I arrived at the clearing at around eleven thirty,' she said, taking a sip of the hot tea and somehow finding her voice. 'I found a tree in which I could hide safely without being seen. What happened that night was one of the most terrible things I have ever witnessed. A group of people arrived in the clearing led by Lady Naithara. There were some very important people in the community at the gathering, including the Lord Provost!'

As she spoke the Laird noticed the sense the shock among the group.

'She introduced the Sheriff,' said Lizzy, feeling relief at finally getting to tell Torean all that she knew. 'She told the group of what he had done to you. Lady Anstruther then went on to summon some kind of being into the clearing. I could not see any form or spectre, but there was a thick stench in the air when she did it. The creature then spoke to the group in a low sinister voice and advised them that you had not been killed, and that they would need to find you quickly if they were to escape his wrath. He was very angry and the group seemed terrified. I remember that as he was shouting he mentioned something about *moving with the moon*, and told them not to summon him again until you and your staff had been destroyed. When the presence had left Lady Anstruther was extremely angry. She shouted at the men that they had best find you and destroy you, and that she would expect an update on their progress the next night. The men decided that they would meet in the clearing again at dawn and dispersed. I went home but could not get any proper sleep. As I dozed my dreams were haunted by foul ghouls. I decided to rise from my bed in order to tell the Laird everything in time that he may join me in the clearing to overhear the men gathering in the morning.'

'Well done, Lizzy,' said the Laird softly touching her shoulder. He could tell that it had taken a great deal of courage for Lizzy to recount this tale to the group and so took the lead from there. 'We went to the clearing as Lizzy has said, and overheard the men saying that they were going to seek you out. They said that they would have to destroy you, but that it was most important that your staff was destroyed.'

Torean noticed that the Laird was not making eye contact with the group. The gruesome details of Lizzy's story had obviously made him ashamed of his niece's actions.

'As soon as they had left the clearing,' the Laird continued, 'we headed for Wilson's farm. I knew that I would need an old friend to help me figure everything out.'

'Yes,' Torean said thoughtfully. 'We were alerted to your situation by a small friend who I believe was with you in the clearing this morning.'

Lizzy and the Laird were looking at one another in confusion.

'However, due to his *nature* we did not know anything about what was said there.' Torean was smiling to himself at his friends' confusion. 'Anyway,' Torean continued, going back to the matter in hand while Lizzy and the Laird looked from one to the other. 'The story you have told has confirmed my calculations. Lady Anstruther and her band intend to make their move upon the new moon, which gives us around a week. I will need to start doing daily meditations to try to make the calculation more accurate. Unfortunately there is little we can do in the meantime, except to keep ourselves out of sight of the men who aid her. I had also suspected that she had recruited some important members of the community. We will need your help in order to know what they are planning and where they intend to strike. Your information has been very helpful. We know that the creature we are dealing with is not in physical form yet, and that he is obviously weakened, hence him not wanting to be summoned unless strictly necessary. Angus, old friend, I am sorry that this has come upon your family. Naithara has obviously been consumed by something which is too big for her to control. While this may not be a comfort to you, it should make it easier for us to defeat her.'

The Laird looked troubled. He went to speak but was glad when he was interrupted.

'Old friend,' Wilson said sensing Angus' shame. 'Now is the time to tell us how you are involved in all this?' Deep down Wilson was also extremely curious. 'We would not normally demand such information,' he said, trying to make Torean understand that he would not usually pry into his private affairs. 'But considering the circumstances we have no choice.'

'Yes,' Lizzy added, 'and who is this boy who travels with you. I do not know him. Although he looks like he could be a member of your family.'

'Well to start at the beginning,' said Torean, feeling like he did not know where the beginning of such a tale would be. 'The whole thing relates to my staff. The MacKay family was entrusted with this staff to stop evil forces using the power which resides in Cairn Holme for their own ends. Tom here is also a MacKay. He has his own staff and has come here from *elsewhere*, to help me with this fight. He is a child I know, but he is a MacKay. He is strong in more ways than he knows.'

Tom smiled as Torean said this. He had been nervous in the group until now. He knew that the three who had arrived had not trusted him to be among the conversation.

Torean continued, 'The staff helps to channel the power of the valley in order to protect it. I understand that this all sounds rather far fetched. In spite of this, I would hope that after what Lizzy has told you of the creature whom Lady Naithara is helping, you would be able to believe me now. Naithara has summoned some unearthly spirit which intends to use the earth-power which resides in the valley to rise again.'

'Good God,' said Wilson, staring at Torean wide eyed.

'So you have carried this burden all these years?' said the Laird.

'Yes,' Torean replied. 'Although it is not a burden, it is my destiny. I have never had any other option, but I would not have chosen differently. Although after what happened to my son, I wish it was not always so hard.'

Adaira looked up at these words. She found it hard to hear Torean talking about Abhainn. Until a few days ago she had come to terms with the accident which had taken her young husband's life. Now she knew that what was now tearing her life apart had also taken his. The greatest part of her resentment came from the fact that Abhainn had kept this part of his life from her. She thought they shared themselves completely and did not like to think that he had something so important that he didn't think he could trust her with.

'Torean,' said Lizzy inquisitively. 'I do not mean to interrupt, but there is still something which I do not understand. You mentioned someone was in the clearing with us who provided you with information about our whereabouts. I did not see anyone in the clearing other than the men working with Lady Naithara?'

'Ah,' Torean said smiling. 'The little friend of whom I speak is with us now. Come, little one,' Torean whispered, glancing skyward. Suddenly the little bird hopped into the group, stopped in the middle and looking around he began chirping at Torean, hopping round in a circle in order to let everyone in the group get a good look at him. It was like he was presenting himself so they could thank him for being so brave.

'The bird!' exclaimed Lizzy. She couldn't believe it.

'Well I'll be damned,' said the Laird. 'I thought this little fellow was going to get us found out this morning!' The Laird chuckled under his breath, 'Helping us all along were you?'

The bird jumped on the spot in front of the Laird as though he was also laughing at the old man's comments.

'So as you can see,' said Torean, who was now also laughing, 'we do have some things on our side. It has helped our spirits greatly friends that you have taken this risk to venture here to see us.' Torean was beaming at the three.

'So, what do we do now?' Lizzy asked.

Tom spoke at this point. It was the first time he had spoken since the three strangers had arrived. 'It's a pity that we do not have anyone in the clearing tonight to hear what has come of their exploits today.'

'You're right,' Torean said. 'Perhaps we should send our little friend on one more errand? He won't be able to provide us with the detailed information Lizzy has, but he should at least be able to show us a picture of what has taken place. Tom, come with me and we will make it so.'

Tom nodded and the two went off into the darkness with the little bird hopping behind them. It was almost as if he had understood their conversation and knew that he was also part of what going to happen next.

Lizzy watched the pair go off and wondered what they were going to do.

Aneirin could see the puzzled expression on her face and said, 'They need to use the staves to communicate properly with the bird. I dare say he didn't want to overwhelm you by doing this in front of you. Besides, I think that he is used to keeping this information to himself. This has been a secret for my grandfather his entire life. It may be too much for him to share everything about the staff in one night.'

Lizzy smiled and nodded. 'I'm glad to see you are well, Aneirin. I was so scared when I heard what had happened to your home.' She reached over and touched his hand.

Aneirin blushed and hid his face as he smiled, grateful for her concern. They had known one another all their lives; he was so comforted to have her with them. It felt like a life time had passed since he had seen her. The days of him visiting the big house and making excuses to stay and talk with her seemed so long ago. It was like remembering someone else's life. Could so much have happened in a few days? 'I'm sorry that I haven't visited you in the last week or so, I think my granda was trying to keep me away from the house because of what was going on.'

'Don't worry,' she said smiling, 'although I did miss your visits.'

Torean and Tom returned to the circle. Torean once again had been drained by the enchantment and was supported by Tom as he sat down again among the group. 'It is done,' he said wearily.

The Laird and Lizzy were looking at one another, concerned by what the enchantment had done to Torean. They weren't sure if that was the effect the staff had upon him. How could he fight Naithara if it sapped his energy in this way?'

'Hopefully,' he said as Tom helped him to sit down, 'he will return by morning with news of what he has seen. In the meantime, I suggest that we should try to get some sleep. Once we know what has occurred tonight we can discuss our next steps further.'

The Laird stood up, 'Yes, I am tired.' The man was holding his lower back and trying to stretch. 'Although I do not think that we have brought quite enough for us all to make camp?'

Wilson smiled and opened his bag, 'Don't worry on that front. My Mary is very creative when she's packing a bag. Once when we went away she tried to sneak her sewing machine into the trunk!' At that he pulled out three blankets and passed one to each of them.

They all started to laugh, amazed that Mrs Wilson could have managed to fit enough supplies into the small pack which Wilson had carried on his back.

As they lay down to go to sleep Tom thought he would never get any rest. He wished he could be there with the little bird to overhear what was happening in the clearing with Lady Naithara. As he eventually dozed off, he had visions of a tall and fearsome woman towering over a group of men. In his mind she was a terrible pale creature with dead eyes. He saw her standing by a roaring fire, her face lit only by the flames from torches surrounding her. She was shouting in rage that her men had not found the MacKays already. His heart pounded like they were animals being hunted.

* * *

As the little sparrow arrived in the clearing, feeling exhausted from his journey, the band was already assembled and Lady Naithara was holding court at the head of the group. He was relieved that he had made it in time. To him they were strange big creatures, always so serious. His understanding of human behaviour was basic. He could not understand the loud noises that they made, but he could sense emotions from them. He knew that this group of people was malevolent and that the group up in the hills was good.

'Well, I hope you have good news for me?' she said in an impatient manner.

'My Lady,' said the Provost being extremely subservient. 'It is not a simple matter.'

This does not sound promising, Hamish,' she said in a voice that sounded like a cat playing with its prey.

He didn't like being on this side of Lady Naithara's wrath. He was not used to being spoken to in this manner. 'We have found that they were staying in Longford's Pass.' The Provost knew that he didn't sound as confident as usual. 'And we believe them to now have separated. I have sent two of our group after the woman and the boy, as we believe that they have fled the valley.'

'Thank you, Hamish. And you believe this will help?' said Lady Naithara, impatiently looking at her impeccable nails.

'Well, we had thought that if we could capture the woman and the boy they may be good leverage against the old man.'

'Yes, I suppose this is true,' Naithara responded in an almost bored tone. 'What else?'

'We started to go up further into the hills to seek out Torean, but had to turn back in order to meet you here, my Lady.' As he finished speaking, the Provost lowered his gaze and looked at the ground awaiting Naithara's response.

'I see,' she said thoughtfully. 'This looks as though I will need to get involved personally. We have around a week in which to remove Torean MacKay or there will be dire consequences for us all. My master's punishments are as awesome as his rewards can be sublime. We cannot set out into the hills again tonight. However, we will need to go back to where you finished tomorrow morning. I expect you all here at six o'clock. Ensure that you bring enough supplies to stay in the hills overnight. We shall need to live as he is living in order to smoke him out, I feel.'

'Yes, my Lady,' said the Provost grovelling.

'Go now!' said Naithara angrily. His behaviour made her livid. Somehow she had hoped that these idiots would be able to take care of this quickly, but it was proving more complicated. Naithara was fully aware that the wrath of her master would be great if this were not taken care of quickly.

As the men started to leave the clearing the Lord Provost lingered behind in order to speak with Naithara privately. He had always felt that he had a special place in her service. Like most fools intoxicated by power, he somehow thought that someone like Naithara actually cared about her servants. 'My Lady, if I may?'

'Yes, Hamish?' she said curtly. 'Please bear in mind that my patience is short this evening.' She was in no mood to listen to his whimpering. She was longing for someone to punish herself.

'I apologise, my Lady, but I am worried about the Sheriff Michael MacDonald. He has proven himself to be extremely untrustworthy and I sense in him that he is not completely committed to this cause. I merely wish to warn you of my misgivings. I know that you would not want someone so un-important to hinder the success of your plans.'

'Thank you,' said Naithara. 'I will bear this in mind. Michael was useful when I was hoping to achieve this through more conventional methods. Perhaps now this has become more complicated he is not so suitable. As such he is dispensable.'

At these words a greedy smile came over the Provost's face. These were exactly the words he had been hoping for. He knew he would be able to dispose of the Sheriff soon. He simply needed him to make one more mistake. He stroked his moustache. *It shouldn't be too hard. The man is a walking mistake.*

'I would like you to watch him and report to me if you think there is any chance of him betraying us,' she continued. 'The last thing I need is him involving someone like my uncle in this.'

'Yes, my Lady,' said the Provost, grovelling once again. 'Thank you for your ear, I seek nothing but to serve.' He backed away slowly, slightly bent forward in a bow.

'Yes, yes,' Naithara said impatiently. She was not in the mood for such pandering. She swept from the clearing and back to the house. She would need to find a way to leave the house early tomorrow morning without her uncle noticing that she was missing. Hopefully the old man would be as absent as he had been the day before. He sometimes disappeared into his study and was hardly seen for several days. She was hoping that this would be the case now. It was strange that he could be so consumed by books, yet he had never discovered the power which lay beneath his fingertips. *The fool, he would probably be too afraid to use it even if he had.* With these thoughts she smiled and walked on, focused on her goal of ensuring that her master would have no call to doubt her abilities again. She would be the one to finally realise the power which her family had rested upon for so long. It would make her immortal.

As he watched her leave, the Provost was already thinking of any way he could find to remove the Sheriff from the picture. He knew that his rightful place was at Naithara's side. The last thing he needed was to have this idiot involving himself in something he was incapable of achieving. When Eiric rose to power, he wanted to be the man at Naithara's side. Nothing was going to get in his way.

Chapter Twelve
The Great Unknown

Tom woke early the next morning to find that most of the group were already awake and packing their things. Aneirin was sitting up next to him looking out over the valley expectantly. From his expression Tom already knew the answer to his question. 'Has the bird arrived back yet?'

'No, but granda has said that he hopes he will be here soon.' Aneirin was obviously also impatient for news of what had happened and was scanning the sky for any sign of the small creature. It was a cold morning and Aneirin could see his breath in front of his face as he gazed towards the sunrise.

Tom decided to walk around the clearing at a brisk pace in order to heat himself up. It was so hard sitting waiting for news. He had never felt so impatient.

Suddenly, the little bird appeared over the horizon and the group immediately rushed to gather round. Torean and Tom nodded to one another and advanced holding their staffs. They didn't waste time separating themselves from the group. Together they raised their staves, 'Suaimhneach,' they said in unison. As before, Tom felt himself being suddenly drawn into the consciousness of the little creature. In a flooding rush of images he saw the same group as before gathered around flaming torches. While he could not understand what they were saying, he could feel a great sense of urgency. He was extremely frustrated. He felt angry at himself for not being able to hear the words being said. He couldn't even be sure whether the sense of urgency came from the group of men, or whether it came from the little bird. The group did not talk long, and soon scattered in different directions. As this image faded, Torean and Tom retreated from the bird's consciousness and turned to face the group.

'Well?' Lizzy said, looking extremely worried.

The little bird was hopping on the ground behind them chirping repeatedly. The little creature was desperate to know whether his mission had been a success.

'Well done, my little friend,' Torean said smiling at the bird. 'You have served us well.'

At this the bird hopped excitedly on the spot, obviously pleased that he had conveyed his message successfully.

Tom couldn't look round at the bird. He was forlorn. 'I hope you gained more from that than I did,' he said woefully, leaning his head on his staff in frustration. He was despondent because of how difficult it was to glean a clear understanding of what had transpired from such a small creature.

Torean looked at him, understanding his frustration. 'Well boy,' he said clapping him on the back. 'I understood enough. They did not look happy. And the fact that they all scattered in different directions tells us that they did not move to find us again last night. I would guess that they are setting out again this morning. Hopefully we will be safe here for a while longer.'

Tom felt relieved that Torean had understood more of what the bird had tried to convey. However, he felt extremely frustrated by his lack of focus and skill when communicating with animals. 'All that this teaches me is that I still have a great deal to learn,' he said looking at the ground.

'Don't worry, lad,' Torean smiled. 'It is a very hard skill to master to be able to understand such base images. All I did was logically ascertain what information I could from what the bird witnessed. Besides, we all have a great deal to learn. When you have learned everything there is to know, you're dead.'

Tom tried to smile, but he was frustrated. He wondered whether he would be able to communicate with the little Nuggie if he appeared to him again.

'Do you think it's wise to stay in one place, Torean?' Wilson asked worriedly. The faces of the whole group seemed to turn, and by their expressions suggested that Wilson had simply said what they were all thinking.

'Well,' said Torean, for the first time addressing the whole group. 'I would not be too hasty to wander around while I do not know where our enemy is heading. Plus, I would doubt that they would think of coming here directly after Longford's Pass. While you may know me well enough to guess my tactics, I do not believe that they do.'

'How can you be sure?' Lizzy said exasperated.

'Well, dear,' said Torean, 'I cannot be sure of anything. All they can be sure of is that I will not have fled this fight. They will try to smoke me out, and I must ensure that we prevail. One thing I am sure of is that the three of you should all head back into the town as quickly as possible.'

'We cannot leave you!' Lizzy burst out in anguish, trying to protest against Torean's statement. She couldn't believe what she heard. They had come too far to abandon them now.

'No, my girl, this is not safe for us as it is,' Torean said, trying to placate her. 'Plus, while our little friend here did well to gather the information he did, we really need someone to be unseen among our enemy in order to aid us fully in this fight. We need you to gather further information and try to keep us informed. I'm sure our little friend here will be invaluable in passing information.' The little bird hopped around again, obviously pleased that he was to have a further role in the adventure.

'I'm afraid, Lizzy, that I agree,' the Laird said, putting his arm around her. 'While my niece is used to me disappearing for days among my books, I am sure she will become highly suspicious when you are not there busy around the house. If we return now it is plausible for me to say that I sent you to the next town on an errand yesterday. Plus as Torean rightly states, we can hopefully get some information which can help keep him and his family safe from harm. Well, safe that is, until their final confrontation. I fear, old friend,' he said turning to Torean, 'that when it comes down to it, we will unfortunately be ill-equipped to help you when that time comes.'

'My dear friend,' said Torean emotionally. 'You have already provided a well needed form of aid, that of comradeship. In times such as these it's comforting to know who one's friends truly are.'

Lizzy was not happy about the decision. She had risked so much to try and get this far. Despite this she fought back her anger, because ultimately she could see that the men were right. They would not be able to help Torean at all if Lady Naithara and her men discovered that they too were aware of their plans. She knew, however, that she would find the next week very difficult worrying about whether Torean and his family were safe, especially Aneirin. They had always been close since childhood and the thought of losing him was unbearable to her. Despite the fact that Lizzy was already employed at the Laird's house, there was barely two years between the pair. Somehow she had always felt destined for Aneirin.

Wilson, who was a father of daughters, could see that she was troubled. He also was not so old as to not recognise when someone was in love. He stroked her chestnut hair and said, 'Come, my dear. We had best get going soon. If Torean's enemies are on the move this morning, we do not want our departure to lead them to this hiding place.'

Lizzy looked around the group, she was trying her best not to cry. She stopped and focused on Aneirin as a tear tumbled down her cheek. 'Take care of each other,' she said focusing on his blue eyes. 'I can't bear the idea that there is nothing more we can do to help you.'

'Dearest Lizzy,' Adaira smiled, 'Torean has spoken truly. You have already helped us all. The thought that even now in this dark time we have friends has raised our spirits enormously.'

'Forsooth, my mother is right,' Aneirin added. He also only had eyes for Lizzy. 'I know that you have helped me to see that while all seems lost there is still hope. And with our little friend here, I'm sure we can keep in contact. I have a feeling that you will be seeing him regularly. When you do, think of me. You can't get rid of me that easily, Lizzy McCann.'

Lizzy smiled shyly. He always knew how to make her smile. 'Well, I look to the day that we can all sit down together, when this is finally all over.'

Torean smiled at her with fondness. 'Remember that, Lizzy. This will be over soon, and with God looking over us, we shall prevail. Also, remember that you can be of help to us. We will need someone to be our eyes and ears. I cannot say how we will contact you, but I believe we shall need your help if we are to defeat this evil.'

Lizzy felt slightly comforted that their return to the village may help the family in the long run. She hugged Torean tightly and he kissed her head.

'Lizzy, thank you,' he said.

She blushed. The MacKay family had been like her own since she was so young. She just hoped that she had done enough.

With that the three went around the group and embraced the family members. Lizzy stopped at Tom and said, 'I may not know you, but I can see that you are a MacKay. I will think of you as I do all the rest. Take care of yourself, young Tom.'

She then took Tom into an embrace. It made him feel that he too had someone who cared for his plight. He felt a rush of emotion for the girl who he now knew had helped them more than once. He simply said, 'Thank you, Lizzy.'

After their goodbyes the group set off sadly from the family and headed back down the mountainside, taking the same route they had come by the previous day. They hoped that by doing this they would be less likely to encounter the pack that searched for Torean and his family. Hopefully, as they had discussed, Naithara and her men would make their approach from Longford's Pass.

As Tom watched them leave he hoped that they would make their journey back safely without being discovered. He could not stop himself from thinking about the fact that at that very moment their enemies stalked the hills seeking them out. He knew that the family was all aware that Devil's Ford would not be safe for long. They had nowhere to hide.

Torean looked round at the remaining members of the group. It seemed so small now that the others had gone. 'Come,' he said. 'We cannot sit here idle. We must discuss where we should move to next. I would wager that while we are safe for now, this place will not be safe for much longer. Our enemies may not know me as well as our departed friends there, but there are limited places in these hills where one may find shelter. We still have just under a week until they strike, and we cannot risk failure now.'

The group sat down in a circle and began to discuss the matter.

'Where shall we go?' Adaira asked wearily. She was already exhausted, and the thought of having to move on again drained away the hope their friends had brought them.

'Well,' said Torean. 'Tom was the one who brought us to Devil's Ford. Have you any further ideas boy?'

Tom was shocked that they were all looking to him to advise them. 'Eh, well,' he stammered trying to think of places they could go. 'I'm not sure. I suppose I would say that wherever we go, we should probably head in the same direction as your friends who have just left. If we know that Lady Naithara and her band are headed from Longford's Pass it would be folly to try to head back the way we came in order to find shelter.'

'Good start, boy,' Torean said nodding. 'So the question that leaves us with is where we can go if we head in that direction. We obviously cannot take their route down the mountainside as it leads too close to the town and we dare not be seen. I am sure that news of what has happened to us will have spread, and most people will probably believe the official version that Aneirin is a criminal on the run.'

'There are caves further up in the hills,' Aneirin said thoughtfully. 'Although from what I know of them, they cannot provide great shelter, and the temperatures at that height would not be easy to survive at night even in the summer.'

'Well, they may be our only option,' said Torean sternly, rubbing his now extremely whiskery chin. 'Also remember that through our lore we have ways of providing heat if need be. Good thinking boy. I believe the caves you speak of are up by Hermit's Way. It is best that we all know where we are headed. If we are attacked before we can move on, we need to know where to meet. If not, we could end up scattered.'

Adaira suddenly looked like she was going to cry again. 'Torean, please do not talk that way. If I am going to be able to survive this I need to believe that we can be together and be safe.'

'Unfortunately, dear, that is something that I cannot promise you.' He touched her hand. 'Nevertheless I will do everything in my power to ensure that we stay together. I believe that we can be safe here for one more night. If we move on tomorrow morning, that leaves us with roughly five days until they move. If we can survive in the hills for a further four days we will need to head towards to town to be in place when they strike. Hopefully Angus and our friends will be able to help us with safe passage to where the group hopes to meet. For the moment we will make it through today here, and head for Hermit's Way tomorrow morning.'

'So which way should we go?' Aneirin asked.

'Well,' the old man said, picking up a stray stick from the ground. 'If we head this way,' he continued drawing a crude map on the earth. 'The area has two points of entry. So if we were attacked we could separate in order to lose them. Tom do you know these paths?'

'I have some knowledge of them, but it is not as good as your own. I have never ventured in these hills unaccompanied and my grandfather was always the navigator.'

'I know them well enough,' Aneirin said. 'I suggest that we pair up. If we have to separate, I will go with Tom and granda you should take mum. That way we know that at least one person in each pair is confident of where they are headed? It also means that there is one staff bearer in each pairing should we need to defend ourselves.'

'That sounds like a plan,' Torean said, patting him on the back. 'Don't worry, lassie,' he said noticing Adaira's expression. 'Hopefully there shall be no need to separate. We have been safe here so far. We are just being prepared.'

The group all nodded to one another, the decision had been made and they all knew what was expected of them. It gave them a sense of purpose for the coming day, even though they knew it would still be extremely long. Tom, Aneirin and Torean went to an open space in the camp to practice with the staves and Adaira busied herself going through their remaining supplies to gauge whether they had enough food and water to keep them going for a further four days. They all knew it was going to be a long day. It felt like they were waiting for danger.

Tom was grateful when Adaira sent him and Aneirin in search of some fresh mushrooms. But this was short lived when Aneirin pointed out that this must mean supplies were low. The two of them trudged through the countryside and Tom didn't like the idea of spending the next week eating mushroom stew.

* * *

At dawn Naithara and her followers gathered in the clearing by the aviary and set out for Longford's Pass. As they walked towards the hills, the Lord Provost made sure that he walked by Naithara's side. He was a very proud man, and he positioned himself there as he believed himself to be at Naithara's right hand. Also, following his discussion with Naithara the previous evening, he was determined to ensure that the Sheriff was in no position to jeopardise the Lady's safety and the success of their mission. He looked like an ever faithful dog at his mistress' side.

'I should have come with you yesterday when you went to search,' Naithara said while walking. 'I believe that with my advanced powers I will be able to sense where Torean is. You men must have been like children fumbling in the dark yesterday.'

'Not quite children, my Lady,' said the Provost in his usual slimy manner. 'Nevertheless, your presence was missed. I am sure with you beside us, we cannot fail.'

She smiled at him. 'My master has given me skills that will help me to feel Torean when he is using his staff. This should act like a compass to help guide our way.'

'You are a marvel, my Lady,' the Provost said grovelling. 'I am ashamed that we have let you down thus far. I feel in my heart that this time we shall be successful.'

'I hope you are right, Hamish. A great deal depends upon it,' she said sullenly. The strain of the past days was evident on her face. 'There are no words to describe the wrath my master shall bring upon us all if we fail.' She seemed to be staring into the distance with a look which could almost have made one feel pity. 'Yet, fear not, he is also generous,' she said, now smiling, as though she had snapped out of her maudlin. 'When we are successful and he has gained the power he needs to take physical form we shall all be handsomely rewarded.'

'Indeed Lady, indeed.' replied the Provost distantly. He was looking out over the valley ambitiously. Unlike the Sheriff he had had no doubts whatsoever about his actions. He felt that this was the opportunity his life had been building towards. At last he would receive the power which was rightfully his. He would also gain what he viewed to be his rightful position, from which he would be able to inflict all manner of punishments upon the deserving. He walked on imagining how he could rule over the dirt-grubbing poor with an iron fist. He envisioned his position within Naithara's court of being her Chancellor. How he hated those poor snivelling idiots who believed that the world owed them a living. He would weed them all out when he was in his position of power.

They reached Longford's Pass by mid morning and the Provost took Lady Naithara through everything they had surmised the day before upon their visit there. 'After examining the area yesterday, we believed that the group may have separated. Torean having headed further into the hills, while Adaira and her son would have fled the valley. While he is foolhardy and would not abandon this fight, we believe that he would not put his family in any further danger.'

Naithara considered his words, closed her eyes and murmured some words under her breath which the men could not make out. After a few moments she opened her eyes and addressed the group. 'While I can understand the logic of your findings, I do not believe that this has been the case. My own searching has revealed to me that the band left together.'

The men looked at one another, their expressions held both fear and awe at her immense power.

'I believe they all headed into the hills,' she continued, pointing towards the path which led further in to the hillside, and to Devil's Ford. 'For some strange reason it feels like there were more than three of them.'

'Perhaps that is the horse you are sensing, my Lady? The boy and his mother did escape on horseback.' The Sheriff said meekly. He regretted having spoken almost immediately.

The Lord Provost shot him a look which showed that he obviously believed this perception to be utter nonsense.

The Sheriff slunk back dejected by the Provost's constant contempt.

'Perhaps you are right,' Lady Naithara said brightly. 'It could be the horse. There was definitely something or someone else with them.' She then turned and lowered the bag she had been carrying to the ground. 'For now I think we should all eat a light meal and discuss where we believe they could have headed from this point. I would be happier if I thought we had a definite sense of direction.'

The men sat down and took various rations from their packs. As they sat eating they discussed among themselves where they would go if they headed into the hills for shelter. The murmuring among the group did not seem to provide anything conclusive. Most suggestions were shot down, several of the men had no idea at all where they would go if they were trekking out into the hills and were simply sitting shaking their heads.

After they had finished eating, Lady Naithara stood among them and spoke. 'We have not yet come up with anything which I would deem to be a plausible suggestion. As our time is short, I think that we should take the path from here into the hills. As we walk I will use my senses to see if I can detect a direction we should walk in. I realise that it is not ideal, but we cannot sit here hoping that one of us will have a flash of inspiration.'

'We must be careful, my Lady,' said the Sheriff. 'There are few places along that path we can hope to find shelter if we do not find the MacKays before nightfall.'

'Be quiet fool!' said the Provost. 'Lady Naithara has senses you could never comprehend. She will smoke out Torean quickly, and if that does not happen today, she will be able to find somewhere we can lay our heads for the night. The last thing we need is your nay saying.'

'Thank you, Hamish,' said Naithara, holding up a hand to stay him. 'You have great faith in me, and I will prove to you that your faith is well placed. However, if we are to succeed, we must understand that we all have the power to overcome this obstacle. I would not have chosen any of you if you were not capable of such a task.'

The men looked around one another and smiled vainly. Patting one another on the backs, the group then headed off down the path which would ultimately lead them to Devil's Ford.

The Sheriff had thought to himself that this may be the place where the MacKays were hiding, but after being berated for voicing his opinion earlier he thought it best to keep quiet. He had decided that it would be best to blend into the group as they walked. As he walked he thought, *with luck this will all come to nothing and by tomorrow evening I can be back in my home. Then I can try to figure out a way to get myself out of this mess.* The Sheriff was in many ways a coward. The fact that he had managed to get this involved in something so dangerous was a mystery even to him. Although what he was feeling was not simply cowardice. Since he had understood Naithara's feelings towards him were not romantic, he felt like he had woken from a daze. He felt a great sense of guilt. Somehow he couldn't help thinking how his father would be ashamed if he could see him now standing among these men. Remembering how his father had known Torean MacKay so well, made him feel sick to his stomach.

Time passed quickly on the bright and sunny day. Lady Naithara walked at the head of the group. Occasionally she would stop and raise her hand for the group to halt. She would close her eyes and murmur under her breath in order to find a sense of direction. Swaying on the spot, holding her sacred stones in her hands, she would allow her arms to move freely and they pointed in the direction in which the group should continue. The Sheriff thought that she looked like a human divining rod. He would have laughed at the sight had he not feared her so much.

After the third or fourth time doing this she cursed under her breath.

'This blasted wind is not helping me.' She looked dishevelled and tired; her blonde hair was hanging in wisps from the clasps holding it in place. 'I can sense the power, but the way it is carried on the wind it makes it hard to determine which direction it comes from.' She was looking around herself in an extremely frustrated manner, like someone who was being swarmed by insects. The men were scared to make suggestions for fear that she would use her powers against them. She was being bombarded by traces of magic that were resonant of Torean's magic, but she did not understand how it could all be coming from him. The wind made it seem to surround her. It made it extremely difficult to pinpoint a definite direction for the group to head in.

The Sheriff, who was the only one among the group to have seen Torean use his staff, thought that the wind, being so changeable may have been his doing. He had seen what the old man had done in his cottage with the smoke from the fire.

After a few minutes the Minister decided it was time for someone to speak. 'We have several hours before the light begins to fade, my Lady, there is hope yet.' The quiet, gently spoken man, who looked completely out of place among the group, was looking at Naithara admiringly and hoping that this would help to quell her temper. Even though he was among Naithara's group he still looked like a gentle man of god.

She smiled at him. 'We will keep going for a while longer. When the light starts to fade, I will focus my energy upon finding us somewhere to shelter for the night. Hopefully we are on the right path and if we cannot find them today, we will be able to move on them early tomorrow morning.'

They group trudged on for a further two hours and seemed no closer to their goal. Michael was growing weary and finally plucked up the courage to speak. 'The light begins to fade, my Lady,' he said hoping that he would not be struck down for speaking so. No-one responded to his statement, so he carried on. 'We should think of shelter if we are to survive to search another day.'

The Provost glared at him with eyes that suggested he could quite happily slit the Sheriff's throat in his sleep. He opened his mouth to berate Michael, but Naithara sighed and he thought better of it.

'You are right, Michael,' she said wearily. 'It will do my master no service if we freeze to death on this mountain path.' She closed her eyes and focused again. In her head she could sense the wind passing through the trees. She allowed herself to be enveloped by the patterns of the breeze. From this she could sense which areas were open with ravaging gales, and which were more sheltered. After a few moments she said, 'This way men, at least with this task my path is clear.' Leading them down a path among the trees, she said, 'Fear not, you will sleep safely tonight.'

She led them into a clearing which was sheltered by some trees on the east side. This kept the worst of the wind away and allowed them to light a fire in order to cook. The shelter from the wind also helped the weary travellers find some warmth. The men huddled around the flames trying to get some heat, and soon mugs of steaming tea were being passed around. Sitting as they were, they looked like a pitiful bunch. Tired and blistered, many of the men at this point were questioning their reasons for being there. Unlike Naithara, this was not their first day trudging through the hills seeking out their elusive goal.

After their meal they sat around the fire and the Provost led the conversation, trying to focus the group's attention on where Torean and his family could be. He was acutely aware that if they were not careful the men would lose their faith under such circumstances. He thought if he brought them back to the task in hand it would help to distract them from any thoughts of desertion. 'We must use every resource we have. I want you to put yourself in his place. Where would you hide if you needed somewhere safe in these hills? Remember that this would also need to be somewhere which was still within reach of the valley.'

'I have a thought but I dare not utter it,' said the Sheriff sarcastically. In his tiredness, he spoke with a tone which he would not normally dare use. However, having sat listening to the Provost drone on, he felt that he couldn't help himself.

'That is probably best, Michael,' said the Provost with contempt. 'Your other thoughts have produced nothing fruitful thus far.' The Provost's voice was thick with bile.

Lady Naithara looked round at the Provost. 'Hamish, you are too harsh. We should all have the right to speak. While Michael has made mistakes, he is used to dealing with criminals. He may know how a man like Torean thinks.' She smiled at the Sheriff. 'Speak, Michael,' she said kindly.

He hesitated for a moment. Naithara had not been so pleasant to him for several days. For a second he wondered whether he had misjudged her affection for him, and looked at her across at her in the firelight, once again noticing her beauty. Nonetheless, a small voice in his head thought that this may mean that she was simply becoming desperate. She had only ever been nice to him when she had wanted something. 'Well,' he said deciding that he had best continue now he had started. 'I was thinking. If I wanted to hide somewhere which would provide a good vantage point, but would not be an obvious place to go to, I would probably chose Devil's Ford.'

The Provost laughed aloud. 'Hah, you see, my Lady? Every word he speaks is folly. What idiot would go to Devil's Ford? Especially with his family and a horse in tow, it would be suicide!' The rest of the group nodded in agreement with the Provost.

The Provost beamed at the Sheriff, delighted that the whole group agreed with him.

Lady Naithara began to smile. The Sheriff was now waiting on her mocking him also. He was surprised when she held her hand up to silence the Provost. 'Very good, Michael,' she said sincerely. 'While it does seem improbable, I believe that Torean would take such a risk if it would provide him with somewhere we would not think to look. I think he would stay there believing himself to be safe from our eyes. We can show him that this is not the case. The decision is made!'

The Provost tried to interject, 'My Lady!'

'Enough, Hamish!' she shouted fiercely. 'We have no other leads. Do you have any better suggestions?'

'My Lady, please!' the Provost stuttered. 'You must see reason. I may not have any plausible suggestions, but to risk all of our lives on the say so of someone who has failed us before is madness. Do you honestly believe that Torean would have risked the life of his family venturing to such a place?' The Provost was pleading with Lady Naithara hoping to make her see sense.

'I say that we rise before dawn and start the walk to Devil's Ford,' she said completely ignoring his plea. 'With luck, we can catch them in their beds! Now, I think it best if we all try to get some sleep. We have an early rise in the morning.' The fact that she had now decided upon a plan of action seemed to lift a great sense of defeat from her. She smiled around the group as though they were on a childhood camping trip.

The men seemed to hesitate, looking to the Provost for guidance. Naithara noticed this and was infuriated. 'You fools!' she bellowed. 'Do you look to Hamish for guidance? Have you forgotten who it was that brought you all together? He may have the courage to speak against me, but he does not have the power to give you what you desire. If you do not wish to incur my wrath or that of my master, I would advise that you all re-think your positions. I am no mere woman to be treated in this manner. Those of you who would rather follow Hamish may leave here now.'

The men stared at the ground in shame, and then slowly moved to lay out their blankets. There were several of them muttering to one another in protest at the thought of making the journey to Devil's Ford. However, none of them dared to utter these thoughts to Lady Naithara for fear of being made an example.

As he lay down to go to sleep Michael was deeply troubled. If he was wrong with his suggestion then he would have led this group along a very treacherous path. He knew that the Provost would surely find a way to dispose of him under such circumstances. It was also clear that it was too late to run. He knew that he would need to follow this path to its end. On the other hand, a part of him secretly hoped that he was wrong about the MacKays. He already regretted his actions at Torean's farm and did not relish the idea of the three family members being murdered while they slept. As he watched the group settling down and one by one drifting off to sleep he found himself wondering how on earth he had allowed himself to end up in this predicament, and how, if possible, he could get himself out of it. The whole situation felt hopeless. He lay down on his bedding and closed his eyes. He somehow knew that he would not drift off as easily as the others.

Chapter Thirteen
A Severing Conflict

At that very same moment Tom was also lying trying to get to sleep. They were both un-knowingly looking at the same sky, both feeling extremely nervous about what was to come the next day. Tom was worried about their journey the following morning. He was not completely sure of the route to their next destination, and didn't like relying on someone else to get him there. He also couldn't help wondering about where Naithara and her men were. They must be in the hills somewhere, camping just as he and the others were. The thought of them lying in wait somewhere close by made him feel very cold, even though he was wrapped up tight in his blankets.

As he lay there he closed his eyes and started going over everything in his mind that he would need to remember for the following morning. Suddenly he heard a noise coming from the undergrowth. His eyes thrust open wide he laid as still as stone. Could they have found them in the night? How could they have made such a journey after nightfall? He felt his fear subside as no further noises came. He sat up and looked in the direction the noise had come from just in time to see a small head appear through the long grass. It was the Nuggie. Tom felt a rush of relief, the little creature had returned as Torean had predicted. This time the animal appeared more confident as it left the undergrowth and approached his bedding. It looked like the same creature. Nevertheless Tom couldn't be certain it was the same one. Its dark grey skin was stretched over its oblong head. Large jet black eyes looked at him warily and its large floppy ears bobbed as it crept forward. He noticed that there were whiskery hairs growing in large tufts from its ears, and it had similar whiskers growing on its chin. It somehow seemed older than the creature who had visited him before.

'Shassy saw?' the small creature said, just as it had before.

Tom slowly reached for his staff, the little animal's eyes opened in fear and it began to back away. He was able to get it in time and quietly muttered, 'Suaimhneach.' As he felt the power flow through him he muttered, 'Do not be afraid, little one. Can you repeat your question?'

The animal turned its head on one side and after a few moments said in a little high-pitched voice, 'I am Low-Paw, I was sent to find the staff wielder.'

'Do you need help?' Tom enquired.

'We have sensed your presence among the hills and came to present ourselves.'

'It's a pleasure to meet you, Low-Paw. Was it you who visited me before?' Tom asked.

'No,' the little animal said sternly. He looked slightly insulted by Tom's suggestion. 'That was my cousin, Bright-Teeth. His lack of success meant that he was deemed unfit to make further contact with you. Do not fear, he will be punished for his cowardice.'

'No!' Tom said, his voice louder than he had intended. He saw Torean stir in his sleep. He stayed silent until the old man had rolled over again. 'Don't punish him. I didn't know what he was, and so didn't know how to react to his visit. The fault was mine.'

'You are most gracious, staff wielder, I shall pass on your words to our elders,' Low-Paw said, bowing to the ground so low that his nose almost touched the earth. As he did so his long ears flapped forward and brushed the dirt. He rose again and said, 'What danger has brought you among the hills, staff wielder? Our tribe does not regularly have visitors such as you.'

'Well,' said Tom. 'We are in hiding until we can rise to fight against an evil force which threatens the valley. We will be able to move soon to eliminate it.'

'We suspected that there was danger,' the strange creature said, rubbing its whiskery chin with his long fingers. 'Our elders had sensed a foul magic upon the winds. The same way they sensed your presence among us. I shall return to them with the information you have given me and allow them to deliberate.'

'What will they deliberate over?' Tom asked, confused.

'Whether to join you in your fight or whether we should run. Our tribe has been in this valley for many centuries, and I believe that most of our elders would choose to defend it. Even so, there are those who do not wish to become involved in the matters of the Humamans. However, if we leave we run the risk of exposure. Cairn Holme is a special place. We do not know whether our people can survive outside of its protection.'

'Humamans?' Tom mused. 'You mean Humans?'

'Yes, as you say, humamans.'

Tom shook his head. 'Well, I thank you for your visit. I wish you well, and hope to see you again.'

'It has been my honour, staff wielder. I shall tell my people of your grace and your glory.' With that the little creature raised its hand and blew a sparkling dust towards Tom's face. He felt a dizzy sensation come over him and he flopped back onto his blankets with a dull thud.

Tom felt someone shaking him vigorously. He turned and found that Torean was trying to wake him up. He then saw that it was still dark. 'What time is it?' he asked groggily.

'It's just before dawn. I think we should make a move,' Torean replied.

Tom could see that Torean looked troubled and did not question him. He rose from his bed and began to pack up his things. 'Are they coming?' he asked worriedly.

'I can't be sure, but I have a bad feeling.' Torean said seriously, raising his head and sniffing the cold air. Without another word he turned and walked away towards the centre of the camp.

'Torean,' Tom called after him.

'What, boy?' he asked impatiently. 'We have no time to spare here.'

'I know,' said Tom. 'I just wanted to let you know that the Nuggie visited again last night. They wished to know why we were among the hills. They are debating whether or not to fight with us.'

'Really?' Torean asked, now interested despite his need for haste. 'That is extremely unusual. They usually keep well away from our kind. Anyway,' he continued after a few moments thought, 'put this from your mind for now. We must concentrate on getting safely to our next destination. We can discuss this further when we arrive.'

Tom nodded, quickly packed up his bedding and followed Torean to the centre of the camp.

Adaira and Aneirin were already awake and were nearly ready to depart. 'I thought we were waiting until dawn?' asked Adaira looking towards Torean.

'I know, my dear,' he said picking up one of the bags, 'but I feel that we cannot linger here.' He then turned to Aneirin. 'I would like you to ready Onero. We must leave here swiftly.'

The group then worked quickly in silence to prepare for their departure. Adaira passed Tom some dry, now stale bread, 'I know it's not much, son, but it will need to do for now. We don't have time for anything hardier.'

Tom smiled. 'Thank you, Adaira,' he said gratefully. He knew that this situation wasn't good, and reaching for his staff he tried to focus his senses to see if he could feel what was troubling Torean. As he did so he felt scared, but wasn't sure whether that was simply down to the situation they were in or whether he was sensing something else. The whole family was nervous and he could feel that way above anything else which was in the surrounding area.

After a short time the group gathered at the edge of the camp. Torean looked around them. 'We must head off now. I think we should travel as quietly as possible for a time. We would not wish to alert anyone to our presence, and also the ground we will walk today is treacherous under normal circumstances. In this light we cannot afford to lose our concentration.' The group nodded silently in agreement. They all felt afraid.

Torean then walked into the centre of the camp, raised his staff and muttered under his breath. The wind rose and leaves and grass started to swirl around him. As the dust settled Tom noticed that, as had happened at Longford's Pass, all the signs which would have shown that someone had camped in the area had been wiped out.

He returned to the group and they had one last look around them before heading off. Suddenly Tom felt a buzzing sensation in his head. It had been the same sensation he had felt back at the farm when the Sheriff and his men had arrived. 'Someone's coming!' he shouted to Torean.

'Yes,' said Torean trying to be quiet. 'I felt it too. We must flee now!'

They were too late. Naithara and her men burst suddenly into the clearing. 'Seize them!' Naithara shouted, pointing towards the panicking family.

Tom froze in panic. Luckily Torean had already turned to the band with his staff and started casting protective enchantments. The winds rose and it was hard for the band to see where Torean and his family were.

Torean turned, 'Go, Now! I will hold them off from here. Remember where we must meet.'

Aneirin stayed were he stood, 'I will not leave you, granda.'

'Go boy!' he shouted trying to make himself heard over the wind.

Tom turned to Adaira, 'You should go, and I promise I will get Aneirin out of here.'

She looked at him for a moment, her eyes wide with fear. Completely torn, her instincts told her to flee the fight, but could she leave her son? After a few moments fear got the better of her and she turned and fled the clearing the way the group had agreed to leave taking Onero with her.

Tom turned back round to look for Aneirin. He was still standing at his grandfather's side, readying himself to fight the oncoming men. Torean was using his staff to fend off three men who were trying to reach him.

Tom forced his way through the wind and grabbed Aneirin's arm. 'Aneirin, we must go. If we are to all to survive we cannot stay here.'

Aneirin turned to him. 'You are a coward!' he bellowed over the roaring noise of the wind. 'You should be at my granda's side. Give me your staff if you're too afraid to fight!'

Tom felt ashamed. He should have been helping Torean to fend off the men.

Torean turned to them both quickly; he could not spare much time to speak to them. The old man was using all his strength to keep the men at bay, 'Both of you go, now!'

At that Tom noticed that Lady Naithara was casting enchantments of her own. She had her arms raised, arched like a bird and was making a narrow path through the winds Torean was using to keep the band at bay. Tom knew that Torean would not have the strength to keep up the winds and stop Naithara for long. He turned to Aneirin, 'Stand behind me. I'm going to try to help.'

Aneirin looked at him doubtfully. 'We cannot leave him, Tom.' He was grateful that Tom did not want to simply flee and leave his grandfather to his death.

'I know,' he shouted. 'Just get behind me.' He turned back to Torean and raised his staff. Then, summoning his courage he said, 'Beathaich,' and could feel the power rush through him. For a moment he didn't know whether he would be able to stand it. How had Torean kept this going for so long? It was like his heart was on fire with the pressure. In spite of this he centred his thoughts and focused himself. He stood steady behind Torean.

The old man turned to him. 'About time, boy,' he yelled over the din.

Tom's intervention had greatly increased the power behind Torean's enchantment. Tom saw that Lady Naithara had been knocked back by the power of the wind attacking her group and was now lying on the ground. The men had started to scatter unsure of what their next move should be.

Torean turned to him again. 'I want you and Aneirin to get out of here; if we go separately we'll have a greater chance of getting away. We will meet in the place we discussed.'

Tom nodded and turned to Aneirin. 'We have to make a move. Your grandfather wants us to run, and then he is going to follow.'

He could tell that Aneirin was not happy about the idea, but the boy nodded and said, 'Let's go.'

With that the two turned and ran in the same direction Adaira had fled in several minutes earlier. Tom tried to keep his part of the enchantment linked for as long as possible, even so once they had turned to flee he felt the link between Torean fade until it was no more. He had never felt so afraid, even when the cottage had been on fire. His heart was battering against his ribcage as he raced through the hillside. His senses also told him that after he had broken his bond with Torean the enchantment continued. He hoped that Torean would not completely exhaust himself buying time for their escape.

The two boys fled, stumbling into the undergrowth together, running and tripping over tree stumps and bushes as they ran. To Tom it seemed endless. He never wanted to stop running; the thought of being caught filled him with immense fear. At the same time he had never felt so completely exhausted. They did not stop their frantic pace until they were both completely out of breath. 'Can we stop?' Tom asked, slowing to a stagger. He had a stitch and knew that he would end up falling if he didn't take a break.

Aneirin stopped and bent doubled-over, trying to catch his breath. 'Yes,' he panted. 'It's probably best. We will need to get our bearings. I ran so hard getting out of there I haven't paid any attention to where we are.'

Tom, looking around himself suddenly realised that he had done the same thing. Peering around in the early light of dawn he thought that he too was not sure of where they were. 'Damn,' he muttered to himself and dropped down onto the grass. 'We had best try to find the path again soon. We definitely can't afford to lose our head start on them. When Torean leaves they will follow him.'

Aneirin looked around himself for a few moments. 'I think I know where we need to walk. Follow me.' Aneirin then motioned for Tom to be silent and he slowly started walking through the undergrowth back the way the boys had come minutes before.

Tom stood up and stretched, there was no time to lose. He followed after Aneirin hoping that he was right.

As Tom caught up with him Aneirin stopped dead. He looked round at Tom and put his fingers to his lips to signal that they should both be quiet. Someone was coming through the undergrowth ahead of them. The figure came close by them and went past onto the mountain path northward.

After the figure had passed Aneirin turned to Tom, 'That was only one person. Perhaps it was my granda?'

'Maybe,' Tom said thoughtfully. 'But if it was Torean, the others will not be far behind him. Should we hide here for a while?'

'Not far at all,' a woman's voice said behind the boys. 'Seize them!' she shouted.

Before the boys could move they were grabbed on either side by arms which came out of the undergrowth. Naithara's men tied their arms roughly behind their backs. One of them took Tom's staff and went to pass it to Lady Naithara.

'The staff!' she shouted exhilarated. 'The old fool was stupid enough to give it to the children hoping to protect it.' She reached out a hand to touch the staff and a spark of blue light flew from it and caught her hand. 'Ah!' she shrieked in pain. 'I think we will need my master's help to destroy such a powerful object. Hamish, perhaps you should carry the staff for now. The old man must have passed it to the children hoping they could escape with it. I think we should head back. These two should act as perfect bait to lure Torean out. When he does come to us, we will have his staff and he will be defenceless against us.'

Aneirin and Tom looked at one another. As long as Lady Naithara thought that Tom's staff was the one which belonged to Torean there was still a chance. Tom tried to reassure Aneirin, but before he could speak the two boys were dragged forward and the group started their decent down the mountainside.

'Well,' Naithara sneered at Aneirin. 'Let's see how long it takes your fool of a grandfather to come looking for you. When we get you back, you and your little friend here are going to tell me everything you know about this staff, whether you like it or not.'

Aneirin spat on the ground next to her feet, 'We will tell you nothing, witch!'

The Lord Provost hit Aneirin hard across the face with the back of his hand, and his lip began to bleed. 'Be quiet, you filthy maggot. Do you not know to whom you speak?'

Not allowing Aneirin to respond he then pushed him forward and the group continued their journey. Aneirin tripped as he was pushed but managed to keep his balance. Tom and Aneirin did not speak to one another again. Tom's mind was racing trying to think of anything that Torean had taught him which would allow him to get his staff back. He was painfully aware that there was nothing he could do to help them unless he had the staff in his possession.

* * *

Torean ran up through the mountain pass, his lungs breathing hard. He had thought he would see the boys in front of him, but hoped the fact that he hadn't, meant that they had simply had too great a head start. After ten minutes he had to stop. He was panting and bent over double. Checking behind him he decided that he had lost Naithara and her men and took the rest of the way up the hillside at a slower pace. He was careful as he walked; he knew that he would need to watch his footing. It would be folly to rush his way up the hillside when one wrong footing could cause him to fall.

In what seemed like no time at all he reached the area known as Hermit's Way. The area was riddled with caves and he began to look around for the group. Frantically looking around he could not see anyone, but thought that they may have hidden with the horse in one of the caves in case Torean had been pursued. He decided to call out. 'Aneirin, Adaira? Are any of you here?'

Slowly Adaira emerged from one of the caves leading Onero beside her. Her eyes were red from crying; she had obviously been hiding in the cave petrified at the thought of what had happened to the rest of the group. 'Is Aneirin with you?' she asked worriedly.

'No,' Torean said wearily. 'He and Tom fled before me. Are they not here yet?'

'No,' Adaira muttered. She looked as though blind panic was setting in. If the boys had left before Torean, they should already be there. 'They're not here! They should be here! Where could they possibly be?'

'Don't panic yet, lassie, there could still be a good reason why they are tardy. They could have taken a different path from us,' Torean said, in a voice which sounded like he was trying to convince himself more than Adaira.

'They should be here!' she cried. 'What will we do if they do not arrive soon? I know that Aneirin knows these hills, and young Tom seems to know Cairn Holme equally well.'

'Calm yourself,' Torean said. He was racking his brains trying to think of a way to contact the boys. He knew that there must be a way to find out where they were. Then an idea came to him, 'I will call our little friend and ask him to search the hillside for us, he will be much quicker than we would be on foot, and he seems to have a knack of knowing exactly where we need him to be.' Torean, feeling slightly relieved that he had thought of something to help, turned and closed his eyes. Raising his staff he said, 'Suaimhneach, little one.' He hoped that the little bird was close by. They hadn't seen him at all that day.

He and Adaira searched the skies for the little bird hoping that he would hear Torean's summons. After a few minutes, which felt like hours to the pair, the little bird circled above them and landed next to Torean. Again Torean raised his staff and focusing on the little creature repeated, 'Suaimhneach. Find them, little one.' He focused his thoughts on the two boys, and hoped this would be enough to guide the little creature to its new task. The bird wasted no time and flew away from them and into the hillside.

'What do we do now?' Adaira asked mournfully.

'All we can do,' Torean said, dropping to the ground from the exertion of communicating with the bird. 'We wait. No good can come of us leaving here at this time. If we leave this place and the boys show up, they would then leave in search of us. Hopefully our friend will bring us news of where they are and we will be better placed to get them here safely.

Adaira dropped to the ground next to Torean and he put his arms around her. She sobbed gently against his chest and Torean did all he could to comfort her. However, he also found himself weeping. He had done his best to keep his family safe. Despite this, once again, as it had been with his son, the staff may have cost him another loved one.

After a time, the two looked up as though worn out by weeping. 'Torean, do not torture yourself.' Adaira said kindly. She knew that he was thinking about his son. 'I know that you blame yourself for my husband's death. In all honesty, I blamed you myself when you explained the situation. Nevertheless, what you do with your staff is important. If anyone is to blame for these things it is people like Lady Anstruther. I pray that my son will not be lost like his father.'

Torean felt immense gratitude for Adaira's words, but could not think of anything to say to her which would fully convey his emotions. So, in silence, they sat and watched the sky. Both terrified at the prospect of what could have happened to Tom and Aneirin, and both hoping that the little bird would return soon and tell them where they could head to find the boys.

The two must have dozed off and were awoken in mid-afternoon by the twittering of the little bird that had returned and was hopping around them frantically. 'He's here!' said Torean.

'The boys!' was all Adaira could say.

Neither of them felt joy, it was more a sense of relief mixed with nervousness about what was about to be revealed to them.

Wasting no time, Torean once again raised his staff and said, 'Suaimhneach.' His consciousness was then flooded with the images the little bird had seen. He saw the boys being led down the hillside with their hands bound behind their backs. He could tell that Aneirin looked like he had suffered a blow to his face, but otherwise they looked unharmed. He couldn't rationalise it, but a great sense of panic washed over him. Their worst fears had been realised. He couldn't stand it. Torean was finding the images unbearable and so he pulled away from the little bird and staggered away from both he and Adaira. He didn't want to have to say the words aloud. Surely it couldn't be true? If he just didn't say it then it wouldn't be true.

'Torean?' Adaira asked frantically. Moving forward towards him, she grabbed him by his tunic. 'You're frightening me. What did you see?' She then grabbed him by the shoulders and shook him violently. 'Where is my son?'

Torean, unable to look Adaira in the eyes simply stared at the ground and mumbled, 'They have him. They have them both.'

Adaira did not speak. Her mouth opened and closed and releasing her grip on Torean she stumbled backwards. Her hands over her mouth she dropped to the ground and began to wail.

Torean who could not think straight, simply dropped to the ground beside her. Taking her into his arms he rocked her back and forth. He then looked to the sky and cried aloud. 'I'll find you! When I do, you had better run!' His voice echoed around the hills.

At the sound, the little bird frightened, had taken flight and disappeared into a nearby tree. He wanted to help the staff bearer, but he couldn't understand their loud noises. He knew that he had brought them grave news, and thought how he would feel if one his chicks were taken from his nest.

'Torean?' Adaira asked manically through her tears. 'What shall we do? I can't lose him. Not after Abhainn. Not again…'

'We'll get them back,' he said firmly. 'They have taken the boys in order to lure me in. If they want me to come to them that is exactly what I'll do.' He took Adaira in his arms and stroked her hair. 'Do not worry, I will get him back. I'll get both the boys back, and I'll make every last one of them pay.'

Adaira rocked back and forth in his arms mumbling over and over to herself. 'I just want him back. Please bring him back. I can't lose him too. Can you bring him back?' She was like a distraught child.

Torean knew that there was nothing he could say to her just now. He needed to give her time to take in the news, he needed some time himself. Then they could decide what they should do next.

Chapter Fourteen
A Prisoner of Fortune

It was late afternoon and Tom and Aneirin were being led down the hillside towards to village. Lady Naithara stopped the group at a safe point before they became too close to town and they all had a short rest. 'Stop men. We can rest here before finishing our journey. I think we should cut off at the first fields and go around the village. We don't want too many questions asked regarding these two,' she said, pointing at the boys dismissively like they were an inconvenience.

'You won't be able to hide your evil long, witch!' Aneirin spat at her.

Again the Provost struck Aneirin across the face. 'Silence you wretch!' he said spitting at Aneirin's feet. 'Do not speak of things you know nothing about. You will be snuffed out soon enough, and no-one will ask any questions. You are worth nothing, never forget that.' He turned away from Aneirin deliberately standing with his back to him to show that he no longer wished Aneirin to feel that he had the option to address the group.

Tom turned to Aneirin and quietly said, 'Don't worry. We'll get out of this, just keep your head down.' Looking round to be sure that none of the men were listening he continued, 'If they take us back to the Laird's house we'll be able to make contact with your friends. Surely they can help us.'

Aneirin looked over at Tom, 'I hope you're right.' Spitting blood onto the ground he continued, 'If not, you're going to have to figure out a way to get that staff back. We're powerless without it.'

Tom looked up at the man carrying the staff, frustrated. It was amazing that the staff had been part of Tom's life for such a short time; still it filled him with bile to watch someone else manhandling it. It was like someone had taken away something which was now an essential part of his being. It had been passed to the Sheriff to carry on the way down the hill as the Provost had been put off by the way it had reacted to Naithara's touch. For a moment he panicked as he noticed that the Sheriff was looking at him as well. Had he been listening to the boy's conversation? Looking into his face he realised that the Sheriff was not looking at him with the same hatred and distaste the others did. He looked scared, almost like he wanted to help them. Tom broke his eye contact with the Sheriff and looked at Aneirin. 'That may be possible. I'll need to work on it, but there might just be a way.'

Aneirin looked confused, but didn't have a chance to question Tom further, as he was then dragged to his feet by one of the men and they continued their journey back towards the village. Neither of the boys had been offered any water throughout their journey and were both starting to feel weary with thirst.

In silence the two boys walked along, while Tom was trying to rack his brains to think of a way to communicate with the Sheriff without the others noticing. Torean had mentioned to him a way of communicating with others through thoughts, if you were in close quarters, which worked in a similar way to that of communicating with animals. But he would need to be in possession of the staff to be able to do this. He was so frustrated.

At this they reached the entrance to a field which Tom knew to be close to the village. He somehow felt safer knowing that he was in familiar surroundings.

The group paused and Lady Naithara said, 'I think we should split up. We will look rather conspicuous walking through the village in such a large group. It would be impossible to get the boys through the village un-noticed if we alone looked conspicuous.'

'What do you suggest, my Lady?' said the Provost hopefully. 'I will gladly take charge of the boys.'

Aneirin noticed that the Provost had a glint in his eye when he said this. His look made Tom think that it would not be good for either of them if they ended up alone with this man. He looked like he had been waiting for an opportunity to torture them like animals. He could almost imagine the Provost as a child torturing small rodents. This was a man who hadn't needed Naithara's power to be seduced. He was already evil.

'No,' Naithara said, smiling. 'Although thank you, Hamish.'

The Provost's face dropped, he wasn't going to get to have his fun.

'I believe,' she continued, 'the easiest way to deal with our little guests until nightfall would be for the Sheriff here to take the boys and the staff and lock them in one of his cells. No-one would question the Sheriff leading the two boys back through the town.'

The Provost was obviously angry at the thought that Lady Naithara wished to put the boys into the Sheriff's care. 'My Lady, the Sheriff has done nothing but cause problems. Are you sure he is capable of such an important task?'

'Hamish,' she said touching his shoulder. 'I know you wish to protect me. Even so, do not forget that it was Michael here who suggested that we go to Devil's Ford where we did in fact find Torean and his family. I believe that his position does make him better at thinking and communicating with such types.' She turned to the Sheriff. 'Michael, do you think you can manage this?'

The Sheriff, who looked rather forlorn at the thought of being given any form of task, stumbled slightly over his response and then said, 'Of course, my Lady.' He would have quite happily agreed with the Provost on this count if it would have gotten him out of such a responsibility. Just when he thought he was going to get away from this situation he ended up being dragged back in. In spite of this, without another word he took both of the boys by the shoulder and began to lead them away from the group. Somehow, even now when he felt nothing but fear for Naithara, he could not deny her.

Lady Naithara shouted after them in what Tom thought was a strangely innocent tone considering what they had been discussing. 'Midnight, Michael, bring them at midnight to the usual place.'

The Sheriff raised a hand into the air to indicate that he had heard her instruction and carried on walking without looking back. This somehow made him feel more detached from the situation.

The Provost watched them leave and was livid that such an important task had been given to such a fool. He could have gotten information from the boys if they had been entrusted to him, and had a little fun along the way. The Provost hoped that the Sheriff would lose the boys before midnight. Maybe then Lady Naithara would see that he was useless. Maybe then she would let him dispose of the Sheriff in the way the Provost had been desperate to for days now. He would like to see the look in Michael's eyes when he throttled his fat little neck, eyes bulging.

Michael and the two boys made their way into the village and towards the Sheriff's offices at the far end of the town. Tom could not believe their luck. If any of Naithara's men were going to help them get out of this, he thought that this Sheriff would. After much consideration he ventured to speak to the man. 'Sir,' he said testing the water.

The Sheriff made no response.

'Please don't do this,' Tom continued. 'We are only children, we don't know anything.' He sounded as sincere and childlike as he possibly could.

'Don't speak, boy!' the Sheriff snapped. 'It would be easier all round if neither of you spoke!' He didn't want to converse with the children. He didn't particularly like children as it was, and definitely didn't want them trying to convince him of their innocence. He just wanted this over with.

Tom and Aneirin looked at one another. The way the Sheriff had spoken to them was different to the way the other men had addressed them. His words sounded as though he was a man full of despair; a man who was trying to blank out exactly what he was being expected to do. Tom thought that this made him more like a man that could be worked on.

After a short walk he led them into his offices and up to the front desk where a young man in a crisp shirt and tie sat. The boy wore spectacles and was avidly reading from some papers he had in front of him. Tom thought that he couldn't be any older than twenty, and looked like he believed his position to be very important.

The boy looked up as they entered. 'Sheriff MacDonald,' he said, rising from his chair. 'I was starting to worry that something had happened to you?'

'Don't worry, David,' said the Sheriff impatiently, waving his hand to indicate for the boy to sit back down. 'I was out apprehending these two young scallywags. They were worrying sheep on a farm up by, goading the poor dog on.' As he said this he waved his hand vaguely in order to negate the need to specify exactly where this had taken place. 'I think some time in the cells would make them consider the error of their ways. Don't you, boys?' He was now looking at them, obviously terrified that they may not go quietly.

Tom could not see any sense in making a scene at this point. He doubted that the young man David would be able to help them very much, or would even believe them if they did tell him their fanciful tale. He simply nodded.

Aneirin, seeing this, looked at his shoes trying his best to look penitent.

'Shall I take their details?' David said eagerly, he was now excited at the thought of getting his hands on a pair of criminals. It didn't happen very often in the small village.

'No, boy, that won't be necessary,' the Sheriff said, again feeling impatient at David's lust for detective work. 'I have already taken the details of their parent's names and will be informing them in due course.'

Dejected at the thought of not getting to apprehend two criminals for questioning, David went back to reading through the papers on his desk. *Perhaps I should have tried to gain a position in a bigger town. Nothing ever happens here. The fool McDonald is only the Sheriff because his father was before him,* he thought to himself.

The Sheriff led the two through towards the back of the offices and put them inside a cell. Motioning for them to sit down, Tom and Aneirin sat on a long bench at the back of the cell.

'Look boys, I know this is hard,' he said wringing his hands, 'but if we all just do what we're told I'm sure everything will be fine.' He wasn't sure whether he really believed what he was saying, but what else could he say to the children.

'That's easy for you to say,' Aneirin said sarcastically, obviously not convinced by the man's statement.

'Being cheeky is not going to help things, you little whelp!' the Sheriff replied angrily. He was trying to be patient with them, but what did they expect? Didn't they understand the position he was in? He couldn't simply open the door and tell them to leave.

'I believe what my cousin here is trying to say,' Tom motioned towards Aneirin, 'is that we are prisoners here. We have done no wrong, Sheriff, as you know. There can be no charge against us. You seem like a good man, you could let us go. We would disappear. Your mistress need not hear from us again.'

The Sheriff stared at the ground, 'Look young man, do not call her my *mistress*. This situation is complicated. I cannot let you go, if I did then…' he trailed off.

'We could find a way to protect you,' Tom said kindly

'You protect me?' the Sheriff laughed darkly. 'You are children. What could you possibly do to protect me?'

'Perhaps you don't need to do anything so obvious as to let us leave. All you need to do is to leave the staff within reach.' Tom added nodding at the staff the Sheriff still held in his hand.

The Sheriff suddenly looked at the staff as though he had forgotten that he had been holding it at all. *What use was the staff to this boy?* he thought. They were children, what could they possibly achieve with the old man's staff?

The boys looked at one another, several moments had passed and the Sheriff was still standing looking at the staff blindly. Aneirin shuffled his feet which seemed to break the daze the Sheriff had entered.

'Boys,' he said pausing. 'I don't want any harm to come to you. But I cannot let you or this staff out of my sight. I will ensure that you are fed, and I will take you to Lady Naithara this evening as instructed. You have had a long day; I would suggest that you both try to get some sleep. Are you not tired?' He didn't wish to carry on this conversation further, as he was starting to feel sick.

With that he swept out of the cell and closed the door. As they heard the lock turn in the door Aneirin looked up at Tom. 'Great work, I think we'll be out of here in no time.'

Tom looked at the ground. Aneirin's attitude wasn't going to help them. 'I thought perhaps we could convince him to help us. I know from the way he's behaved that he doesn't believe in Lady Naithara's cause the way the others do. I think he just feels trapped and now can't think of a way out.'

'So what do you suggest?' Aneirin snapped, getting more frustrated. 'You saw the way he reacted. He doesn't believe that two young boys would be able to protect him from the wrath he would face if he let us go. To be honest, I have no idea how we could protect him either!'

'Perhaps,' Tom said thoughtfully. 'But that doesn't mean that we still can't use this situation to our advantage. We will see him again when we are brought our food. I doubt he will let anyone other than himself have contact with us in case we decide to start shouting about why we are here. I also don't think that he will use a great deal of force if we tried to escape.'

'We will need to get your staff back if we try to escape. We won't be able to defend ourselves out there without it,' Aneirin added.

'You're right, we will need the staff,' Tom said dejectedly.

Several moments passed in silence as the boys tried to come up with an idea which would help them to get out of this situation. They needed to find a way to escape and get the staff back.

'There is a window in the door there,' Aneirin said, pointing to a small square window inset in the cell door. 'If you go up on my shoulders you could look out to see if you can see the staff anywhere in the main office.'

'Good idea!' Tom replied. 'Please, let the staff be visible from here,' he said to himself. 'If we can't locate it before we make our escape things could become very difficult.'

Aneirin went over to the door and crouched down to allow Tom to climb onto his shoulders. Once they were sure that Tom was in place he slowly stood up using the door to help support some of the weight. Once standing up fully Tom quickly scanned the room through the small window. He could just make out the desk at the front of the station where the young man was sitting. Tom noticed that the boy had nodded-off, that could be helpful. Looking in the other direction he saw the office which Sheriff MacDonald occupied. Just inside the door, which was lying open, he could see the staff sitting inside an umbrella stand. 'Aneirin, you can put me down now,' he whispered.

'What did you see?' Aneirin asked expectantly.

'He has the staff in his office. It's just left of the room across the hall. The door is lying open, we just have to hope that it stays that way when he comes in here later on.'

'Did you notice anything else?' Aneirin asked, obviously hoping that there had been some more information which would aid their escape.

'The man on the front desk is asleep,' Tom said excitedly. 'If we could incapacitate the Sheriff somehow and if we could do it quietly, we may be able to escape past him without attracting too much attention.' Tom, even as he said this, had a puzzled expression on his face. How were they going to incapacitate a grown man when they had no weapons?

'The only thing we have in here is the bench and that bucket over there,' Aneirin said, pointing towards the make shift toilet in the corner.

'I suppose that will just have to do. It's a long shot, but we can't just sit here and wait to be taken to Lady Naithara this evening. Can we?'

* * *

When Torean and Adaira had finally received the news about what had happened to the boys it had been mid afternoon.

Adaira, who was frantically untying the horse said, 'We must go now! I cannot wait here while they have my son Torean.' She had a crazed look on her face.

'Adaira, stop,' Torean said, now looked extremely drained. The old man had been racking his brains trying to come up with their best next move. 'I do not want to sit here and wait either. However, we'll never make it down to the village before nightfall.'

'What are you suggesting?' Adaira barked angrily, her voice hoarse from crying. 'That we camp here and risk losing them in order to save our own skins?' She was starting to cry again now.

'Of course I'm not suggesting that, Adaira.' Torean hated seeing her this way. He felt that this whole situation was his fault. 'Remember, we are no good to the boys if we are dead. If we set off now, we could be back at Devil's Ford by nightfall. At least then we are cutting some time from our journey back into the village.'

Adaira was not happy at the thought of them only completing such a short leg of their journey when her son was in such dire peril. But she at least felt comforted by the fact that they were going to get moving immediately. She hated the thought of sitting still and worrying about where her son might be, considering what may be happening to him. The whole situation made her feel physically sick.

The two headed off down the mountain side with Torean leading them and Adaira following behind leading Onero down the rocky path. Neither of them spoke to one another on their way down the trail. There seemed to be no words to communicate how they were both feeling. Adaira had thought that things could not get any worse after losing their home. The thought of losing Aneirin was unbearable. If she lost him, then the last part of Abhainn she had left would be gone.

Torean also felt that he had inflicted enough pain upon his family. He would not permit anything to happen to his grandson, not after losing his boy.

The journey seemed to take so much longer than it had that morning when they had all been fleeing through the countryside. Torean felt somehow grateful for the journey. He was not looking forward to setting up camp in the last place they had all been together. In spite of this, he could not see that they had any choice. No matter how tempted he may feel to rush after the boys, he knew it would be folly to try to set out down the mountainside at night. If the weather turned, or they made a wrong footing it could be fatal.

When they arrived at Devil's Ford Adaira tied Onero to a tree. It was the same spot where they had been camped previously, and she set about lighting a fire and preparing a meal for Torean and herself. It was like they had never left. She was not hungry, but out of routine, and also to delay the time when she would have to stop and think about what was happening, she went through the motions of preparing them food. As she was doing this she thought about the fact that it somehow felt like so long ago that the four of them had been camped there together. The day had changed everything. When they had lost their home it had been hard, but they had still had one another.

Torean went out into the trees and returned shortly with a dead rabbit. He had not gone hunting out of hunger, but more so he could avoid seeing Adaira's face. It was hard to see her in so much pain. He sat in silence and skinned the small animal, preparing it to add to the broth which Adaira was preparing.

He was then surprised that the smell of the food as it cooked made him feel hungry. It wasn't until the meal was being prepared that Torean had realised that neither of them had eaten at all that day. It hadn't seemed important. Why would you eat at such a time?

The two sat and ate their meal in silence. As they finished Adaira took Torean's bowl from him and said, 'So do you have a plan?' Her voice was slightly hoarse from the exertions of the day.

Torean looked up and said, 'Not exactly.' He had never felt this tired in his life. 'I think we need to get to the outskirts of the town and head for Old Wilson's farm. He is aware of our situation and it will give you somewhere safe to wait until I can get the boys back.'

At this Adaira shot him an angry glance. 'If you think I am going to sit in a house nursing a cup of tea waiting for you to save my son you are gravely mistaken.'

'I just want to try to keep you safe, my dear,' Torean pleaded.

'It's a little late for that, Torean,' Adaira said in a tone which she immediately regretted. 'We are all involved in this,' she added in a kinder voice. 'I will not sit and wait for bad news. I already lost Abhainn. I may not have been able to control that, but I will not allow the same fate to befall my son.' Adaira had lost her forlorn look and now appeared to have a steely determination.

'I will never forgive myself for what happened to Abhainn,' said Torean, wiping a tear from his eye. 'And believe me, I understand your feelings on the matter. If I cannot sway you, then we must do this together. Nevertheless, I still think we should head for Old Wilson's first. I will need somewhere to gather my thoughts on how best to proceed, and he may have information on what has been happening in the village in our absence.'

I will trust your judgement there,' Adaira said after a brief silence. 'For now we must try to get some rest,' she conceded. She too felt weary to carry on talking on the subject.

At that Torean noticed that some fairies had entered the clearing. It was as though the tiny creatures could sense their grief.

Adaira had never seen fairies before and couldn't help but look up in awe.

They fluttered between the two like little fire flies. Dancing in an intricate formation, the creatures moved in a way which suggested they knew exactly how graceful they were. The beautiful light show seemed to bring them both out of themselves, and the two sat holding hands both watching the skies. The little brown creatures were gone as quickly as they had come, but they seemed to remind the pair exactly what they were fighting for.

After a short spell of silence Torean continued their conversation. 'We should rise just before dawn to ensure that we can be on our way as early as possible.' He felt slightly more positive. 'I think we should head from here down past Longford's Pass. While it is not the route the group took town into the village yesterday, it will bring us out at the right point to head for Wilson's place without being noticed.'

Adaira nodded.

'Goodnight, Adaira,' he said to her fondly. 'I will get your son back for you.' Once again Torean had a tear in his eye.

'We will both get them back,' said Adaira touching his hand. 'And when the time comes, I want to see the look of defeat in her eyes. We cannot permit her to succeed, not after this,' she said vengefully. 'If it takes my last breath I will make her pay for what she has done to our family. And if she has laid a hand on my boy I will strike her down personally.'

'Don't worry on that account, my dear,' said Torean heartened by her words. 'When the battle comes, I will wreak vengeance upon those who have caused us this pain. But for now we must content ourselves with the knowledge that they will not harm the boys while they are useful to them.'

'Yes, that's true. Goodnight, Torean,' Adaira said. She was comforted by the thought that the boys should remain reasonably safe while the group needed them to lure Torean from the hills.

With that the two of them lay down near the remnants of their fire and tried to get some sleep. They had not feared lighting a fire that night. Somehow it felt like they had nothing left to lose. It was not easy for either of them to doze off despite their exhaustion. Be that as it may, if they were to have enough strength for the coming day they knew they had no choice. As such they both lay dozing instead of properly sleeping throughout the night, both anxious to be up and on their way.

'*Cabhair*,' Torean softly said as they lay down. This incantation usually relieved the suffering of those around you. He didn't know whether it would work in this case, but wanted to do anything he could to help Adaira find some peace.

As Adaira dozed, she saw a mixture of images. She saw the boys in pain being dragged along the ground by the group. The images were interspersed with flashing pictures of small fairies. They weaved in and out of her dreams posing with their slim bodies and white blonde hair.

Chapter Fifteen
The Long Wait

Lizzy was impatiently pottering around the house distractedly carrying out her morning chores. They had arrived back the previous afternoon and she was already finding it unbearable waiting for news about Torean and his family. This was made doubly difficult by the fact that she knew the first news she was likely to receive would be discerned from Lady Naithara's mood when she returned from her trip into the hills.

Their journey the previous day had been reasonably uneventful. They had travelled quietly, partially because they did not wish to alert anyone who may be in the hills that they were travelling, and partially because they were all rather frightened by the prospect which lay ahead. The events of the previous days had all been rather a lot to take in. This had consisted of Lizzy believing Torean dead, only to find out that this was in fact not the case. She had then discovered that her mistress was in collusion with evil spirits, something which was incredible in itself. Finally she had found that a man she had known all her life, Torean MacKay, was in fact some kind of sorcerer.

Lizzy just keep calm. You have done everything you can to help, she thought to herself.

When they arrived back she had busied herself catching up on chores in the house. Although the estate was of a reasonable size, recent lack of money within the Laird's family had meant that she was the only servant in residence. She managed to avoid unwanted conversations with the cook who came in and had asked why no-one had given her prior notice to the fact that the family were going away for an overnight stay. Lizzy had simply told her that she had not had any notice herself. This didn't seem to pacify the grumpy old woman, but there was nothing else to be said. Lizzy found herself almost laughing with amusement at the thought of how the cook would have reacted if she had told her what had really happened.

Putting all the thoughts of the previous day aside she went into the kitchen to prepare some mid-morning tea for the Laird. Taking a tray up to his study she knocked on the door and waited.

'Enter,' said the familiar voice from inside.

She opened the door and entered quietly. 'My Lord, I am just bringing you some tea.' She looked at him waiting for a response. Despite their adventures of the past few days, being back in the house had made Lizzy revert to her normal formality with the old man.

The Laird's study was a fairly large room with an open fire. There were shelves containing many books, and in the corner, a large desk behind which the old man sat.

As Lizzy entered the room, the Laird could tell by her expression and the tone of her voice that she was getting extremely frustrated. 'My dear,' he said kindly. 'I know this is difficult but we must try to be patient. I assume that my niece has not made an appearance as yet?'

'No sign, my Lord,' Lizzy said despondently.

'Well, she should be back today. I would not imagine that her group would stay in the hills for more than one night. It would cause too much suspicion,' the Laird said taking a cup from Lizzy. 'Thank you, my dear.'

'If I may be so bold,' she said cautiously, 'what are you doing while we wait?'

'Lizzy, my dear,' the Laird said patiently. 'I believe we are beyond the point where you should feel you cannot freely ask me such questions. If you must know, I am going through some old books and papers from the library,' he said, picking up huge bundles of papers tied to together with string. 'My great grandfather amassed quite a large collection of texts, many of which involved the occult. He was, shall we say, a keen observer? I am working on the assumption that my niece learned something about her arts from the works in this house. I cannot see where else she would have learned about the power held within Cairn Holme.' He suddenly looked angry as he turned over pages which lay strewn on the desk in front of him.

'Have you ever read such books before?' Lizzy asked, slightly frightened at the thought of books containing evil being kept in the house.

'No, my dear,' the Laird said, trying to reassure her. 'Although I was aware that they were in the library, I personally have never had any interest in such subjects. In all honesty I had forgotten about them until this situation arose. I realise that we will be highly unlikely to be able to help Torean when he has to fight this evil, but I thought it wouldn't hurt to try to obtain any information possible about what this could mean.' He had an expression on his face which showed that he didn't believe he would find anything worthwhile, but that he had to be doing something. The old man had always fallen back on books his entire life. In all other situations they had provided the knowledge he needed, or more importantly, the comfort he had needed. He was desperately seeking some of that now.

'Yes,' Lizzy said looking hopeful. 'It comforts me to know that we are not just sitting here waiting for bad news.' She turned and headed back towards the door. 'I had best let you get on with your work. If you require anything just ring the bell.'

'Thank you, Lizzy, you are most kind,' he said smiling at her fondly. 'If you can let me know when my niece returns I would be most grateful. Although, please ensure that you do so subtly. She will have gone off on this mission with the hope that I would not notice her absence. I believe it would be best to keep up this pretence for the time being.'

'Yes, my Lord,' Lizzy replied exiting the room. She walked down the stairs and looked at the clock. It was eleven thirty. She wondered when Lady Naithara would return. If her journey took a similar length to the one they had taken the previous day she should hopefully be back in the early afternoon.

Lady Naithara made an appearance later on the afternoon, just before four o'clock. Lizzy tried to appear as though she did not find this unusual.

She took Naithara's coat from her and enquired whether she would like to take tea.

'Ah,' said Naithara wearily. 'That would be wonderful. I have had quite an eventful morning; can you please bring it to my room? I would like to have a late afternoon nap.'

'Of course, my Lady,' said Lizzy following her up the stairs.

When Lizzy entered the Lady's room carrying a tray containing a pot of tea and some fresh crumpets, she noticed that Naithara had drawn the curtains and was sitting up in bed by lamp light.

'Thank you, Lizzy,' she said smiling. 'You are a godsend.'

Lizzy sat the tray on Naithara's lap and enquired innocently, 'You look rather pale, my Lady. I hope that you are not coming down with something?'

'Do not worry about me,' said Naithara, picking up the teapot and pouring it into her cup. 'It is simply exhaustion. I have had a busy morning.'

'What were you doing?' Lizzy enquired further.

'Erm,' said Naithara trying to come up with a plausible explanation. 'Well, come now, Lizzy, a young lady is allowed to have some secrets,' she said, hoping to lead Lizzy away from further questions by suggesting that she may have a young beau.

'Of course, my Lady, forgive my impertinent question,' Lizzy said with a slight curtsey. 'I hope that your ventures were fruitful?'

What a strange question? Naithara thought. Then she dismissed this thinking that Lizzy must have believed her suggestion about meeting a young man. 'Yes,' she replied trying to look demure. 'They were very fruitful indeed.' She thought to herself, *more fruitful than you can imagine my dear.*

'Will you be dining with us this evening?' Lizzy said, hoping to glean any form of information she could about Naithara's plans for the rest of the day.

'Of course,' Naithara replied matter-of-factly. It was like a verbal game of chess, she knew she must be careful what she said to avoid making the girl suspicious. If Lizzy did notice her sneaking out the in the night she may be curious, perhaps it would be best to mention her late night rendezvous following the story of her imaginary beau. 'Can I trust you with a secret Lizzy?' she enquired.

'Of course you can,' Lizzy said, feeling slightly apprehensive about what Naithara was about to divulge.

'I will be going out tonight,' she said using an extremely silly voice. 'I have arranged a secret meeting with my love tonight at midnight. Will you keep this secret from my uncle?'

'Yes, my Lady,' Lizzy said, trying not to look too relieved. 'I would be glad to keep such a secret, new love is so exciting.' She did her best to appear in awe of Naithara.

'Yes it is,' Naithara said smugly. She was happy that this silly girl seemed to be lapping up her every word. 'Now, Lizzy,' she continued. 'If you don't mind, I am weary. Can you wake me in a couple of hours?'

'Yes, my Lady,' Lizzy said, curtseying and backing away towards he door. 'Enjoy your nap.'

'Thank you, Lizzy,' Naithara said, sipping her tea.

Lizzy closed the door softly behind her. It took all her strength not to gallop down the hallway to the Laird's study. She slowly walked away and back to the staircase. Now out of sight of Lady Naithara's room she could contain herself no longer. She held her skirts to stop her tripping and took the stairs two at a time until she was on the next landing. Slightly out of breath, she took a moment to compose herself and then knocked on the Laird's study door.

'Enter,' the Laird said nonchalantly. He knew he could not sound anxious in case his visitor was his niece. As the door opened and Lizzy entered he looked visibly relieved.

Lizzy closed the door behind her and stood at the door.

'Well, my girl?' the Laird asked impatiently. 'Don't just stand there, come in and take a seat. Tell me everything she has said.'

Lizzy crossed the room and took the seat opposite the Laird at this desk. It felt strange sitting across from him here, she had never been in this position before. She took a deep breath before starting and said, 'It's hard to say.' She wasn't really sure where to begin. 'She is tired, and has gone for a rest. She fed me a story that she had been out meeting a secret lover. She also confided in me that she is sneaking out of the house tonight to meet this mystery man at midnight.'

'Interesting,' said the Laird.

'What do you think it means?' Lizzy asked feeling frustrated.

'Well,' the Laird mused stroking his chin. 'It is worrying that she doesn't seem to be in a dark mood. This suggests that their mission had some level of success.'

'Oh God, no,' Lizzy muttered, putting hands to her face.

'The fact that she has told you about this fictitious meeting with a lover this evening suggests that they are meeting again tonight. She obviously thought it best to tell you about this so that if you saw her leaving the house you would not be suspicious.'

'So what do we do?' Lizzy asked pleadingly.

'All we can do just now is make sure that we follow her this evening and try to find out what is happening. Did she mention where she was going?'

'No,' Lizzy said, now angry with herself for not asking this question when she had the Lady's ear. 'Will it be the clearing beyond the aviary again?'

'Probably,' the Laird replied. 'We know that they have met there more than once. It would seem strange to try to find somewhere else secluded to have their gathering. Nevertheless, it would probably be best for us to follow behind her just in case. I would suggest that we leave the house around eleven fifteen and wait in a quiet part of the garden. When she leaves through the scullery door, we should then be able to follow close behind her to ensure that we don't miss what is happening. We will need to be careful to ensure that we find somewhere close by to watch, but somewhere we cannot be seen.'

'If it is by the aviary,' Lizzy mused, 'we can hopefully hide where we did before.'

'We shall see,' the Laird replied. 'For now, we must carry on as normal. Go through this evening as though nothing unusual is going on.'

'I wish we could contact Mr Wilson,' Lizzy said.

'Unfortunately that is not practical given the timescales involved,' the Laird said, frustrated at the prospect himself. 'We shall need to go along, and then update Wilson with anything we hear tomorrow.'

* * *

Back in their jail cell, the two boys were going over the plan they had formulated to try to overcome the Sheriff when he entered the room. They had dragged the bench over to the wall next to the door. It was against a wall so that when the door opened the person standing on the bench would be concealed.

'So,' said Tom pacing up and down. 'I'll stand on the bench holding the metal bucket. When he opens the door, I will hit him over the head with it.'

'Do you really think it will knock him out?' Aneirin asked doubtfully.

'Maybe not,' said Tom feeling frustrated. 'Although even if it doesn't knock him out it should stun him, hopefully that would give you enough time to be able to make a run for his office and retrieve the staff.'

'Wouldn't you be better to get the staff?' Aneirin said starting to feel nervous.

'You are faster than me,' Tom said. 'Anyway, don't doubt yourself. I'm sure you could use the staff if you had to.'

'I hope you're right,' Aneirin replied, his voice full of doubt.

Suddenly they heard the lock turning in the door. Tom rushed to take his place on the bench and waited. His heart was pounding as he lifted the heavy metal bucket over his head and waited. It was only a bucket, but it felt like a tonne weight as he stood there, his arms beginning to shake.

The Sheriff opened the door. He was holding a tray which had a jug on it, some mugs, a loaf of bread and some cheese.

As the door closed over behind him, Tom took his chance and brought the bucket down over his head. It hit the man with a dull thud and he fell to the floor sending the tray flying.

With the mugs bouncing loudly on the hard cell floor, Aneirin nodded to Tom and shot out of the door towards the Sheriff's office.

The blow had not knocked the man out, and he was now lying spread on the floor concussed, trying to figure out what had happened. Tom didn't waste anytime and leapt from the bench towards the cell door.

The Sheriff, however, was too quick for Tom and staggering to stand up, managed to grab Tom's arm as he tried to get out of the door.

The Sheriff had left his office door open. Aneirin rushed into the room and retrieved the staff. His heart beating fast, he turned round and headed back out of the office door just in time to see Tom appear in the door way. He then saw Tom being yanked back into the room.

Aneirin froze as he saw that Tom was not free of the Sheriff. He was trying to think of anything he could do with the staff to help free Tom, but in his fear his mind had gone completely blank. Time suddenly seemed to stand still, all he could hear was his heart beating loudly in his chest.

'Run!' Tom shouted to him desperately.

This tore Aneirin from his daze and he sprinted towards the front door. He had no idea what he was doing, he couldn't leave Tom behind. But he knew if he turned back they would both be caught.

David was sitting behind the desk in a daze as Aneirin ran past him.

Aneirin burst through the front door looking left and right in the street and decided to head towards the Laird's house. He then thought, you fool! Thinking better of his first choice, he decided it would be better to hide somewhere until the Sheriff had gone rather than to be seen running up the street. He turned left and then took the nearest side street he came to. He wouldn't last two seconds against a grown man. Out of breath he crouched down and sat shaking, clutching Tom's staff in his grasp. It took all of his control not to vomit on the street where he sat.

Back in the cell, the Sheriff spun Tom round and hit him hard in the face. The man had not wanted to be in this position, but he couldn't believe that the little wretches had attacked him. He had finally had enough. Even if he was making this child bear the brunt of the anger he really felt towards Naithara and the Provost he didn't care. He was not going to give the Provost the opportunity to gloat at his failure.

Tom fell to the floor with the blow and hid his face in his hands. He was like a frightened animal, and the blow had stunned him so that he no longer thought of running.

The Sheriff then quickly slammed the door on Tom and shouted to David, 'Lock that blasted door!'

The boy, who had been dozing until the sudden commotion, was still dazed looking around the office. Nothing like this had ever happened before.

'Move now!' the Sheriff screamed at him.

The Sheriff burst out into the street and looked around him. He cursed at the top of his voice, 'Damn you, you little fiend! I'll find you!' He then turned right and ran up the street towards the edge of the village and the hills. He assumed that the boy had tried to head back to where his family was likely to be.

Aneirin was hidden behind a bin in an alley up the side of the local tavern. He heard the Sheriff's footsteps running in the opposite direction and felt relieved. He slowly crept out of the alley way and looked up the street in the direction the Sheriff had ran. It was starting to grow dark, and he thought he had best head towards the Laird's house and find Lizzy.

Tom was lying on the cell floor feeling sick. Wiping the blood from his lip, he looked at his hand and couldn't control himself any longer. He began to weep uncontrollably as his panic set in. He had no way to escape on his own. He had never wanted to be with his grandfather more. After everything he had achieved since arriving with Torean and his family, he suddenly felt like a frightened child again. He was alone and he was helpless. Unless Aneirin made it, he may also have lost his grandfather's staff. He hadn't felt fear like this since he had lost his father. He sat back against the bench and took a deep breath. He knew he needed to steady himself. Tom shook his head and looked up towards the only light now in the room, which was coming from the small window in the cell door. He definitely preferred adventures when he was safe enjoying them from the right side of the pages.

Chapter Sixteen
The Condemned Man

Lizzy and the Laird sat together in his study watching the clock. It was past eleven and the evening had dragged waiting for them to find out what had happened during Naithara's trip into the hills. Dinner had been a long affair. Despite the Laird's valiant attempt to seem jovial and light hearted, Lizzy could still sense that there was a great uneasiness in the room.

As soon as they had finished eating their food the Laird was desperate to leave his niece's company, worried that he may say something to make her suspicious. 'Well, my dear,' he said smiling across the table at her. 'I hope you won't think me rude if I pay you my leave? I am in the middle of reading through some rather fascinating papers on ancient fishing rights.'

'Of course, uncle,' Naithara replied smiling.

'Hah,' the Laird said jovially. 'I see that you find the pleasures of an old man amusing. I must say that I can understand why a young lady would not be entertained by such subjects, eh Lizzy?' He now winked over at Lizzy.

'Yes, my Lord,' she said with a slight curtsey. She was worried that the Laird was trying a little too hard to seem nonchalant.

Naithara rose from her chair. 'Don't worry, uncle. I do not question the workings of your mind when I know that I could never match your intellect.'

Lizzy thought that this too seemed a strange comment for Naithara to make. She usually acted as though she believed she needed to try to control the Laird's behaviour because he was incapable. Perhaps she too was nervous this evening that the Laird would pass comment on the fact that she had been absent from the house the previous evening.

As such the three went about their business as best as possible and the evening passed extremely slowly.

The Laird nodded and stood up, saying to Lizzy, 'Well, my girl, I think it best we make a move. We have to be in front of her when she leaves the house. Go to your room and fetch your travelling cloak, I will meet you in the scullery.

Lizzy dashed from the room and hurried up the narrow staircase which led to her living quarters. Grabbing her cloak quickly she rushed back down the stairs to meet the Laird.

He was waiting for her in the scullery when she entered and motioned for her to be quiet. He then opened the back door and the two of them silently moved out in to the garden. They chose a spot behind a large tree, hoping that its shadow would render them invisible to anyone leaving the house, where they waited patiently.

Ten minutes after their arrival they heard the back door open for a second time and Lady Naithara ran out into the night. They allowed her to leave the immediate area before giving chase quietly across the grass. They moved with stealth being careful to make their journey in stages. They had to move between things like trees and bushes to ensure that they were not left out in the open should Naithara choose to look behind her.

After a time they were relieved when they realised that Naithara was in fact returning to the clearing by the aviary. This meant that they knew where they could hide and still have a good vantage point to watch the group. When they arrived they managed to quietly take up their previous position behind the boxes next to the aviary itself. The area was very quiet, all the birds were asleep and the Laird thought that they would need to be careful at this point as any noise could result in them being found out.

Naithara went around the clearing setting up the torches as she had before and then waited in the shadows for her guests to arrive.

Slowly the men arrived one by one, cloaked as before. The scene made for a gruesome sight. They were like evil spectres gathered to carry out foul deeds. The group, now back to its full compliment after the return of the two who had gone on the fruitless mission to try to catch Adaira and her son, stood and whispered to one another in hushed tones, now awaiting the arrival of the Sheriff with his prisoners.

Before long the Sheriff appeared in the clearing dragging Tom along behind him. He was a sorry sight. The blow the Sheriff had dealt him had already come up as a large bruise and he had dried blood on his face and shirt.

The group muttered to one another as they saw him approach.

Naithara looked livid, 'What is the meaning of this, Michael? Are you delivering our boys one at a time, or has something happened?'

'Well,' stuttered the Sheriff, who was terrified by what his punishment would be. 'There was a minor incident earlier today.'

The group was now no longer muttering, but was cursing at the Sheriff.

Lizzy looked at the Laird terrified. 'Naithara said *boys*,' she whispered. 'That means they got Aneirin too. What have they done to him?'

Lizzy felt an arm around her shoulder and looked up to smile at the Laird gratefully, when she realised that it was not the Laird who was comforting her. She almost gasped aloud, but was stopped by a hand reaching round over her mouth.

'I'm here. I told you that you couldn't get rid of me that easily,' Aneirin's voice whispered in her ear.

Lizzy wasn't sure whether she felt completely terrified, or overjoyed that Aneirin seemed to have evaded their clutches.

Meanwhile, Naithara was holding up her hands to quieten the group of men. 'Michael,' she said looking at him with utter hatred. 'Prey, tell us about this *incident* which befell you this afternoon. I assume by the looks of things that it involved beating our boy here to within an inch of his life?'

The Sheriff was terrified. How could he explain to her that one of the boys had escaped? 'They attacked me, my Lady. One of them got away, but I managed to keep this one.' He gestured towards Tom who was down on his knees with his hands bound. The Sheriff's sadly hopeful expression was almost pitiful.

'I see,' said Naithara gravely. 'We shall summon my master and see what he has to say.'

'Please,' the Sheriff begged.

'Silence!' Naithara bellowed. 'While you have kept one of the boys, it is not even Torean's grandson. Who is this little wretch?' she asked, looking at Tom as though he was a disgusting piece of excrement.

'My Lady,' continued the Sheriff, unsure of why he was still talking, 'the boy says that he is Aneirin's cousin.'

'Cousin, eh,' said Naithara. 'Well hopefully such a distant relative will be enough to lure the old man from the hills.

With that Naithara swept round and began the chant. The other men joined in and the winds began to rise. As before the clearing was suddenly filled with the thick presence which came with Eiric.

'What do you have for me?' the deep disembodied voice called.

'My Lord,' said Naithara grovelling. 'We have a boy, a relative of Torean MacKay. We hope to use him as bait to lure the old man to us.'

There was no response.

'We also have his staff,' Naithara said, hoping that this would placate her master.

'Show it to me,' he boomed.

'Of course,' Naithara muttered.

At once Lady Naithara's face changed. Eiric had entered her body in order to use her eyes. Tom noticed that her face now appeared very long and angular, and her eyes looked like those of a wolf staring through the dark.

He looked at Tom and muttered.

Agony flowed through the boy's body, leaving him writhing on the ground.

'You have found a staff bearer alright, but you do not have his staff. Who is responsible for this?'

Before the Sheriff could speak in his defence the Provost spat venomously, 'The fault lies with this wretch!' He was pointing at the Sheriff.

A light flashed through the air from Naithara's eyes striking the Sheriff in the chest. Like a puppet with its strings suddenly cut, the Sheriff fell to the ground dead.

They were all afraid, all except the Provost. The men in the group were looking from one to the other now terrified that they could be next to feel Eiric's powerful wrath. The Provost was looking at the Sheriff's broken body enraptured by the sight. He almost looked like he envied the powers which Eiric could command.

Lizzy hid her head in Aneirin's breast disgusted by what she saw. She could not control her fear. If this being had just killed the Sheriff without a second thought, what was he going to do to Tom?

'Let me see the staff wielder,' said the voice, which seemed extremely out of place coming from Naithara's mouth.

Tom was dragged forward, his face ashen white.

The Provost pulled Tom's hair to force his face upwards.

'Where is the staff?' the voice screamed, its piercing eyes drilling through Tom's soul.

Tom didn't know the answer. He knew that Aneirin had the staff, but not where he had taken it when he had fled the Sheriff's offices. He couldn't have said so aloud, he was far too afraid. He didn't know where to look. He couldn't look at the ground without seeing the Sheriff's blank eyes looking up at him.

Her master was livid. 'You have brought me this mute boy!' As he spoke he exited Naithara's body. She crumbled to the ground.

Naithara began to beg, she was on all fours on the ground. 'Master, the boy will draw the old man.'

'That is not good enough! I gave you a simple task.' The voice seemed to be swirling around the clearing now as it spoke.

Naithara cowered. She knew that she dare not speak for fear that this would make matters worse.

The winds rose around them, it was extremely loud. Tom watched as the leaves began blowing up around the clearing into a whirlwind.

As quickly as the winds had begun there was complete silence. It was the kind of silence which could almost seem deafening after such an incredible noise.

'You have been faithful,' Eiric then said in a voice much quieter than he had used before. 'I will therefore grant you mercy.'

'Thank you, my Lord!' Naithara exclaimed, raising her hands towards the heavens.

'You will have two more of your days to fix this. Call me here again when twelve o'clock chimes.'

'Yes, my Lord,' Naithara stuttered, looking at the ground.

A wind rushed around the clearing once more and died away. Eiric was gone.

The group stayed where they were standing. No one spoke for what seemed like a long time.

The Minister approached Naithara and warily put a hand on her shoulder. 'My Lady,' he said hesitantly. 'What should we do with erm, with the Sheriff?' He pointed to where the body was still lying on the ground.

Naithara looked up, her face tear stained. 'I don't know,' she said sounding like a small child. 'Do you have any ideas?'

The Minister walked over to the body and looked at him for a long time. He walked back to Naithara. 'There isn't a mark on him,' he said trying not to show his disgust at the situation. 'I will get one of the men to help me. I think we could take him back to his house, put him in his bed. I will go by in the morning to visit him, and find him dead in his bed.'

'Thank you,' said Naithara.

The Minister put out a hand and helped Naithara to her feet. 'I think you should return home. You will need your rest if we are to start bright and early tomorrow morning to fix this.'

She smiled at him. 'Thank you.' She rose to her feet and suddenly noticed Tom still standing near where the Sheriff was lying. 'Ah,' she said despondently. 'I forgot about the boy. With the Sheriff gone, I'm not sure what to do with him.'

The Provost overheard this and stepped forward. 'I will take him, my Lady.'

'Thank you, Hamish,' she said smiling. 'That would be very helpful. If you can find somewhere safe to keep him, we will need to gather again tomorrow night. I will contact you tomorrow with more details. I think we need to do something to lure Torean out of the Shadows. I will go home and consult my texts. There must be an enchantment to lure him here.'

'Of course, my Lady,' the Provost said bowing his head. 'I am honoured that you have trusted me with such a task.' He turned to towards Tom with an extremely evil look upon his face. He was going to enjoy playing with this little wretch. She needed him alive, but that still left him some room for a little fun.

The group slowly dispersed from the clearing. The Minister and another man were carrying the Sheriff's body away while the Provost grabbed Tom by his scruff and dragged him away.

After they had all gone Lizzy, Aneirin and the Laird emerged from their hiding place. They were all absolutely petrified.

'We can't leave him with that man,' Aneirin exclaimed, looking like he wanted to follow them there and then.

'Aneirin, my lad,' said the Laird. 'I don't like the Provost either. However it would be extremely dangerous for us to try to rescue him tonight.'

'We can't just leave him?' Lizzy whispered, feeling sick.

'We don't have any choice for now. I suggest that we go home and try to get some rest. We should then head off to Wilson's farm as soon as possible tomorrow morning. We are going to need to come up with a plan to get young Tom. I also have come across something among my books which we will need to discuss.'

'What?' Lizzy cut in hopefully.

'Not tonight, dear,' the Laird replied wearily. 'I think we have seen enough tonight. I do not have the stomach to discuss these matters further.'

'Where will I go?' Aneirin asked looking around him.

'Come back with us,' the Laird said putting an arm around him. 'I know it's not ideal, but I think you can sleep in the outhouse in the garden. Naithara will not know you are there, and it means that Lizzy and I can fetch you on our way through the gardens tomorrow morning. You would be safer at Wilson's house than you would be here in the centre of town.'

'Thank you,' said Aneirin gratefully.

'Not at all, my boy,' replied the Laird. 'Now come, let us get some sleep if we can. We are going to have a very busy day tomorrow.'

With that the group headed back towards the Laird's house. They had given Naithara a fifteen minute heard start which meant that she should be safe inside the house by the time they entered.

Meanwhile Tom was being dragged up a dirt path towards a dark house on the outskirts of the village. The place suited the Provost. It had a definite dark air of evil.

The Provost pushed him through a door into a large kitchen and Tom fell to the floor.

'Be quiet, you little fool!' he whispered loudly. 'If anyone hears you bumbling about, you will regret it.' The man then walked towards the sideboard and lit a lamp which sat upon it. He dragged Tom to his feet and led him towards a door at the far end of the room. When the door opened it revealed a narrow staircase spiralling downwards. He pushed Tom down the stairs in front of him and Tom struggled to keep his balance with his hands bound.

As they entered the cellar Tom noticed that there were many bottles of wine arranged in an intricate rack which stretched the length of the ten foot room.

The Provost threw him to the floor and sat the lamp on a small table in the corner of the room. 'I think we're going to have some fun now,' he grinned at Tom and touched his meticulously groomed moustache. 'Do you think I should have a glass while we work? Hmm? It would make it so much more enjoyable. Something spicy I think.' He walked towards a rack and took out a dusty bottle considering its label carefully.

He sat down the bottle and approached Tom slowly. He pushed him onto a small chair in the corner of the room and stood over him smiling. Tom was petrified. He didn't want to imagine what this man would do to him. The Provost disappeared in the shadows and reappeared holding a long slim knife. He moved the knife in his hand letting the light catch the blade. Tom watched petrified as the man then approached him and stroked the blade against his face. He didn't like how much the man liked what he was doing.

'She needs you alive tomorrow, but that doesn't mean she needs you to be in perfect condition.' He was grinning at Tom hungrily.

With a swift move he kissed the blade against Tom's skin and the boy felt a searing pain across his cheek. Hot blood trickled down his face and onto his neck. It took everything he had not to scream from the pain, but he didn't want to give the Provost the satisfaction.

Suddenly a woman's voice came up the stairs in the kitchen. 'Hamish? Is that you?'

'Damn,' cursed the man.

'Are you in the cellar?' she continued. 'What are you doing down there?'

'You,' he whispered to Tom. 'Stay quiet. If you do not, I will cut off every one of your little fingers. You don't need them to help to lure the old man in.'

Tom said nothing, he was petrified. He simply hoped that the woman would distract the man from what he had been going to do for him.

'Coming, darling,' the Provost said in a sickly sweet voice. He sat down the bloody knife and ran up the stairs with the lamp, closing the cellar door behind him.

Tom who was now in complete darkness heard a key turn in the lock as the door closed. He could still hear their voices in the kitchen although the sound was muffled.

'What were you doing down there at this hour?' said the woman.

'Just checking something about one of my vintages,' he replied convincingly. 'The Minister didn't believe me that we had a Chateau Ausone. I was looking it out so that I can show it to him next time he visits.'

The woman shook her head and tutted at him. 'You and your wine, are you coming to bed now?'

'Of course, my sweet,' he replied putting an arm around her.

Tom heard the footsteps die away as the pair left the kitchen and looked around him. He couldn't see a single thing. The boy had never been in such darkness. Leaning back against one of the racks he closed his eyes and tried to feel grateful for the fact that the Provost had not been able to carry on with his torture session. In spite of this he suddenly felt a great despair wash over him. How would his friends know where he was? Aneirin may try to return to the Sheriff's office to free him, and he wouldn't be there, the Sheriff. He couldn't exactly say that he felt pity for the man, but it was the first time Tom had seen a man killed in front of him. He was completely alone. If only he had kept his staff he would have felt like there was a part of his grandfather with him. He lay in the dark cold and afraid, with nothing to do but wait and despair.

Chapter Seventeen
The Long Journey Home

Torean and Adaira woke early in the morning in order to start their journey back down the hillside towards the village. They had little to say to one another as they packed up their bedding and saddled Onero. They could feel the boys' absence hanging over them, and knew that it would still be some time yet before they would have any news of what was happening to them.

'When do you think we will reach Old Wilson's farm?' Adaira asked. She was feeling impatient before they had even begun their journey.

'Well, my dear,' said Torean, 'it must be just before seven judging by the sun. So I think we could be there by around lunchtime.' He could feel her becoming impatient. 'The quicker we get going, the quicker we will get there lassie.'

She smiled in spite of herself. It felt strange to smile when her only son was in such peril. It felt almost like she was committing a sin. Should one be able to smile or laugh? Surely it would be impossible to keep up her permanent fear, she was exhausted by it. Since this whole thing had begun she felt like she had aged. She had never felt so drained, this somehow felt even worse than when she had lost her husband. She had been ignorant then of what had actually happened. The one thing that this whole situation had done was to explain what had really happened to her husband. When he had died, the whole thing had felt so pointless. He had gone, and it had happened for no reason. At least now she knew that he had died fighting for a worthy cause. She would use all the strength she had left to ensure that her boy did not die in the same way.

'Come, my old friend,' Torean said quietly, untying Onero's reins from the tree where he was tethered. The horse whinnied expectantly. The old man looked at the horse in awe. It was, as Tom had said, very aware of its surroundings. It was easy for Torean to forget this because of how used to Onero he was. He wondered what it would be like having to deal with an ordinary horse.

Without wasting any further time the two left the camp and it somehow felt strange. They were both desperate to head out after the boys, but somehow leaving the hillside and heading back to the village felt like they were leaving safety. They were heading back into the wolves den. It was a mixture of desperation and apprehension.

The road was hard, and with every step Torean saw the vision he had witnessed through the little bird's eyes of his grandson and Tom being dragged down the hillside.

They walked down the hillside towards the village with the little bird that had stayed with them in the clearing overnight following them from above.

Somehow the little feathered creature felt like his part in this story was not over yet. He didn't want to miss out on the adventure.

When they stopped for a brief rest half-way through the journey the little bird landed on Onero's head. The horse neighed softly to let him know that he was there. In response the bird hopped up and down on his head chirping loudly. It was almost like the two were laughing with one another.

The situation made Torean and Adaira laugh. It was nice to have something which distracted them from what was happening.

Torean felt himself becoming rather attached to the little creature. He had started as a link between his family and the people hunting them, and had become the only connection he had with his grandson who was in great danger.

After a light meal they continued down the hillside and after a couple of hours had reached the bottom of the hillside at the edge of the village. They then turned and headed through the fields towards Wilson's farm. They knew that their route would take them close to where their own farm stood.

As they passed by and could see the rubble of what had once been their home. They couldn't help but stop for a few moments and just hold one another. 'Well, girl,' Torean commented pointing towards the farm, 'the barn is still standing. At least I won't have to completely rebuild it.'

Adaira tried to smile at Torean's words. To her this didn't seem like any great comfort. Until she knew that her son was safe she couldn't imagine being able to envisage them rebuilding their home.

'I know it doesn't seem like much, lassie,' he said, seeing the pain in her eyes. 'We have to try our best to look to the future. This doesn't have long to play out, and before long you, Aneirin and I will be arguing about how best to re-build the place.'

She smiled at him hoping that he was right. His words helped her to see the three of them back together and working to rebuild their home. This gave her some hope.

After one last, longing look at their home they headed off towards Wilson's farm hoping that he would be able to give them some news about what had been happening since Lady Naithara had led Aneirin and Tom away from their camp. For now they had to hope, it was all they had.

Chapter Eighteen
The Gathering

It was early in the morning, just before seven when Lizzy knocked the Laird's door to bring him some tea. Little did she know that at the same time Torean and Adaira were setting out down the hillside towards the town.

She entered the dark room and sat the tray next to the Laird's bed and went to open one of the curtains to let in a little light.

As the curtains opened the old man grumbled and rolled over away from the light.

She moved back towards the bed and spoke to him gently. 'My Lord, it's time to wake.'

'I know, Lizzy dear,' he said, heaving himself to sit upright in the bed. 'I'm just an old man. I expected to be able to relax in my sunset years. Alas, there is always one more adventure.' He smiled and took his cup from her. 'When would you like to leave, my dear?'

'I think we should head off as quickly as possible,' she said looking anxiously towards the door. 'I am going to pop out into the garden before it gets much later and give Aneirin a cup of tea. He must be freezing stuck out there.'

'Yes,' said the Laird thoughtfully. 'Just ensure that you are not seen. We cannot afford for my niece to see you sneaking out there. She would love to get Aneirin back.'

She nodded and quickly left the room.

Rushing down the stairs, she poured Aneirin a cup of tea into the mug used by the gardener and headed outside. She knocked the door and entered the outhouse. As she entered it was hard to see anything through the gloom. 'Aneirin, are you there?'

Aneirin stepped out of the shadows, 'I'm here, Lizzy. Sorry for hiding, but when the door opened I didn't know whether it would be you.'

'You did the right thing,' she said, passing him the cup of tea. 'I thought you might be a bit cold.'

'Cold? Not me,' Aneirin said sarcastically. He winked at her and took the cup gratefully. 'When do we head off?'

'The Laird is just waking up,' she said motioning towards the house. 'I think we should get going as soon as possible. I don't like the thought of you stuck in here risking getting caught.'

'Don't worry about me, Lizzy,' he said touching her hand. 'You go back in and get ready to leave. I will finish this tea and head off. I will get you both a little bit further out among the trees. I don't think it would be safe for Naithara to catch you both poking around in here, I don't suppose you often decide to weed the vegetable patch do you?'

She smiled, it felt so good to have Aneirin close, to know that he was safe. Without speaking she kissed him on the cheek and left the outhouse.

As he watched her leave, Aneirin couldn't help but feel the same way she did. It had been hard being separated from her. He gulped down his tea and put the cup behind a plant pot so it wouldn't look conspicuous should someone enter the outhouse. He quietly opened the door, being careful to ensure that no-one was up at any of the windows and crept deeper into the garden. Making his way for the gate which was situated in the back wall, he wanted to find somewhere just outside the garden to sit in wait for Lizzy and the Laird.

Meanwhile, back in the house Lizzy had fetched her cloak and was waiting on the Laird appearing so they could get on their way.

By the time the old man entered the kitchen it was nearly eight o'clock.

She was beginning to get impatient and didn't want Naithara to wake and find them on their way out. She had been very careful to prepare a cold breakfast for Naithara and leave it on her nightstand with a note explaining that the Laird had sent her to the next village to by him fresh parchment and ink. It was a plausible excuse as the Laird was often running out of his supplies when he got engrossed in his work.

The Laird entered the room and motioned for her not to speak. They both quietly exited through the back door and made their way quietly to the back of the garden. Neither spoke, even when they were outside. They were both nervous at the prospect of being caught.

As they closed the gate behind them Lizzy looked around for Aneirin. 'Aneirin,' she said in a loud whisper. 'Are you here?'

The Laird was looking around at the bushes for the boy.

Aneirin stepped out from behind a large shrub and motioned for them to follow him.

They walked on in relative silence until they had gone a good way from the house.

'Did you sleep okay, boy?' said the Laird.

'As well as can be expected,' Aneirin replied. 'While we have been living rough for some time, I could not stop thinking about Tom, I detest the Provost. I only hope that he has not done something despicable to him.'

'I know what you mean,' the Laird said. 'He does not have a good reputation. However we must hope for the best. Hopefully, once we have a good chat with Wilson we will have devised a plan to free him.'

'I wish we could contact my granda,' Aneirin said, looking at the staff he carried.

'I almost forgot about that,' said the Laird, now also looking at the gnarled cane. 'Do you know how to use it?'

Aneirin looked sheepish. 'Not really,' he replied. 'In truth this one belongs to Tom. I have practised with it, but I am not accomplished. If my grandfather were with us he would know what to do.'

'I wouldn't worry on that account,' said Lizzy looking over at him. 'Torean will not sit idly by once he knows what has happened to you. I am sure we will see him sooner than you think.'

Aneirin smiled. 'I hope you're right,' he mused. 'We need him now more than ever. You know, although I felt no love for the man who kept Tom and I in a cell, I feel greatly affected by the Sheriff's death.'

'Unfortunately, death never gets easier,' the Laird retorted. 'I was never a great fan of Michael McDonald. He was nowhere near the man his father had been. Nevertheless, to see him snuffed out in such a way was greatly distressing. For me it has helped to hammer home what we are really fighting here. We cannot any of us be careless or it could cost us our lives.'

Lizzy was now feeling disturbed by the men's words. She had lain in bed the night before unable to see anything but the blank stare which had been in the Sheriff's eyes.

Suddenly Aneirin stopped in his tracks. He was staring into the distance in silence.

'What's wrong?' said Lizzy. She stopped herself from saying anything more when she realised what Aneirin was looking at. They were now able to see the burned remains of the farm in the distance. She walked towards him and took his hand in hers.

'It looks so strange,' he muttered. 'When my mother and I ran for the hills the fire hadn't started. I could see the smoke rising when we reached Longford's Pass, but it still makes it seem so definite to see the place where I was born as a ruin.'

'You will rebuild it,' Lizzy said, brushing the hair from his eyes. 'It will all be over soon.' Still holding his hand she led him on. She knew it was not good to stand there and dwell on such things.

They walked on and were soon walking up the dirt road which led to Wilson's farm. As they reached the house they all somehow felt a sense of expectation.

Wilson opened the door and ushered them inside without a word.

Sitting around the table as they had several days before, Lizzy thought it felt like a life time ago when they had decided to head out into the hills after Torean and his family.

'Well,' said Wilson. 'I'm surprised to see you here, Aneirin. You must tell me everything that has happened.'

Aneirin explained what had transpired finishing with the story with how the Sheriff had been killed and that Tom was still a prisoner. Wilson's wife set down cups and a pot of tea and joined them at the table. She looked pale, which did not sit well with such a normally rosy person.

'I'm not sure where to begin,' Wilson said. 'I suppose we need to try to get the boy out. Do any of you know anything of Torean's whereabouts?'

'No,' said the Laird. 'We are hoping that he will make himself known to us soon, although I'm not sure how.'

'You say the Provost has him?' Wilson questioned.

'Yes,' Lizzy said. 'He led him off last night. I assume he will be in his house?'

'It would be the most obvious place to keep him,' the Laird mused. 'Even so, I am not sure how we would be able to free him.'

'If we could head there and you could make some kind of distraction, I could try to get in and find him?' Aneirin proposed.

'I'm not sure that's a good idea boy,' replied Wilson. 'It sounds like you had a narrow escape, and they are bound to be looking for you since they believe you to have Torean's staff.'

'I agree,' said the Laird. 'If we are to do this, I think it would be folly to put you in harm's way.'

Lizzy, who was relieved that they were not going to allow Aneirin to put himself in danger, felt guilty as she imagined Tom tied up, perhaps beaten? 'I could go?' she proposed. 'Could I use the pretence that I am there on behalf of the Laird and gain entry to the house?'

'You could, lassie,' Wilson said, 'but I am not sure what you would do once you were in there. He is unlikely to be keeping him anywhere obvious. I doubt that the Provost's family is aware of what he has been doing. If he can keep the boy from his wife, he would not be easy to find when you had little time to look.'

'I suggest,' said the Laird, 'that we all take some time to try to think of a way to get in there.'

A long time seemed to pass and they were all getting frustrated by their lack of progress. The atmosphere was broken when Mrs Wilson realised that it was gone twelve and stood to prepare them some bread and cheese for lunch.

As she worked about the kitchen a knock came to the back door. Wilson rose from his chair looking nervous. 'I think you should all hide,' he said looking around the room for a suitable place. 'I do not usually receive guests at the back door. If you were followed today Aneirin could end up being taken again. God knows what they would do to us if they found out we were aware of their plans.

Mrs Wilson ushered them all into the larder in the corner and closed the door before motioning for her husband to open the back door.

He then turned the handle and opened it in silence.

From inside the larder the three could not hear anything which was being said. They were tightly crammed together and felt scared that the door could suddenly burst open in front of them revealing their enemies.

The larder door slowly opened and Mrs Wilson, smiling, told them it was safe. As they stepped out into the light of the room once more it took Aneirin's eyes time to adjust. He suddenly realised that his grandfather and mother stood in front of him. He dropped the staff in his hand and ran towards them. It was such an amazing feeling to see them again.

The three stood for several moments in an embrace. Torean was the first to speak. 'If you are to become a wielder of the staff, my boy, you need to learn not to throw it on stone floors.'

Aneirin laughed, a tear rolling down his cheek. 'Sorry, granda,' he said taking him into a tight embrace.

The family stepped apart and the group gathered around the wooden table once more. 'Where is Tom?' Torean asked, all the joy from finding his grandson suddenly gone from his face.

'They still have him, granda,' Aneirin muttered. 'The Provost has him.'

'This is bad,' said Torean leaning his head against his staff. 'I brought the boy into this. I need to get him out of there.'

'That is exactly what we have been discussing,' said the Laird. 'Our only options are to try to get into the Provost's house, or to try to retrieve him when they meet again tonight.'

'We may have the advantage if we try to do it tonight,' said Torean. 'They do not know that we are aware of where they meet. I'm sure they would not expect to see us there?'

'They killed the Sheriff, granda,' said Aneirin looking worried. 'They killed him like he was a fly. Do you think that we can stand against them? Especially since luring you to them is exactly what they want.'

'Well,' the old man said thoughtfully. 'If we can't stand against them now, I doubt we will be able to defeat them in the end. All we have to do is get in, grab Tom and get back out again.'

'How do you suggest that we do that?' Adaira said feeling frustrated.

'I can't be certain that it would work,' replied Torean. 'Although I think that I can provide a decent distraction with my staff which may allow Aneirin here to sneak in and free the boy.'

Aneirin nodded. 'I think it's the only chance we have.'

Lizzy tried to interject.

'No, Lizzy,' Aneirin said. 'We have been sitting here all morning trying to come up with a plan to free him. I think this may be our best shot.'

Lizzy looked crestfallen as the men began to discuss how they would approach the clearing. Wilson suggested that he could bring his gun to cover Aneirin when he went in after the boy. After a few minutes Lizzy suddenly remembered something. 'My Lord,' she said turning to the Laird. 'I have just remembered, last night you said you had discovered something regarding this matter?'

'I believe you're right, my girl,' the Laird said touching her shoulder. 'I had completely forgotten.'

'What's all this, Angus?' Torean asked thoughtfully.

'When we returned from our journey into the hills,' the Laird continued. 'I decided to do some research among the books in my library to see what I could discover. My grandfather had had a somewhat unhealthy interest in the occult. I thought that this must have been the place where my niece stumbled upon her information regarding this, Eiric.'

'What did you find?' Adaira questioned impatiently.

'Nothing at first,' said the Laird. 'There were a great many papers on contacting the dead and making poisons. However, I then stumbled upon writings which mentioned an ancient text which contained the spirit of a demon known as Eiric. I would guess that my grandfather, after reading this must have sought the book out. The text advised that the entity was imprisoned within the book many centuries ago. He was a very evil creature which had once roamed the lands around Cairn Holme in the days when the magical creatures lived among us. The text advised that if someone were in possession of the book, they could potentially free Eiric. And that the only way he could be completely destroyed would be if the book itself was also destroyed.'

'Why didn't the person who bound him in the book simply destroy it there and then?' said Aneirin.

'Good question, boy,' said the Laird. 'From what I can gather, it would take a very special type of magic to destroy the book. The sorcerers in those days took their power from calling up spirits; I believe they were known as Shades. It would take something which could harness the power of Cairn Holme to destroy the book.'

'Like the staff,' Lizzy said thoughtfully.

'My thoughts exactly,' said the Laird.

'My friend,' said Torean. 'You may just have given us what we need to win this fight.'

'How do we get hold of the book?' Aneirin asked.

'That is tricky,' Torean mused. 'I think it may come down to either Lizzy or you, Angus.'

The pair looked nervous.

'The book will surely be in your home somewhere if Naithara has been using it to contact her master. Where would she keep it?' Torean questioned.

'In her room,' said Lizzy without having to think. 'I have often entered her room and felt an uneasy presence. I think she has contacted this spirit from there.'

'Excellent,' replied Torean.

'What do you suggest?' Lizzy asked.

'Firstly,' said Torean, 'I think that none of you should be seen. One of the few things we have right now is that they do not know we have your help. If we are to have somewhere to shelter and any chance of retrieving this book, you cannot be noticed. I think that Wilson should stay here, and you should both go back to the house.'

Lizzy looked distraught. 'I cannot stand sitting around waiting any longer.'

'You don't have any choice,' said Torean impatiently. 'You will need to return to the house today. I will then need you to return here tomorrow morning as you have today, so that we can regroup and plan for the final fight.'

'Are you confident that you can do this?' Adaira asked. She didn't like this plan at all. She had only just gotten her son back and did not like the idea of putting him in jeopardy again.

'We cannot be sure of anything, my girl,' he said touching her hand. He could sense her fear. 'But young Aneirin has proved himself most capable so far since he and Tom were captured. Do you think you can get Tom if I can hold them off?' he asked his grandson.

'Yes,' Aneirin said firmly. He had not been able to rest since Tom had been dragged off by that monster. They had to help free him.

'Then it is decided,' Torean decreed looking around the group.

'Good luck, my friend,' said the Laird rising from his chair. 'We will be praying for you this evening.'

'Thank you,' Torean replied, rising from his chair and embracing the

Laird. 'We will see you both in the morning, and with any luck we will have young Tom back safe and sound.'

Lizzy sat in her chair unable to move. Aneirin approached her and stroked her hair. 'Don't worry Lizzy. Everything's going to be okay.'

'I thought you were safe,' she mumbled.

'None of us are safe, not until this is over. If it were me instead of Tom imprisoned in the Provost's house, you would think nothing of him doing this for me.'

She knew he was right and rose to follow the Laird back to the house. It was going to be another long night waiting for news of what had happened.

The two headed off from the house and left the others to prepare for the evening ahead. As they walked back to the house neither spoke very much. They had left that morning with high hopes of what would come of the day. Despite the fact that they had now seen Torean and knew what lay ahead, Lizzy felt extremely apprehensive.

Chapter Nineteen
The Unexpected Cavalry

It was very dark as Torean and Aneirin crept into the clearing. After a great deal of persuasion Adaira had agreed to stay behind at Wilson's farm. Torean understood that it had been very hard for her to part with Aneirin again, but he couldn't do this alone, and he didn't want his enemies to know about their friends. It also took him back to the days when he and his son had fought together. Aneirin had his father's determination.

They sat among the bushes feeling very cold and very nervous. Aneirin had not brought Tom's staff with them because Torean had decided that it would be better for now to keep up the pretence that there was only one staff. He had felt slightly relieved because his grandfather didn't know he had been practising with the staff, and he didn't feel particularly confident. Aneirin had mentioned that Eiric had said that Tom was a staff wielder, but the group did not seem to realise that this meant there was more than one.

They sat together in silence, unable to speak in case the enemy arrived and they inadvertently revealed their position. After what seemed like a very long time they noticed movement among the trees. The group was beginning to gather and were lighting their torches as before. Very soon Naithara strode into the clearing and stood in the middle with an expression that made her look like she was meditating. She had her hands clasped together in front of her and was looking towards the sky with her eyes closed.

Torean knew that she was trying to sense his presence and hoped that the wards he had placed around Aneirin and himself would not give them away. Had he just been standing there holding the staff without protection they would have been shining like a beacon in the dark.

One of the last people to arrive was the Provost. He was dragging Tom behind him. Tom tripped and stumbled as he was led along. He had never felt so tired in his life.

Aneirin noticed that Tom was bound as before, and saw the untreated gash on his face which now added to his bruising. He felt a rush of relief to see him again. Aneirin had expected the Provost to have tortured Tom. He hoped Tom had managed to escape his wrath with nothing more than the cut on his face.

His train of thought was broken when Torean motioned to him to move off towards the bushes behind where the Provost had positioned Tom. The old man then moved off in the opposite direction hoping to draw the fire away from the boy. Their only hope was for Aneirin to be able to get in and grab Tom quickly while the group was distracted.

Naithara then looked up to address the group and silence descended. Aneirin froze, now paranoid that he would be seen.

'The old man is close at hand,' she crooned, looking around the men. 'I can taste his fear. As I surmised he has come for the boy. I suggest that we are all patient and await his arrival.'

The men stood in silence for a few moments, and then began looking from one to the other unsure of what exactly they were expected to do.

'Do you not intend to summon Eiric to our aid?' said the Minister feeling a little fearful at the thought of facing Torean without their master to protect them.

'No,' Naithara said impatiently. 'My master was extremely angry last night. I do not intend to call upon him until we can confirm that we have defeated the old man.' She knew that if Eiric was disappointed again he may take more than one man's life.

Tom was standing with his head bowed looking at the ground. He had never felt so alone. He was sore all over. Although the Provost had not had the opportunity to give him any more *special attention*, he had been lying on a stone floor in the dark unsure whether he would see the light of day again. Suddenly he noticed something out of the corner of his eye. Summoning his little remaining energy he slightly lifted his head towards where the movement had come from, but saw nothing. The grass was moving but it could have simply been the wind. He thought he heard a low whispering. He then saw something in the opposite direction and when he glanced he did see a figure in the shadows. It was Aneirin among the bushes. He looked towards where Aneirin stood without raising his head any further and saw that Aneirin was signalling to him. Unsure of what this meant he felt a rush of courage and decided that it was now or never. Again without lifting his head he sidled towards the Provost slowly and before the man could react kicked him sharply in the groin.

The Provost doubled over with pain, then reached out for Tom but did not manage to get hold of him.

The group who were momentarily distracted by this did not see Torean emerging from the bushes. With his staff held aloft he shouted, '*Criothnaic!*'

As he did the ground surrounding the group began to tremble violently. Several of the men fell to the ground and Aneirin knew this was his only chance and wasted no time. He ran towards Tom and quickly tried to untie him.

'Thank God. I thought I was going to die here,' Tom said.

'Less talk,' Aneirin whispered, his face screwed up trying to untie the knots. 'If I can't get this, can you run with your hands bound?'

'Right now,' Tom whispered loudly, 'I think I could run just about anywhere.'

Naithara had turned away from Torean and noticed Aneirin. She quickly bellowed to her men, 'Get the boys!'

Torean however, reacted too quickly. He ran extremely fast for a man of his age, trying to place himself between the boys and the group. Spinning around with his staff held aloft he cried, 'Amail!' There were spells being cast by Naithara flying around him.

Suddenly the winds in the clearing rose and seemed to be pushing the group back from where the boys stood. No matter how hard the men pressed they could not penetrate the gale. The torches in the clearing blew out with the strength of the blast and suddenly all around them was darkness.

Torean was beside the boys. 'Hurry, we must use this to get out of here quickly.' His voice sounded extremely strained from trying to keep up the spell.

Aneirin struggled quickly to try to free Tom and make a retreat.

'Let's just go, Aneirin,' Tom said, feeling panicked. 'I think I can keep my balance.' He just wanted away.

Meanwhile Naithara stood in the middle of the clearing trying to focus her energy. All of a sudden the winds from Torean's enchantment disappeared as though they had never been and the torches relit themselves. Naithara stood perfectly poised with a self-satisfied smile on her face. She then motioned her hand and shouted, 'Men after, what the…' she was abruptly cut off by confusion.

It had gone un-noticed to both sides in the dark, but a large group of Nuggies had entered the clearing and positioned themselves in a crescent moon shape surrounding Torean and the boys.

Tom instantly knew that they had been the first movement he had detected among the trees.

'You shall not harm the staff wielder!' shouted Low-Paw from the centre of the group. He held up his hand towards Naithara and the other Nuggies followed his example. They all began to hum a deep vibrating sound, and suddenly a shield of piercing blue light rose up around the group. It surrounded them and looked like a curved wall between the two camps.

After a few moments Naithara broke out of her confusion and shouted to her men, 'After them! Are you afraid of these little rats?'

The men looked at one another for a couple of moments unsure of what the little creatures had created, but started to move slowly forward.

Low-Paw turned to Tom and said in a strained voice, 'You must go staff wielder. We can hold them off but not for long.'

'Will you be okay?' Tom asked. He did not want these little creatures to sacrifice themselves on his behalf. There had been enough death.

The creature simply smiled, 'Do not doubt us master. We have fought worse animals than these throughout our history. Like all of their kind, they underestimate the strength of the ancient powers.'

Tom, not wanting to waste the advantage that Low-Paw and his Nuggies had bought them, shouted his thanks hoarsely and the three ran blindly out into the night.

They had only been running a few seconds when Tom heard an

explosion behind them. Terrified that Low-Paw had been injured, he turned round to see that a couple of Naithara's men had been sent flying backwards when they had tried to penetrate the shield surrounding the little creatures. He couldn't believe that the Nuggies had come to his aid. He hoped one day he would be able to show his gratitude to them.

The Nuggies were still holding their own against the group of men. Once Long-Paw was sure that Tom and the others had been given enough of a start into the distance, he signalled to them to make their next move. The creatures raised their little hands higher into their air, and Low-Paw uttered, 'Wait for my mark, men.'

Naithara's men were looking at the shield created by the Nuggies trying to find a way through the wall. They heard Low-Paw speak, but, unlike Tom, they had no connection with the little animal and simply heard some garbled sounds.

Low-Paw waited until enough of the men were up-close to the shield and shouted, 'Now!'

Suddenly the force field fell. It looked like a wall of water which had been held, was now released upon the men. The force of the flowing energy sent them flying backwards. As though floating on water they were all dragged back from where they had once stood which gave the Nuggies ample time to disappear in the undergrowth.

With the light from the shield gone the clearing seemed strangely dark. The men noticed that in the sudden lack of light they were almost blinded and could not make out in which direction the little creatures had made their escape.

Naithara was now completely consumed by her rage. Power surged through her and exited from her finger tips. It was white hot. How could the old man have slipped through her fingers once more? How could he have managed to take her only bargaining tool with him? She knew that her master would not understand her failure. How could they have lost the staff wielder? The men around her cowered away, fearing that they may be struck down the same way the Sheriff had been. While they continued to be in awe of the power Naithara was able to command, the last few days had shown them what failure could reap. As she raged, they all, one by one, turned and fled for their lives.

After a few moments Naithara stopped her angry tirade and dropped to the ground. She looked around the empty clearing, and for the first time thought that they may not achieve their aims. She looked like a lost child.

Only one man had remained behind - the Provost. He knelt down beside her and put his arm around her. Naithara had shown weakness tonight, something which the Provost did not like. He wondered whether it was perhaps time for him to assert himself in order to ensure that their venture was successful. He had always wondered whether a woman was capable of such a task.

Chapter Twenty
The Longest Wait

Feeling heartened, Tom ran through the night without another look back. He was free. After feeling so hopeless he was now back with his friends. This filled him with a new found energy. He felt like he could have run for days. However, it was one of the first times since this whole adventure had begun that he suddenly felt naked without his staff. As the Nuggies had said, he was a staff wielder. It was now a part of his being. Running endlessly as he now was, he was absolutely free. Continuing the fight and not having his staff now felt like he was missing a limb.

The three slowed from their run after they were sure that the group was not following them.

After a few seconds Aneirin stopped beside a tree where Onero was tethered. They had left him there in case they needed to make a hasty escape.

Tom, leaning against the tree and breathless, looked around and suddenly noticed that Torean was struggling. His heart sinking, Tom shook Aneirin to alert him and the boys ran almost having to catch the old man before he fell to the ground. As he held Torean's arm Tom noticed that his hand was covered in blood. 'Torean, what happened?' he questioned.

'Granda?' Aneirin asked, now petrified.

'Don't worry about me, boys,' the old man replied trying to hide his pain. 'It was a stray spell, nothing serious. I've just lost a bit of blood and I'm feeling rather drained. Just get me to Wilson's and I will be fine.'

'Lean on me,' Aneirin said, putting his grandfather's uninjured arm around his shoulders.

Tom ripped the sleeve of his shirt for a tourniquet and wrapped it around Torean's arm above the wound to help stem the bleeding.

With some help from Tom, Aneirin helped his granda onto the horse and then climbed up in front. 'Tom, are you alright to follow on foot?'

'Of course,' Tom panted. He was utterly exhausted, but knew that he would have to push himself a little bit further to reach the farm and safety.

They were glad to be together again, but both boys were worried about Torean. They knew that they had no hope of surviving this fight without him. They journeyed on in silence, both desperate to get to Wilson's farm and get Torean some assistance.

Tom was banging on the door at the farm and was now starting to feel desperate. Under other circumstances he would have felt strange about making such a noise at someone's door in the middle of the night. Not on this occasion. He was weary, scared and just wanted to be inside the house with the cold night closed away.

Wilson opened the door; he and his wife had sat up with Adaira waiting upon the group returning. When he saw Tom's ashen white face, he was glad to see the boy, but he knew that all was not well. He pushed the boy aside and saw Aneirin holding Torean up. He ran to his old friend and lifted him in his strong arms, carrying him quickly into the house.

Tom went to Aneirin in order to help him inside. The boy was exhausted from carrying his grandfather's weight.

'I want to say thank you,' Tom said sheepishly.

'Tom, you don't have to,' he said smiling wearily. 'You would have done the same for me. For now I just want to get inside and do all I can to make sure my granda is well.'

Tom suddenly felt weak. Aneirin caught him and helped him over the threshold. He then closed the door and walked into the kitchen with Tom leaning on him for support. The group was a sorry sight.

Wilson had Torean stretched out on a bench while Adaira and Mrs Wilson fussed around him with wet cloths and bandages.

'Is he alright?' Aneirin asked, sounding all too much like a little boy again.

'Don't worry, son,' his mother replied, looking scared by Torean's condition herself. 'He's weak, but I think he'll be fine.'

'Will he be fit to fight?' Tom muttered as he lowered himself into a seat painfully. He was still extremely stiff from his time spent in the Provost's cellar.

'I sure hope so,' Torean groaned. 'This is nothing.'

'I think you should get some sleep,' Mrs Wilson said.

'I can't leave him,' Aneirin moaned.

'Neither can I,' Tom added, although he was clearly exhausted.

'Go,' Torean muttered.

'Aneirin,' his mother said sternly. 'You have played your part tonight. We cannot survive with you both exhausted.' Turning to Tom she smiled, 'It's good to have you back safe, boy.'

He looked at her and tried to smile. Having never felt so tired, he didn't need a lot of persuasion. He just wished that his own mother was with him.

'Go to bed,' she continued. 'Lizzy will be here in the morning and we will need to make plans.'

She knew just what to say to sway her son. Going to bed would surely make Lizzy arrive sooner. She was the one who made him happy. Aneirin rose from his chair groaning, kissed his mother and left the kitchen to head upstairs to bed.

Tom did not rise from his chair and plucking up the courage said, 'If it isn't too much trouble, could I possibly have something to eat? I haven't eaten in over a day, and I think that my hunger may keep me from sleep.'

'Of course you can,' Mrs Wilson said, leaving Adaira to finish tending to Torean. She was ashamed that she had not offered the boy anything before now. It was then that she noticed the cut on Tom's face. 'Forgive me, my lamb, with Torean in this state it was easy to forget why this whole thing happened tonight. It looks like they beat you. Is it bad?'

'No,' Tom muttered. Talking about it made him feel strange. He felt numbed by the whole experience and he didn't feel fear even though the Provost had not had time to hurt him. 'I was lucky on that front,' he continued. 'I can assure you that my lack of injury is not due to the Provost's want of trying. He fortunately never managed to have any length of time alone with me. Otherwise I fear I would have been in a much worse state.'

Mrs Wilson set about cleaning his face before she made him some supper.

'He is an evil man,' Wilson mused. 'I have always thought there was something about him. Even as a child he used to sit and pull the wings of insects, he enjoyed causing pain.'

'Well,' Torean said, leaning up on the bench as Adaira propped a cushion behind him. 'At least this little fly got away. We had rather an eventful night.'

'So it would seem,' Mrs Wilson said, ruffling Tom's hair as she sat down a large bowl of steaming broth and a plate of fresh bread which was still slightly warm.

Tom wolfed into his food, he had not felt this hungry in a long time. The food disappeared very quickly and left the boy feeling satisfied and drowsy.

'Off with you,' Wilson said, noticing Tom now struggling to keep his eyes open. 'We can discuss your adventures in the morning. For now I think our young friend here speaks for us all with his sleepy expression. It is late and this battle is far from over. We should all get some rest.'

'Good night,' Tom said, rising from his chair and following the path Aneirin had taken out of the room. 'Which room is Aneirin in?' he enquired, suddenly aware that he had no idea where he was going.

'Straight up the stairs, first door on the left.' Mrs Wilson beamed.

'Thank you,' said Tom, who wasted no further time and started up the stairs outside the kitchen door.

'You know,' Mrs Wilson said looking at the empty doorway. 'The resemblance is uncanny. He could be Aneirin's brother.'

'Yes, the family resemblance is remarkably striking,' Adaira responded. She was pleased to have Tom back. She had become rather fond of him since he had appeared in their lives. He was a very sensitive boy.

'Torean,' Mrs Wilson said, now turning to him. 'I think you should sleep down here tonight. It would not be wise to move you, plus it will be warmer down here with the heat from the dying fire.'

'Thank you, my dear,' said Torean taking her hand. 'I am indeed grateful for not having to move. I shall be very comfortable where I lie.'

Adaira rose from the chair next to where Torean lay and kissed him on the head. 'Will you be okay without me?' she asked, feeling a little wary at walking away and leaving him when he was in such a condition.

'Go, girl,' he smiled. 'Get some sleep. I will still be here for you to fuss over in the morning.'

With that the group broke up and headed for the stairs and to bed. They would still have another two days before their next encounter with Naithara. During that time Torean and the boys had to ensure that they were not seen, and Lizzy and the Laird would need to think of a way to get hold of that book.

When Tom woke he could hear the group down in the kitchen talking. He had no idea what time it was, but felt like he had slept for quite some time. He quickly rose and pulled on his clothes so that he could find out what was being said in the house below.

As he entered the kitchen he noticed that the Laird and Lizzy were now also among the group gathered around the table.

'The little creatures were all gathered around us,' Aneirin was saying to Lizzy and the rest of the group. 'Tom spoke to them, although I don't know what they said, it just sounded like noise.' At that he noticed Tom was standing there. 'Here he is. I'm sure Tom can tell us what the little animals were doing.'

Mrs Wilson rose from her chair, 'Let the poor boy sit down first, Aneirin.' She turned to Tom and showed him where to take a seat. 'I have some tea fresh in the pot if you would like, and I'll put some bread over the fire to toast.'

'Thank you,' said Tom, gratefully taking the large mug of tea from the woman. 'That sounds wonderful. Thank you for having me, I haven't had a sleep like that in what feels like a very long time.'

Mrs Wilson beamed at him. 'You're very welcome, lad. Such manners in a young man, you'll go far, my boy!'

'So,' said Aneirin impatiently. 'What were the little creatures saying to you?'

'They are called Nuggies,' Torean said from his makeshift bed on the bench. 'Tom has met with the little creatures before, that is why he could communicate with them. It was quite impressive that your link with them remained even when you were without your staff.'

The group turned to Tom now even more intrigued.

'What Torean has said is true,' Tom said, feeling strange to have them all looking at him. 'The little animal leading them is called Low-Paw. He visited me at night when we were staying among the hills. When I met with him he said that his elders were planning to have a gathering to decide whether they should help us or not. From last night, I assume that they chose the former. I must say I'm grateful that they did. We may not have had such a lucky escape otherwise.'

'What did he say to you in the clearing?' Lizzy enquired, fascinated at the thought of little mythical creatures coming to their rescue.

'He simply said that we should run,' Tom continued. 'He said that his men couldn't keep up the shield they had put around us for much longer. I didn't want to squander the opportunity they had given us, so we ran off. I hope they got away from there okay.' As he finished he felt worried about Low-Paw and his friends. He knew what Naithara was capable of.

'I wouldn't worry on that front,' Torean said, sensing Tom's upset. 'I think our little friends will have had an escape route planned. Plus people like Naithara always underestimate the powers which naturally magical beings possess. I would doubt she would even order her men to chase after them. It would be our escape which would have filled her with anger.'

Tom felt relieved at Torean's words. He hoped the old man was correct.

'This is all very fascinating,' said the Laird. 'I have read of such creatures before, but had no idea that they were real.'

'They're real alright,' said Aneirin smiling. 'They saved our bacon.'

'Indeed,' Torean said shifting uncomfortably. 'They have always been here, although these days they choose not to allow themselves to be seen. They could sense that young Tom was a staff wielder and decided to reveal themselves to him. It is a great honour, my boy.'

'Yes,' Tom mused. 'I hope I see them again so that I can show them my gratitude.'

'That, you cannot guarantee,' Torean replied. 'They are a highly secretive people. The fact that they chose to risk exposure last night must have caused a great deal of upset among their kind.'

Tom knew that Torean was probably right, but he still hoped that he would see the little creature again, crawling out from the undergrowth.

'I suppose all that is left to discuss is what we do from here?' Lizzy said, breaking the group's reverie.

'Well,' Torean said thoughtfully. 'I think it would be best for us to hide out here until the time of the battle. I don't think that Naithara will come here looking for us, and the main thing we need to do is wait until they strike so we can destroy Eiric. Also, as you have found out Angus, in order to achieve this we need to destroy the book which holds his soul together. There is very little point in us succeeding in banishing him on this occasion if he will use someone else to attempt to rise to power again in the future. We will need you both for this,' he said, motioning to Lizzy and the Laird.

'It won't be easy,' the Laird mused.

'I can search her room?' Lizzy responded almost to herself. 'She's used to me going through her belongings. Lady Naithara's not exactly a tidy person. She always leaves things lying around which I have to tidy away. I'm sure she would not think twice if she found me among her things.'

'That may be the simplest option,' Torean said thoughtfully.

'I don't like the idea of putting you in harm's way, my dear,' the Laird said, racking his brains to think of another way around the situation.

'I think,' Lizzy rebutted, 'that this may be the best way to have a look around without arousing her suspicion. What would she think if she found you in her bedroom?'

'True,' the Laird said despondently. 'While I would doubt it would be the first thing which would enter her head, she would start to watch me if that happened. It would be unlikely that either of us would have the opportunity to search her room. In that case, it would probably be best for you to go in and at least scout around to see if you can find its hiding place. Then you can report back to me.'

'So,' Wilson cut in. 'We all know what we are doing?'

'Yes,' Lizzy smiled.

Aneirin touched her hand gently, 'Be careful Lizzy.'

'I always am, Aneirin,' she smiled. 'You seem to be the one who gets into trouble.'

'Hmph,' said Adaira. 'I know exactly where he gets that from.'

Torean chuckled in the corner. 'I think you two should head back to the house now.

'Come along, Lizzy,' said the Laird rising from his chair. 'We have work to do.'

'Is there any way we can let them know how we are getting on?' Lizzy enquired, pulling on her cloak.

'That's a thought,' the Laird mused. 'It would probably best for you to come here again tomorrow morning to update them on what has happened.

It is not completely outlandish for you to have gone out on an errand.'

'Thank you, Angus,' said Torean. He knew that they would be grateful of any kind of news by the time the next day came. 'Well my friends, good hunting!'

'I'll see you all tomorrow,' Lizzy said, smiling at Aneirin.

Mrs Wilson rose to show the visitors out.

The kitchen seemed strangely empty without them there.

Aneirin looked around the group wondering what they were going to do while they waited for news from Lizzy. 'What do we do now?' he asked.

'Well, my boy,' said Torean. 'We do all that we can do. For now, we simply sit here and wait. I know that I for one will be grateful of the time to get my strength back.'

The boys sat for several moments, it was going to be a long day. 'Mr Wilson,' Tom said after a while. 'Is there anywhere Aneirin and I could go and practise with the staff, an empty barn perhaps?'

'I'm not sure, boys,' said Adaira. She did not want them to annoy their guests or put the group in any danger.

'Please,' Aneirin said, knowing exactly what his mother was thinking.

'It's been too long since I have held it in my hands,' said Tom looking at them as though they did not belong to him. 'I feel myself needing to focus my power once more.'

Torean looked at the boy sitting before him. He couldn't believe that in such a short space of time the boy who had not understood anything of his destiny had become so dependent upon it. He understood his feelings. When you became used to the staff's presence, you almost ached when it was taken away from you. 'If Mr Wilson doesn't mind,' he said smiling at Adaira. 'I think it would do some good to keep the boys occupied with such a task. Plus, I do not want young Tom here becoming rusty, not when I am not at my full strength.'

'The barn across the way is empty just now,' Wilson said, pointing out of the window to indicate the out-building he was talking about. 'If Torean thinks it is safe enough then I have no problem with you boys going there.'

'Thank you,' said Tom, feeling extremely grateful. 'Where is my staff?' He had scanned the room several times both last night and tonight and had not seen it sitting anywhere.

'They are in the cupboard here,' said Mrs Wilson walking over and opening a door. She motioned to Tom where they were leaning.

He noticed that she was obviously not comfortable touching either of them. While Wilson and his wife had been extremely understanding with regard to their plight, she obviously was still extremely unsure of anything which could control what would seem to her like an unearthly power.

Tom reached out and took hold of the gnarled cane. He felt a great sense of relief come over him as his hands made contact with the wood. He understood now why he never saw his grandfather without the staff by his side.

The two boys headed out into the courtyard and across to the barn, which Wilson had advised them to use. They were both grateful of something to distract them from the long wait which lay ahead. Also after the events of the previous evening, they were also both aware that it may be crucial for Aneirin to have time to practice focusing his energies with the staff.

Chapter Twenty-One
A Spy is Born

Lizzy and the Laird's journey back to the house had been remarkably quick. They were both anxious to ensure that they could achieve something productive with their day. They knew that, while it would seem like a long time for the group back at the farm, they had very little time in order to find the book and remove it from Naithara without her noticing.

Back at the house Naithara was in a foul mood. The events of the previous evening had made her take to her bed and she was lying in a darkened room still in her bed when Lizzy knocked the door to offer her some tea.

'My Lady?' she enquired, cautiously opening the bedroom door into the gloom. 'I have brought you some tea.'

'Thank you, Lizzy,' Naithara's low voice came from the bed. 'Sit it by the bedside. I am not sure I can drink it.'

'What's wrong, my Lady?' said Lizzy, not having to attempt to sound concerned. She needed Naithara out of that room. They were not going to achieve anything if she hid in her bed all day. 'Did something happen with your encounter with your lover?'

'You could say that,' said Naithara sitting up in bed, grateful of the company. 'Suffice to say it did not go well.'

'I am sorry,' said Lizzy, now daring to sit down on the bed beside her. 'I cannot believe that any man would jilt you my lady. You are the most beautiful woman for several counties.'

'Thank you, Lizzy, you are most kind. Unfortunately my looks are not what are important on this occasion. I think I may have lost his heart forever.'

'I doubt that,' said Lizzy, doing her best to cheer Naithara. 'Whatever has happened, I'm sure it can be resolved. Why don't you rise? I can do your hair and we can pick a beautiful dress. You could arrange a meeting with this beau in order to win back his heart?'

Naithara smiled. 'If only things were so simple.'

'Nothing is to be gained by lying here in your bed,' Lizzy said, going to the window and opening the drapes. 'It is a beautiful day. Even if this man is too much of a fool to know what he has, you should now allow him to spoil such a beautiful afternoon.'

'Perhaps you are right,' Naithara said pulling back the bedclothes. 'Some fresh air may help me to think things over and come up with some ideas on how best to remedy this situation.'

'That's the spirit,' Lizzy said smiling broadly. She walked over to Naithara's wardrobe to pick a nice dress for the mild afternoon. 'I think the lilac would look lovely today. I wish I had such beautiful clothes.'

'The lilac dress sounds lovely, Lizzy.' Naithara poured herself a cup of tea. 'Draw me a bath so that I may wash away my melancholy.'

'Of course, my Lady,' Lizzy curtsied and exited the room quickly. She almost ran to the bathroom desperate to have Naithara quickly get through her ablutions and leave the house for a couple of hours. She ran a good hot bath and returned to Naithara's room to tell her that all was ready for her.

'Thank you, Lizzy,' said Naithara, donning her dressing gown and heading for her bathroom. She couldn't believe that this silly little girl was so quick to believe her stories. Although Lizzy had not helped her, a walk in the afternoon sunshine may be exactly what was needed to figure out what her next move should be. While Eiric had wanted the old man removed, it did not necessarily mean that all was lost. She was sure he had been injured upon their encounter.

Once Naithara was in the bathroom Lizzy took her first opportunity to have a quick look around. She checked the trunk where Naithara kept her winter gowns and found nothing. She checked on top of the shelves in her closet to see if there were any books sitting underneath the array of bonnets and hats which rested upon it. She knew that she could not get too in-depth at this stage while Naithara was only in the bathroom, but her impatience meant that she couldn't stop herself from having a quick look.

'Ah,' said Naithara, soothed as she re-entered the room. 'That was exactly what I needed Lizzy, thank you.'

'Of course, my Lady,' said Lizzy, picking up the gown she had selected and carrying it over to the bed where Naithara slept. She helped the lady don the gown and then followed her as she sat down at her dressing table. As she pinned up Naithara's hair, she felt extremely agitated. She knew that she could not rush the job or Naithara may become suspicious, so she did her best to make Naithara's hair as pretty as possible. 'Would you like anything for your walk?' she enquired.

'No, Lizzy,' Naithara said sighing. 'While you have lifted my spirits, my appetite has not yet returned to me. Hopefully a nice walk will restore it in time for dinner.'

'As you wish,' said Lizzy, stepping back to admire her work. She was becoming extremely good at fixing hair, even if standing behind Naithara made her want to throttle the woman.

After what felt like an eternity the vain woman eventually put on a light cloak and headed out into the grounds. Lizzy thought she would never leave. She knew that she would first have to make Naithara's bed and put away her clothes. If Naithara was to return and catch her in her room, it would look suspicious if none of the chores had been done. As quickly as she could she made Naithara's bed and tidied away her clothes from the previous day. She then hastily started searching everywhere she could think of.

At least an hour had passed, and she had exhausted everywhere possible except the writing desk which sat next to the window. Its lid was locked and Lizzy had been unable to search its contents. Finally, when she had decided that if it was in the room at all it must be there, she took a pin from her hair and decided to try and pick the lock. She had never done such a thing. In fact she wasn't even sure she would be able to. She fiddled with the tiny keyhole for what felt like an eternity and eventually heard a little click which meant that the barrel had turned and unlocked the lid. Raising the lid she gazed inside at its contents. She had never seen anything like it. There were strange dark stones with symbols scored on them, black candles which gave off an unholy smell, even when unlit. She thencame across a small leather bound book at the back of the desk. It looked old and worn, its pages yellowed around the spine. Lizzy, building up her courage reached out her hands to touch the musty binding.

Suddenly she heard the door handle turn and had to quickly close over the writing desk as quietly as possible. She moved swiftly across the room and tried to busy herself at the curtains looking like she was dusting the tops.

'Lizzy, I can't believe you're still here,' Naithara commented, looking much better, her cheeks pink with the breeze.

'Yes, my Lady,' she curtsied. She quickly walked over to the bed away from the window, trying to get as much distance as possible between her and the desk. 'It has been a long time since I gave your room the attention it requires, I apologise.'

'Don't be silly,' Naithara said throwing her cape and gloves onto the bed. 'You work very hard, and I am grateful for everything that you do.'

'Thank you,' said Lizzy relieved by Naithara's pleasant mood.

'If you wouldn't mind fetching me some tea, I think I think I am going to read for a while?'

'Of course,' Lizzy responded, trying her best not to dash from the room. If Naithara intended to read her special book she was bound to notice that the writing desk was not locked.

She ran down the stairs and fetched everything Naithara required. Lizzy had to use all her strength to stop her hands from shaking as she re-entered the room and sat down the tea tray. 'I will leave you in peace now, my Lady,' she said curtseying and turning towards the door.

'Thank you, Lizzy,' she said, sitting herself down on her chaise longue. 'I will ring if I need anything.'

Lizzy left the room and ran down to the kitchen. She would need to recover herself before she went back to the Laird to report all that had happened.

Back in the room, Naithara rose from the chair and approached her writing desk. She had been thinking during her walk that the best thing to do would be to summon Eiric and discuss matters. He could be merciful after all, and she wanted to do what was necessary now to ensure that they succeeded. She reached inside her dress for the little key which hung around her neck and took it off. Putting it inside the lock she was surprised to find that the desk was already opened. She felt panicked for a moment, but put these thoughts out of her mind. She had been very stressed during this time, perhaps the last time she had referred to the book she had neglected to lock the desk.

Lizzy now stood outside the Laird's study, smoothed down her hair and knocked the door.

'Enter,' said the Laird's familiar voice.

Lizzy entered the room and closed the door quietly behind her.

'Well?' the Laird asked, wasting no time on pleasantries.

'I found it,' Lizzy whispered as she crossed the room and sat down across from him at his desk. 'It is in her writing desk. I had to pick the lock to get in, and she returned before I could take it.'

'Do you think she will suspect you?' the Laird asked, wondering whether the unlocked desk would give them away.

'I can't be certain,' Lizzy replied. 'We simply need to hope that she will not realise.'

'I think it would be foolish to try to retrieve the book just now,' the Laird mused. 'From what you have said she did not seem to use the book to summon Eiric when she met with her men. We must hope that when the final battle comes the book will not be a necessity. If that is the case, it may be best to wait to take the book that night.'

'Is that wise?' Lizzy asked, now worrying that it may be folly to leave such and important task to the last minute.

'If we take it before then and she notices before the battle she will know who has taken it,' the Laird responded, feeling exasperated. 'I fear we may have no choice. We could take the book once she heads off for the clearing and give it to Torean there.'

'You're right,' Lizzy said. 'I will head for Wilson's first thing tomorrow morning to inform Torean of everything we have discovered. He will tell us whether this plan is viable or not.'

'We can't do anything else for now,' the Laird replied. 'You have done well, Lizzy. It was very brave to do what you have done.'

'Thank you,' Lizzy blushed. 'I have never been so scared. When the door handle turned and I was in the writing desk it took all of my courage not to scream.'

'Well luckily you didn't,' the Laird said rising from his chair. 'For now we will simply have to do our best to maintain a normal routine. We cannot afford to make her suspicious of either of us, especially if she notices the writing desk.'

Lizzy nodded and rose to leave without another word. She knew it was going to feel like a long wait until she could consult with Torean again, and it would be even longer until she would see Aneirin once more.

Across the house in Naithara's room she was crouched on the floor. Surrounded by her candles now extinguished and stones, Naithara's hair, which had been perfectly pinned up, was now strewn about her face. She looked up and pushed her hair back to reveal a tear-stained, puffy face. Her master's wrath had been severe. If things did not go well the following night he had promised more than to simply abandon her without her powers. The demon had assured her that she would have a very drawn out and painful death. She rose from her position on the floor, still shaken, and began to put away her things in the writing desk. Aware of her forgetfulness the last time she made a point of locking the drawer and replaced the key under her clothes. She then lay down on her bed, buried her face among the pillows and wept. What she hadn't noticed in her upset, was that the book was not back among her things. In his wrath the book had been thrown across the floor, and now lay barely visible beneath the base of her bed.

Chapter Twenty-Two
To Wane and Wax

It was very early the following morning when Lizzy arrived at Wilson's farm. She had hardly slept and was anxious to speak to her friends about what she and the Laird had discovered. Part of her felt deeply disappointed that she was not going to be able to tell them that she had the book in her possession.

Before she could even knock the door, Wilson appeared in the doorway and ushered her inside the house without a word. As she entered the kitchen she saw that the whole group was up and awake, they had obviously been anxious to hear from her too. She was pleased to see that Torean was sitting up at the table. He still had a bandage around his arm but was looking a lot brighter.

'Come in,' he said smiling. 'As you can see we have all been waiting to hear you hold court.'

Mrs Wilson showed Lizzy to a seat where she had already laid a place for breakfast and poured her a large cup of tea from the teapot which sat on the heated fireplace.

'If truth be told,' Torean continued, 'it has been a little slow here.

Awaiting your arrival has been keeping us all from going mad.'

'I'm glad to see you are well,' Adaira said, reaching over to touch her hand. 'We were all so worried about you last night.'

'Thank you, Adaira,' Lizzy smiled. 'Things went as well as could be expected I suppose. I located the book but was disturbed before I could retrieve it. I had to pick the lock in Naithara's desk in order to find it, but she doesn't seem to have noticed that the lock was open. If she has checked her desk I assume she believes she left it open.'

'That's fantastic,' Aneirin said grinning. 'I'm really proud of you Lizzy.'

'It was a close call,' Lizzy continued, smiling at Aneirin's words. 'When I returned yesterday Naithara had taken to her bed. The events of the night before had obviously taken their toll on her. I thought we were going to be thwarted before we had begun. She fed me her lies about having a secret lover, and said that she had been jilted. I did my best to appear interested in her story and eventually managed to coax her out of the house to get some fresh air. Knowing I had very little time, I seized my chance to search through her things. She came back to her room and almost caught me with my hand in the drawer of the desk.'

The group gasped at the thought of Naithara appearing at the door when Lizzy was riffling through her things.

'The Laird thinks that we should not make a move to retrieve the book until tomorrow night. He fears if we take it today and Naithara notices it is missing it could blow our cover.' Her tone suggested that she did not particularly like the idea.

'I think he may be right,' said Mrs Wilson. 'You cannot risk being exposed, Lizzy. Without Torean there to protect you, you and Angus would be defenceless.'

'Mary is right,' Torean added. 'If you can retrieve the book tomorrow evening after she leaves you could bring it to us at the clearing. From what we have seen, she does not need the text to summon her master. It is tight, but it should be time enough. We only need one shot to destroy the thing.'

'I don't want Lizzy there tomorrow night,' Aneirin cut in. 'Hasn't she risked enough?' He looked genuinely scared at the prospect of Lizzy having to reveal her allegiance to them by appearing at the clearing with the book. He knew that Naithara's wrath would be great if she thought she had been betrayed.

'I understand, son,' Torean said trying to placate him. 'I know it's dangerous, but it may it may be the only way. All the same it would probably be best if Angus brought the book rather than you Lizzy. I think the boy is right, you have risked enough.'

Lizzy's face looked rather flushed. 'I would have thought I had proved myself by now,' she said angrily. 'It was me and not the Laird who hid in the clearing and discovered her plans. I am not going to sit at home waiting for news while you are all out there fighting for your lives.'

'We shall see,' was all that Torean said in response to this.

Aneirin reached over and touched her hand. 'Lizzy, I don't want to lose you.'

She looked at him not feeling particularly comforted by his words. 'I don't want to lose you either, Aneirin. That's the whole point.'

The group sat silently for several moments with the atmosphere becoming slightly-more heated.

'What do we do now?' said Tom breaking the silence. 'More waiting?' In his adventures there had never been so much waiting. He couldn't remember reading about a brave knight having to sit in hiding and wait for two days before he could act. It was easier to become afraid when you had time to think about what was to come.

'Unfortunately, boy,' Torean sighed. 'Do not wish the fight upon us too soon. It will be here before you know it, and it will not be easy.'

Tom hadn't thought of it that way. He didn't feel like he had been particularly tested with his staff until now. Was he really ready for this?

'Can I stay with you for an hour or so?' Lizzy said, looking at the floor. 'It was so hard being around the house yesterday, having to pretend that everything was normal. Plus, if anything happens to any of you, I would like to have had this time with you.'

'Don't talk that way,' Adaira said. 'We are all going to be fine.' She knew all too well that it was highly unlikely for them to all get out of this one okay. Torean had been injured already and the boys were now both going to have to play a part in the final battle.

The time Lizzy spent with the group went all too quickly. They had sat around telling stories and playing cards. They had even ended up laughing despite their tension.

Once it had turned eleven, Torean thought it was time for Lizzy to make a move. 'Come, my girl, you should be getting back. I'm sure Naithara will notice your absence if her lunch is not prepared on time. Also Angus will be anxious to have you back safe.'

Lizzy sighed and rose from her chair. She had been watching the clock for the last half an hour and was aware that she was going to have to make a move. It had just taken Torean speaking to force her.

When she was ready to leave, she went around the group and hugged them all one at a time. Stopping at Aneirin she took both his hands in hers. 'Be careful, Aneirin.'

He took her into an embrace, 'I'll be fine Lizzy. This will all be over soon.'

Tearfully she headed for the door to start her long walk back to the Laird's house. With one last long look at the group standing around the kitchen table, she wondered whether they would all be together again.

After she had left, the kitchen seemed strangely quiet. Her departure had broken them out of their jovial mood and had them all thinking about what lay ahead once more.

The day passed extremely slowly. At nine o'clock Tom decided that he was going to head off to bed. He hoped that if he could get some sleep it would help the time pass by. As he left the kitchen he noticed Torean standing outside the front door. He opened the door quietly and joined the old man on the front step. 'What are you doing?' he enquired.

The old man was standing with his pipe looking up at the stars. 'Looking at the moon,' he said wistfully. 'It has controlled everything we have been doing for the last few weeks. My calculations were all too correct. It is definitely past its waning. Tomorrow night shall bring a new moon, and with it the window of opportunity our enemies have been waiting for. This is good. They will still be in disarray after our last encounter. I think we have held on well.'

Tom now also stood gazing at the moon. 'Do you think the moon knows?'

'Knows what, boy?' Torean said bemused at such a question.

'Do you think it knows all the suffering we have had during its cycle. I suppose not.' Tom looked at the ground now feeling foolish.

'You're probably right there,' said the old man putting an arm around him. 'Although we cannot judge how the heavens perceive us. We are probably like little ants running around on a stone. Now off to bed with you before you catch your death.' He ushered Tom inside and closed the large wooden door behind them.

Before Tom went up the stairs he turned and hugged the old man. It was a spontaneous gesture. He was missing his own grandfather once more.

Torean patted him on the shoulder. He was deeply touched by the boy's affection for him. 'Now then, you, less of all that. We'll all be fine. I have every faith in you. You have proven yourself to be a true staff wielder. The Nuggies would not have come to your aid otherwise. They didn't choose me, although I can't think why.' The old man was chuckling to himself.

Tom pulled away from Torean smiling. 'Good night, Torean.'

'Good night, Tom,' Torean said with a wink.

Tom grinned. The wink had made him look even more like his grandfather. Without another word he turned and went up the stairs to his bed to try to get some rest. The next day was going to be an extremely long one. He would need to be well rested.

As he lay in bed he went over the words of power he knew he would need to remember, *amail* to distract their enemies, *beathaich* to support Torean when he was fighting. Then there was the all important, *aicheadh coirbte*, which he would need to finally destroy Naithara's evil. He was determined that he would not let Torean down because he forgot his incantations. With the words drifting through his thoughts he dozed off to sleep. In his dreams he saw his grandfather's face. He was smiling at him, encouraging him to do his best.

Chapter Twenty-Three
The Final Stand

The next day had been extremely long, although as darkness began to fall Tom found himself feeling extremely nervous. The group had become rather quiet over the last few hours. No-one wanted to discuss what was going to happen.

Mrs Wilson had spent all day trying to convince her husband not to go with them. Nevertheless he had continuously told her that he was not going to leave Torean's side.

'Not all of them will be using magic, my dear,' he said getting frustrated. 'You never know when Torean will need someone to simply take a man down through conventional means. He will need to be concentrating on taking out Naithara and that accursed book.'

'I will try to keep him safe,' said Torean trying to reassure her.

'I'm still not convinced,' she said looking very vexed. 'I married a farmer not a hero.'

Wilson shook his head, he was not going to win her round, but he was still determined to be at Torean's side. He wished he could make her understand.

Mrs Wilson busied herself preparing a meal for the group before they would have to head out. 'You can't go into something like this on an empty stomach,' she said, banging pots and pans.

Tom knew that she was trying desperately to distract herself from what was happening.

When they sat down to eat the meal she had prepared Tom found it hard to eat anything. He was now so nervous that the smell of the food which he would normally have found mouth-wateringly delicious made him feel like he would be sick.

Torean could sense his unease. 'Don't worry,' he said quietly so the others would not hear. 'You'll feel better if you eat something. I can't have you fainting with hunger in the middle of the fight.'

Tom tried to smile at the old man and did his best to look like he was making an effort to eat the food. He hoped moving a lot of it around his plate would make it look like he had eaten more than he had.

After they had finished their meal and helped with the dishes Tom looked at the clock. It was nine thirty already. After all their waiting, the last few hours had flown by. They would need to head out soon to get to the clearing before the others.

As they put on their coats and made ready for the journey, Mrs Wilson appeared looking flustered in the kitchen doorway with a bundle of knitted scarves in her arms.

'It's July,' her husband said impatiently. 'Do you really think we need to be wrapped up like it's mid-winter?'

'It's bitter out there,' she said defensively. 'I don't want any of you ending up with pneumonia.'

That's the least of my worries, Tom thought, feeling queasy.

They thought it best not to argue with her. She was extremely worried and was obviously trying to distract herself from thinking about what was going to happen.

Deep down she was also trying to find any way to delay their departure.

Eventually the group headed out into the night just before ten o'clock. Torean led the front of the group with Tom and Aneirin following on behind. Wilson and Adaira brought up the rear, walking along looking anxious.

Aneirin had tried to convince his mother to wait at home, but she was determined that she was not going to sit waiting in safety while her son was in so much peril.

She had lost her husband to this; she was not going to sit at home and wait to hear that she had lost her son too.

The journey didn't take very long and when they found themselves hiding places amid the clearing Wilson told them that it was just after ten thirty.

'When do you think they will arrive?' Tom enquired.

'I think they could make their way here any time from eleven onwards,' said Torean. 'They will want to be prepared and will probably want to have started the ceremony by midnight at the latest.'

They sat huddled in the darkness, Tom was actually grateful for the large scarf he had around his neck. He felt strangely cold and alone sitting among the group. Part of him hoped that Naithara would have changed her mind and would not go through with the whole thing. Perhaps, since she had failed to destroy Torean, she would be too afraid to risk attempting to bring her master to life. Sitting in the clearing he had last been in as a prisoner, shot a wave of terror through him. The sky above was perfectly clear and the moon shone brightly down.

Back in the Laird's house Lizzy was busying herself with some chores which did not really need done, trying to listen out for Naithara making her exit. Just after ten thirty she heard footsteps in the hall. She rushed to hide behind a door listening to Naithara sneaking out through the scullery. After she heard the footsteps die away she wasted no time and headed for the Laird's study to tell him the news.

As she opened the study door she noticed that the Laird had his cloak sitting over his chair and was pacing the floor looking extremely anxious. In her haste she had not even knocked the door to announce her arrival. 'It is time,' she said slightly out of breath. 'She has just left through the back door. Do you think it's safe to go for the book?'

'It's now or never,' said the Laird with a wink, walking past her out of the study.

She followed him out of the door and through the house until they reached Naithara's bedroom. Neither of them spoke.

As they reached the door they both stopped and looked at one another. Both petrified. 'Here we go,' said the old man taking a deep breath. He appeared almost like he was preparing to jump into cold pool. He turned the door knob and they entered the darkened room.

Even though they knew that Naithara had left the house, they were both wary of lighting a lamp in case she returned and noticed her room lit up. They crept across the floor like thieves and went straight for her writing desk. The Laird took a small pocket knife from his pocket and carefully worked at the lock. After a few seconds the lock in the desk turned and the old man put the knife away. 'It's been a while since I've done that,' he said trying his best to alleviate the fear they both felt. Although deep down a part of him felt like the child he had lost long ago.

They opened the desk and for a moment Lizzy panicked when she realised that the book was not in the same place as it had been when she had last been searching for it. 'It's not there!' she exclaimed.

'It must be!' the Laird said anxiously moving some papers around. Feeling slightly panicked he fumbled around in the dark feeling the candles and stones which lay under the papers Naithara used for writing letters. *Please God, do not let her have taken it to the clearing. She has not used it there before?* They found nothing. Both silent with fear and disappointment their eyes searched the room in desperation. As they turned to leave, something caught Lizzy's eye. 'Is this it?' peering at an object which was barely visible under Naithara's bed. The Laird grabbed the object and held it up the light coming in from the bedroom door.

'Yes,' said Lizzy. 'That looks like the book I saw yesterday. For a moment I thought she had taken it with her.'

'Me too,' said the Laird looking visibly relieved.

They quickly closed the desk and left the room hoping that it would not be too obvious that they had been in there. Out in the hallway the Laird stopped under a lamp and looked at the book.

'My Lord,' Lizzy said impatiently. 'Do we have time for this?'

'Be patient, girl,' he said shortly. 'I simply wish to glance at its contents to ensure that we have the right thing. We will not help Torean at all if we turn up and give him a copy of my niece's journal.'

Lizzy apologised and stood over the Laird, anxious to see in his eyes that he believed they had found the right book. It hadn't entered her head before to think that the book she had found earlier may not be the text they required. She had such little time before, that he hadn't thought to open the book. Not that she would know what she was looking for if she had.

As the Laird opened the book they saw that there were many strange illustrations within. The pictures looked vile. There were flowing pictures of demonic creatures tearing human bodies apart. 'I think this is the one,' he said, relieved yet disgusted. 'The images in the book match the descriptions I found in the writings from my uncle's collection. How he could bear to own such a thing I will never understand.' Wasting no time he hurried back to his study to fetch his cloak. As he ran, he held the book at arms length. It felt like he was holding something dirty, he didn't want to sully himself by holding it too close. Carefully tucking the book into a pocket within his cloak the old man motioned to Lizzy that they should make a move.

The pair headed as quickly as possibly down into the scullery and out into the night. They knew that they would need to be careful getting to the clearing, and that it was not going to be easy trying to locate Torean and his friends once they got there. They simply hoped what they had done would be enough. They both ran, cloaks billowing in the wind.

Naithara arrived at the clearing before the rest of her men. As before, she set out the torches in a circle. She wanted nothing to ruin this ceremony. She had become completely deranged. In her own mind, she had blocked out the fact that Torean still existed. She sang to herself as she set out the lamps. There was no way that her master would fail. He would love her again.

From where Torean and the others were hiding they could see her take her place at the centre of the circle and begin to meditate. She removed her cloak and put it down next to a large tree revealing an elaborate ceremonial robe. The flowing white material, although pure, seemed to make her look even more terrible.

Their tensions rose even though they knew that nothing would happen until the whole group was gathered. The sight of her made them all see what was at stake.

Meanwhile Tom thought he could feel his staff pulsating in his hand with anticipation. It was like a shot of adrenalin shooting through his body. It made it almost impossible to sit still.

One by one the men who were loyal to Naithara began to arrive in the clearing. After around thirty minutes they were all present. The men stood in long dark robes with their faces hidden. The stark contrast between them and the fair white figure in the centre of the circle was startling. It drew all attention to her.

'Shall we begin, gentlemen?' Naithara said sharply, looking up from her trance. She had not looked up once as the men had entered the clearing, but seemed to sense that they had all arrived.

They began to chant in a low murmuring sound. It sounded like monks singing plain song. After the sound had risen to a suitable volume, Naithara began to chant atop their voices, calling once more for her master to come among them. As before the clearing was filled with the thick stench of Eiric's presence.

'Let us begin,' said the low dark voice. 'If we are to succeed here tonight, we cannot waste time.'

Naithara then turned to face the minister. '*Daor umbruma*,' she said in a despicable tongue which did not sound like it came from her own mouth. It was base and animal like.

Tom watched, mesmerized as the man stepped forward and lowered his hood. He then took a knife from within the folds of his cloak and made to slit his own throat.

As he did so Naithara announced, 'The sacrifice of a willing servant shall pave the way to your glory. As the blood touches the hallowed earth under this sacred moon, Eiric shall be re-born!'

As the man's knife rose to his throat Torean stepped from the undergrowth. He raised his staff and shouted, 'Amail!' The only thing he could do right now was to stop this sacrifice.

This caused the winds to rise between Naithara and the minister creating a barrier of shining blue light. As this happened the minister seemed to wake as if from a trance and look at the knife in his hand bewildered.

'Seize him!' shouted Naithara.

Torean then yelled 'Buille!' at the minister, which caused the man to fly through the air and land on the ground concussed. Then nodding at Tom he turned back towards Naithara and her men and yelled, 'Amail,' once more.

Tom rose to stand behind him and raising his staff cried, 'Beathaich!' Their combined strength created a barrier which stopped the group advancing on them. Once again he was taken aback by the strength of the incantation flowing through him from the staff. Somehow this felt even stronger than the last time.

Torean turned to Tom looking strained, 'I am going to need you to keep this incantation going while I try to break through and take a few of them out.'

Tom had never felt more terrified. He was now the only line of defence. Tom simply nodded and did his best to concentrate on the power flowing through him. The shield's span shrunk when Torean's attention shifted, although with immense concentration it still held. *Keep your focus, don't lose this now.*

Meanwhile Torean managed to send a few spells from his staff which incapacitated a few of Naithara's men, who were trying break around the sides of their defences. He was sending spells flying at the men like short sharp bursts of blue lightening.

As he did so the Provost, holding his sacred stones aloft, was sending retaliatory spells towards Torean hoping to stop him. Tom felt his focus waver. He was completely torn between keeping up the defensive spell and wanting to try to help Torean take the men down. Re-focusing himself, the defences held up and the spells merely rebounded on the shield and ended up injuring some of the Provost's own men as they ricocheted.

Meanwhile Naithara was standing at the centre of the group with her eyes closed. This worried Tom. He knew that she was gathering her power to attack them and he didn't know if he alone had the strength to keep the shield up should she attack. He had never felt more like a child.

Suddenly Lizzy and the Laird appeared behind them and were now also facing Naithara and the group. Torean, distracted, turned from his work and shouted across the clearing so they could hear, 'Did you get the book?'

'Yes,' Angus shouted back. 'What should I do with it?'

'Throw it on the ground,' the old man shouted, motioning to them to drop the book.

The Laird retrieved it from his cloak and threw it on the ground in front of them.

'Now stand back,' Torean yelled.

Wilson stepped forward and led Lizzy and the Laird further away from where the book lay.

Torean stood facing the book on the ground and focused his energy. Raising the staff into the air he prepared to destroy the one thing which would stop Eiric from being completely vanquished.

At that moment Naithara struck, the force of her blow sent Tom flying backwards and his protective shield was broken. She did not waste any time and screaming, 'Basaich!' The spell missed Torean's back, but hit the tree in front of him. The tree instantly withered and crashed to the ground. A flying branch hit Torean, square in the chest and he crumpled to the ground.

Aneirin ran to his grandfather's side and was on the ground cradling the old man in his lap.

As Tom turned back to face Naithara's group he was petrified, his courage had deserted him.

Naithara was smiling and the Provost standing next to her was examining Tom like an animal would its prey.

'It's over, little boy,' she said coolly. 'Drop the staff and we may yet let you live.'

At these words Lizzy ran forward to stand at Tom's side. She knew that he felt alone and was not about to let Naithara pick them off one by one.

'You foolish girl,' Naithara said, feeling betrayed at the thought that Lizzy had plotted against her. 'Do you really think you can stand against me? I will swat you like a fly.' Naithara raised her hand to strike Lizzy down.

What she hadn't realised while she had been gloating was that the sight of Lizzy running into the fray had shaken Aneirin from his reverie. Grabbing his grandfather's staff he had risen behind Tom and Lizzy, and was preparing to join the fight.

As Naithara's spell flew through the air, Aneirin dived for Lizzy and managed to throw her out of the way. She lay winded on the ground but was otherwise unhurt. He turned to Tom and nodded. 'Let's do this, cousin.'

Tom felt a surge of courage sweep over him. The momentary distraction of Aneirin's actions had allowed him and Tom the time they needed to act. He whispered to Aneirin, 'Amail.'

The boy said, 'Of course.'

Immediately, Tom turned to face the group and shouted the protective spell. The force field between the two camps was back once more.

It was small, but then Aneirin shouted the same thing. The spell suddenly expanded to form a large arch around the group.

Wasting no time Tom turned to the book lying on the ground and shouted 'Aicheadh Coirbte!' He didn't know whether it would work having never actually tried the incantation before. As the spell shot from his staff Tom didn't think he would be able to channel the power. The staff felt like it weighed a tonne, he was petrified that trying to do this alone had been a big mistake. Be that as it may, the book on the ground exploded in a mass of red flame sending Tom and all those around him through the air.

'No, you fools!' Naithara screamed in agony.

The explosion had caused the shield Aneirin had been controlling to fall. They suddenly became aware of a growing noise in the clearing. It was like the air itself was pulsating.

Swirling around Naithara the spirit of Eiric was screaming in pain as he was destroyed. The noise grew to an unbearable pitch and there was an explosion which filled the clearing with a light which made it seem almost like day.

Tom had no idea how much time had passed when he sat up and opened his eyes. He could see that Eiric's expiration had killed most of Naithara's men. She herself lay like a puppet with its strings cut in the centre of the clearing, blood now strewn across her face and once white robes.

His momentary exhilaration was short lived when he looked around to where his friends lay and saw that they had faired no better.

Wilson was lying on the ground with Adaira holding his head up.

Aneirin, looking round in a similar way to Tom, noticed that Lizzy was lying motionless on the grass. His heart filled with agony, he ran to her frantic with fear that she may be dead. All he could hear was his heart beating as he ran to her limp body. As he cradled her head he noticed Tom looking around the group.

One other person was now also standing among the group. It was the Provost. He alone from Naithara's men looked unharmed.

'After him, Tom!' Aneirin shouted in a rage. 'He cannot live, not after this.'

Tom, now also blinded with grief, tore after the Provost as he disappeared into the trees.

The Provost was throwing rocks at Tom as he fled. He looked like he was trying to cast spells at the boy, but his power had obviously died with Eiric.

With blurred vision from the hot tears on his face, Tom lost him and scratched by the undergrowth and completely weary, he eventually gave up the chase and headed back to the clearing to find out how everyone was.

As he entered the clearing panting with exhaustion, he could see that Torean was sitting up with the Laird's help, although he looked gravely injured.

He could not tell whether Lizzy was dead or unconscious, but Adaira had her head in her lap and Aneirin was brushing her hair from her face. Wilson was now able to sit up but had not tried to move to join the others.

Suddenly Tom's vision became extremely blurry. At first he thought it was because he had been crying. But he then noticed that the group appeared to be becoming less substantial, almost transparent. After only a few seconds everything around Tom seemed completely different. He found that he was lying in his bed staring up at the ceiling in his bedroom. With his face still wet with tears he turned over in bed to see his snow globe sitting atop the tallboy at the foot of the bed. He couldn't believe he was home. He also couldn't believe that he didn't know whether his friends were okay. After all his longing to come home, if felt like he had been ripped from his adventure before he got to read the final page. How could life go on unless he knew what had happened to them all? This couldn't be the end. Then out of a mixture of fear and exhaustion Tom passed out in his bed.

Chapter Twenty-Four
A New Life Revealed

Tom was awoken by movement and opened his eyes to see his mother standing by his bed. 'Happy birthday, sleepy head,' she said beaming. 'It's gone ten o'clock. You had best get up if you intend on going fishing today.'

He felt completely disorientated. He almost felt the need to fight. It all came flooding back to him. He was home, and no time had passed at all since he had left. Torean had been right when he had said the staff would return him where it had found him.

'What is this doing next to your bed?' his mother said, warily picking up the staff. 'Your grandfather's idea of a joke, I'll wager.' She picked up the staff and made for the door. 'Come down for your breakfast, love. Are you feeling okay? You look rather peaky.'

'I'm fine, mum,' Tom managed to say almost out breath. He felt sick. 'I'll be right down.'

She smiled and left the room, closing the door behind her.

Rising from his bed he put on his dressing gown and looked in the mirror. He hadn't seen a mirror since he had left. Staring at his face for a time, he tried to decide whether he looked different. It was then that he noticed he was not wearing his pyjamas, but was still dressed in the shirt and trousers he had been wearing during the battle, grubby and torn. His mother hadn't noticed because he was under the covers when she had come into the room. Strangely he noticed that the cuts and bruises on his face seemed to have gone. *How strange that his return seemed to have healed him, but left him in the same clothes?* He quickly changed into a different pair of pyjamas, put on his dressing gown and headed down the stairs for breakfast.

He hadn't said much during breakfast, unsure of how he could broach the subject and had decided to wait until he was alone with his grandfather to discuss what had happened to him. He could feel them eying him warily. He probably wasn't doing a very good job of pretending to be excited about his birthday.

As they sat by the riverbank he decided to speak to the old man. He felt like he would burst if he could not talk to someone about everything that had happened. 'Granda,' he said warily. 'I need to talk to you about the staff.'

'Oh yes,' his granda mused. 'Well that depends on what you want to know. I don't want to be getting into trouble with your mother.'

'I think it might be a little late for that,' Tom said staring straight ahead of himself.

'What?' the old man questioned.

'I know how to use the staff. I've been away for over two weeks.'

'Good God,' the old man said, stunned. 'You must tell me the full tale.'

After recounting all that had happened to him his grandfather put his arm around him. 'I am proud of you my boy. Although you must realise that when I sat the staff in your room as you slept I had no idea that this would happen. I only meant…'

'Do you think they're okay?' Tom interjected, still worried about what had happened to his friends after he left.

'I can't say for sure,' said the old man. He knew he couldn't reassure him when it may not be true. 'Although I think when we get back to the house there is something I can show you which may help to put your mind at ease.'

Tom was extremely curious about what this may be, but still felt extremely shocked by everything that had happened. A combination of this and how tiring he had found recounting his tale to his grandfather meant that the two of them spent the rest of the afternoon fishing in relative silence.

To Tom this was bliss. He was back with his grandfather. He was safe. This was exactly what he needed after what had happened to him. It would have been very difficult to spend the day with his mother in the house pretending that nothing had happened.

That night after a beautiful dinner and large helpings of cake, Tom made his excuses and headed off to bed.

'Well this is unusual,' his mother laughed, kissing him on the cheek. 'I usually have to pry you away from that fireside. The fishing must have taken it out of you.'

'Yes,' he said smiling. 'I'm tired. Thank you for a lovely day mum.'

'It was a pleasure darlin,' off to bed with you,' she said rising from her chair to go into the kitchen to put the kettle on.

'If it's okay, Helen, I'm going to go and tuck the birthday boy in,' said Evan groaning as he rose from his chair.

The old man followed Tom up the stairs but did not follow him into his room. Tom could hear him through in his own bedroom rooting around in the wardrobe.

After a few minutes he appeared in the doorway and sat on the end of the bed holding a large brown leather book with an ornate metal clasp. 'This is our book of lore my boy,' he said, holding it out for Tom to take.

'Really?' Tom whispered, shocked, taking hold of the heavy volume. 'Aneirin told me that the lore had never been written down. I told him that it really should be in case someone died in battle before they could pass on what they had learned. After all he was like me. Both our fathers were dead. If anything was to happen to Torean or to you before you taught us, the lore would die with you.'

'I know,' the old man smiled. 'When you told me your story today it all became clear. I can't believe that I didn't see it before. Open the book and read the introduction.'

Tom gingerly undid the clasp and swung the book open. His eyes filled with tears as he read the words written within the first pages:

This text contains our family lore. It is our destiny to uphold it and pass it on to those who follow us. I was led to put this text into writing by my young cousin, Tom. While I did not share his love of books, I understood how important this text would be. I hope that one day he may read it and remember me. Aneirin

MacKay.

Tom was flabbergasted. 'I don't know what to say.'

'You are already great among us, my boy,' his grandfather said stroking his hair. 'Aneirin was a great staff wielder himself and in fact built this house we are now living in.'

Tom didn't know what to say. 'Can I read this, granda?' Tom eventually said hopefully.

'Of course,' he smiled. 'Although I would keep it away from your mother, I'm sure if she saw you reading a tome like that she would be curious to find out what you were reading.'

'I will,' Tom promised.

'Knowing who you now are, I would also ask that you do not read beyond the tenth chapter.'

'Why?' asked Tom.

'That will become clear to you later,' said his grandfather. 'Also, it is wise that you do not try to overstretch yourself. You have had a very rushed introduction to our lore. It would be best for you to walk before you can run.'

The old man rose from the bed and Tom leapt up to take him into an embrace. 'I missed you, granda.'

'I know son,' the old man replied. 'It is hard when you are away from those you love. Look at it this way, a new adventure is just beginning. Who knows what mischief you and I can get into now that we are staff wielders both?' His grandfather pulled away from him and winked, 'Goodnight, boy.'

'Good night, granda,' Tom smiled. He hurried to get into his night clothes so that he could read the book in bed. As he lay in bed leafing through the pages, he felt like he was back with Aneirin. He wanted to skip ahead to see what he should avoid, but paid heed to his grandfather's advice. Tom had never had such an eventful birthday in his life. He couldn't wait to see what other adventures would await him and his grandfather.

His grandfather entered his room several hours later. He removed the book lying open on Tom's chest and placed it under the bed. 'Sleep tight, son,' the old man said, stroking his hair. He then looked at his staff, but decided against sitting it next to the boy's bed. He would definitely need a rest.

Glossary of Magical Terms:

Aicheadh Coirbte – The incantation to denounce evil

Amail – To hinder or obstruct your foe, the staff would harness the surrounding elements, for example using the wind, or a nearby river to hold back an enemy.

Amas – To seek out an object, the staff would bring to object to you

Bas – To bring about death, this is extremely costly and one has to be able to control the spell exactly.

Basaich - To make one Wither

Beathaich – Can sustain someone's energy, mainly used when two people are fighting together, it can be used to help boost someone else's enchantment without actually having said the enchantment yourself.

Buille - strike a blow at a foe using surrounding forces, useful if fighting at a distance.

Buireadh – To great a distraction using whatever is surrounding you.

Cabhair – Can relieve any suffering felt by those around you

Càirich - To mend or repair

Cleith – Can conceal that which you wish to hide from an enemy

Coimhead - To see someone and what they are doing, when using the staff the user can use reflective surfaces to see those whom they require, they are limited by distance

Cuairteag – Can create a whirlpool

Daor – To enslave those around you to carry out your bidding

Ioc – A word which can be used to heal people. Must be used sparingly as either uses the energy of the caster or that of living organisms surrounding the caster

Nathura Gathera – the summoning spell, can be used to summon evil spirits, but also used by a staff wielder to summon another MacKay.

Rabhadh – Can send a warning signal, this again can vary as it uses the forces around you.

Srad – Can produce or manipulate fire

Suaimhneach – Can calm animals, it can also be used to communicate with such animals.

ABOUT THE AUTHOR

From Hamilton in Lanarkshire, Clare has a History degree from Strathclyde University and now lives in London with her husband. Having spent some time trying to find some magic in various fields, she is now concentrating on her career as a writer. Clare was drawn to writing by her life long passion for reading and inventing stories. As a child, Clare loved nothing more than curling up on a window seat in her local library and being carried away by a magical story. A fantasy fiction fanatic, she has currently completed her first book 'The Long Staff', and is currently working on the second installment of 'The Staff Wielder Series', called 'The Ancient Exile'. She is at her happiest when she can disappear into a world of her own armed with nothing but a laptop and her imagination.

Other Olida Publishing Titles

THE MAGIC SCALES
Book 1 of the Denthan Series
by Sam Wilding

James's father is missing. With no clue why his dad would run out on him and his mum, he hides out by an ancient stone circle to think. There, James discovers a dead stoat, crushed in an impossibly huge footprint. The mystery of what smashed the little animal leads James into finding Mendel, a wizard from another world called Denthan. Mendel has his own problems though. He's trapped in the body of a goldfish and Denthan's sun is about to die and destroy the planet. James is soon drawn into Mendel's plight and hopes against hope that the goldfish can somehow help him find his dad. Will Denthan be saved? Can Mendel regain his true form? But more importantly, will James ever find his father?

(Children's Fiction / Fantasy / Young Adult)
RRP £9.99
www.olidapublishing.com

Other Olida Publishing Titles

THE SECOND GATEWAY
Book 2 of the Denthan Series
by Sam Wilding

One year on, the zany villagers of Drumfintley are, yet again, all that stand between a peaceful world and certain disaster. When a whole new array of monsters and dark magic begin to emerge from the murky waters of Loch Echty all hell breaks loose. Beneath the Scottish loch, Mendel and James discover the submerged village of Fintley, a huge obelisk and a new crystal key. It is soon clear that they face a greater threat than ever before. In this, the second epic struggle to keep the Peck family together, some souls may be lost for good this time... Will James, Craig and Bero still be able to save us all? Will Mendel, the wizard-goldfish, continue to outwit his oldest and greatest adversary? Will the second gateway take the villagers of Drumfintley on a one-way trip to catastrophe?

(Children's Fiction / Fantasy / Young Adult)
RRP £9.99
www.olidapublishing.com

Other Olida Publishing Titles

RETURN TO DENTHAN
Book 3 of the Denthan Series
by Sam Wilding

Another year on, the missing Harrison children return with Mendel, the wizard goldfish. James Peck is yet again at the helm when the people of Drumfintley are thrown into their most dangerous adventure yet. Mendel's plan is to rescue Cathy Peck, but much more besides… His aim is to bring back a world already destroyed by an exploding sun. They are pitched against Dendralon and a host of new creatures in an amazing array of battles that test the resolve and ingenuity of the Scottish villagers and Mendel alike.
Will James reunite his family at last? Will Mendel manage to save the planet, destroyed two years before? Will they all return to Denthan, Drumfintley and normality? What sacrifices must be made?
(Children's Fiction / Fantasy / Young
RRP £9.99
www.olidapublishing.com

Other Olida Publishing Titles

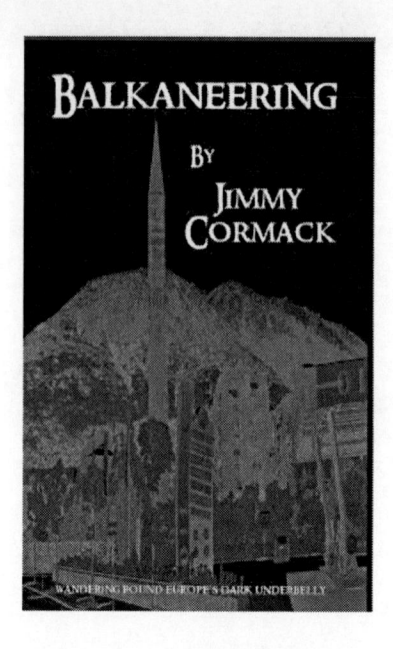

BALKANEERING
BY JIMMY CORMACK

Civil Wars, ethnic cleansing and genocide, mass murderers, liberation movements turned gun-running gangsters and eccentric dictators. And all in recent memory. The Balkans has never had troubles to seek. Jimmy Cormack travels round the parts of Europe the rest of us would prefer to avoid. He examines the history, the geography and the political intrigues that have shaped the region right up to this day. However, he also experiences some lighter moments, meeting a bizarre mixture of misf and dodgy characters and witnesses some wacky, and some near-to-death incidents. (**Literature and Travel / History**)
RRP £7.99
www.olidapublishing.com

Other Olida Publishing Titles

THE EDEN SEED
BY DAMIAN PECK

Matt Malcolm is a devil-may-care marketing manager who inadvertently discovers an ancient seed that has the ability to extend the normal human lifespan by more than nine hundred years, disease free. Representing a huge pharmaceutical company, he blackmails their competitors who pay up to maintain the status quo. Six months on, however, he loses his job and finds his lover murdered. With the only test crop of The Seed destroyed, a trail of destruction is left over Eastern Europe and North Africa as the rival companies and a religious sect called the Seraphim embroil him in the search for the true source of the wonder drug, known as The Eden Seed.

(Thriller, Fiction, Fantasy)
RRP £9.99
buy at www.olidapublishing.com

Other Olida Publishing Titles

WHISKY IN THE JAR
BY ALEXANDER TAIT

"Whisky in the Jar' is an historical novel based on the illicit whisky distilling and smuggling activities that occurred around the eighteenth century on Loch Lomondside. Duncan Robertson is an heroic figure who finds himself ensnared in the conflict between the Highland people and the British military a generation after Culloden. It is also the story of the man who writes the novel. A man fighting his own battle against the mental oppression of agoraphobia, alcohol dependency and the threat of job loss. Where Duncan Robertson's weapons are the broadsword and the pistol, the author uses rock 'n' roll and eastern mysticism. These themes are as vibrantly interwoven as any Highland tartan, with richly colourful characters, romance, suspense and dry Scots humour.

(Literature and Fiction / History)
RRP £9.99
buy at www.olidapublishing.com

Other Olida Publishing Titles

THE CUP
BY ALEXANDER TAIT

In this richly varied collection of a dozen stories, Alexander Tait draws from his rich imagination and historical research to enable his readers to encounter Rock legends of the late sixties, the court of King Arthur and a Roman centurian on the shores of Loch Lomond. Tait's characters are found on Arctic convoys, the beaches of Dunkirk, blitz-torn Birmingham and the surface of the moon. They have been crafted with understanding, warmth and humour. The tales, which range in a time from the crucifixion of Christ to the present day, all deal in their different ways with the eternal battle, within individuals and nations, between good and evil.

(Literature and Fiction / History)
RRP £7.99
www.olidapublishing.com

Other Olida Publishing Titles

Pure Wool

GREGOR ADDISON

"Our wool is pure."

PURE WOOL
by Gregor Addison

. Pure wool is a tale of how conflict arises from mistrust, of violence and sorrow – perhaps, finally, of hope. Life in the valley will never be the same again. When the great flocks clash under the leadership of Broadtail and Bellwether, the lives of both Teg and Cobbler are changed forever. As the collies return to the valley, only old Moses realises the meaning of what they find.

(Literature / Modern Fable)
RRP £6.99
www.olidapublishing.com

Other Olida Publishing Titles

HOLLOW FOOTSTEPS
BY KAREN ROBERTS

The killing of Robert the Bruce's adversary, John Comyn—a Balloi supporter and rival claimant to the crown, cleared Robert's way to the throne in 1306. But King Robert's family paid a steep price after he took the crown. No mercy was shown to anyone who supported him, even women. Something which Marjorie, his only legitimate child by his first wife, would discover.

Hollow Footsteps is a captivating novel with just the right balance of history and fiction. Roberts keeps her readers on their toes, anxiously turning pages, as she expertly navigates the twisted passageways of time and centuries-old intrigue. Whether you're looking for the thrill of the chase or stolen moments of romance, Roberts is sure to deliver.

(Historic Novel, Romance)
RRP £9.99
www.olidapublishing.com